Man

Also by Leah Marie Brown

The It Girls Series
Faking It
Finding It
Working It
Owning It

Dreaming of Manderley

Leah Marie Brown

LYRICAL PRESS
Kensington Publishing Corp.
www.kensingtonbooks.com

LYRICAL PRESS BOOKS are published by

Kensington Publishing Corp.
119 West 40th Street
New York, NY 10018

All Kensington titles, imprints, and distributed lines are available at special quantity discounts for bulk purchases for sales promotion, premiums, fund-raising, educational, or institutional use.

Special book excerpts or customized printings can also be created to fit specific needs. For details, write or phone the office of the Kensington Sales Manager: Attn.: Sales Department. Kensington Publishing Corp., 119 West 40th Street, New York, NY 10018. Phone: 1-800-221-2647.

Lyrical and the Lyrical logo Reg. U.S. Pat. & TM Off.

First Lyrical Press Mass-Market Paperback Printing: January 2018
ISBN-13: 978-1-5161-0113-9
ISBN-10: 1-5161-0113-8

First Lyrical Press Electronic Edition: January 2018
eISBN-13: 978-1-5161-0116-0
eISBN-10: 1-5161-0116-2

10 9 8 7 6 5 4 3 2 1

Printed in the United States of America

Prologue

Last night I dreamt of Jake Gyllenhaal again. It seemed to me that I stood on the balcony of the Hôtel Barrière, Le Majestic, watching him walk the red carpet outside the Palais des Festivals et des Congrès, close enough to see the sun shining on his artfully tousled hair, but separated by an undulating sea of tuxedo-clad paparazzi.

There was Jake, my Jake, serious and self-contained, working the carpet with the effortless grace of an actor from Hollywood's Golden Age—a Cary Grant or Clark Gable. Cameras flashed, reporters shouted, fans screamed, the palm fronds rattled in the Mediterranean breeze.

A willowy blond actress, Hollywood's latest It Girl, joined him, wrapping her toned arm around his waist and briefly resting her head on his muscular shoulder.

He looked down at his wrist, fiddled with his black-diamond-studded cufflinks, before slowly looking through his thick lashes at the crowd, then shifting his gaze up, to where I stood on the balcony of the luxurious hotel. Our gazes locked, my heart skipped a beat, and time seemed to stand still the way it does before a major cosmic shift or in dreams.

I whispered his name in my dream—*Jake*—and he smiled up at me, one of his lazy, lopsided grins. The crowd fell silent, the paparazzi turned their cameras toward me, zooming their lenses in tight. I closed my eyes against the blinding flash of popping bulbs and, when I opened them again, Jake and the paparazzi had vanished.

I was still standing on the balcony. The street below was empty except for a few lovers strolling arm in arm. I sensed I was dreaming, but still felt a sharp stab of loneliness watching the lovers, the kind of loneliness that pierces all the way to your soul and leaves you with lingering effects.

I stared out at the pearly moonlight reflecting off the onyx sea. I heard a noise behind me, but was too transfixed by the otherworldly moonlight to turn around.

And then I *sensed* him, felt the heat of his body before the warmth of his touch. I believe I shivered in the dream, as well as in my sleep. He pressed his lips to my bare neck, and murmured low in my ear, "You *are* real. I feared you were a dream, my darling Manderley."

A cloud passed over the moon, casting the scene in thick, velvety darkness, and then he was gone and I was standing alone on the veranda of my father's Charleston home, alone save for the ghosts of my mother, father, and beloved aunt, floating beside me.

Moonlight can play tricks, even in dreams.

I can never be with Jake. That much is certain. But sometimes, in my dreams, I do go back to those strange, enchanting days in the South of France. Days of innocence and yearning, of sorrow and splendor, when my life as I now know it, began . . .

Chapter One

Text from Emma Lee Maxwell:
Have you gone to any glam parties yet? Have you seen Zac Efron or Liam Hemsworth? Please tell me you are not holed up in your room, reading some dreary old Brontë novel in that sad flannel nightgown? I would die if I had the chance to live in Cannes. Yes, I know that would defeat the purpose. You know what I mean.

Text from Tara Maxwell:
It's tax time and Daddy always filled out my forms. Would you please go on the IRS website, download a 1040EZ form, and fill it out for me? You're so good at all of that stuff.

I am not happy. It is a sparkling sunny day. A soft, sea-scented breeze is blowing on my face and ruffling my long bangs. I am standing on the edge of a cliff in the Côte d'Azur, watching turquoise waves crash on the rocks far below, and all I want to do is let out a high-pitched, mournful cry, like the seagulls circling over my head.

I am not a drama queen. I promise. There are legitimate reasons for my seemingly theatrical ennui. More reasons than nuts in a fruitcake.

Forgive my atrocious manners. I should introduce myself. My name is Manderley Maxwell. Mandy, to my friends. Plain, dirty-dishwater blond, gray-eyed, hard-working, dependable Mandy.

I move in a world filled with pouty-lipped Angelina Jolies, ample-bosomed Scarlett Johanssons, and fashion-forward Blake Livelys, but I am not a bombshell. Not even close.

I will never score a Jake Gyllenhaal, Henry Cavill, or Ryan Gosling. The most I can hope for is a Jonah Hill, an equally reliable guy who tickles my funny bone, even if he doesn't make my pulse race.

Keep the cork on the champagne and the Kleenex in the box because this is not a pity party. It's a reality rave. I know I am strictly B-List, and unless something radical happens in my life, I will remain the hardest working player on the B-list.

Even my job is B-list. I am an assistant to Olivia Tate, big-time Hollywood screenwriter, and, awkwardly, my best friend. It doesn't matter that we both graduated from Columbia University, or that I was editor of *Quarto*, the university's prestigious literary magazine (the same magazine J. D. Salinger once wrote for), I am too busy fetching coffee and proofreading screenplays for my BFF to even think about developing my own writing career.

Then there's my family. After my mother died, my father relied on me to be a maternal figure to my younger sisters, Tara and Emma Lee. My younger, needier, spoiled, more glam sisters. At the age of seven, I was cast as the family spinster. I even wear the requisite tortoiseshell glasses and flannel nightgown. I am one fringed shawl short of spending my days in a rocker, going deaf from the incessant *click-click-click* of my knitting needles.

Two months ago, my daddy and Aunt Patricia died in a freak boating accident one hundred miles off the coast of Sullivan's Island, leaving behind a mountain of debt and years of unpaid taxes we knew nothing about. If it weren't for the trust fund my momma left me, and my job, I would be as aimless and lost as my sisters.

Through the haze of my tears, I watch a black-winged cormorant dive through the air and plunge into the churning sea, disappearing below the surface. I envy the creature. I wonder what it would be like if I copied the cormorant? If I spread my arms wide and dove off this cliff, would the sea wash away my cares?

I am not saying I am the suicidal sort. Not at all.

Though, there are days, like today, when I feel caught in the suffocating cocoon of my life, desperate to wiggle free from the strands and emerge more beautiful, more carefree.

The cormorant surfaces, a fish trapped in its long yellow bill, and floats effortlessly on the crest of a wave, its black, beady eyes seemingly focused on me. He's taunting me, silently challenging me to show a modicum of the daring he showed.

I shift my gaze from the unnerving bird to a clump of grass at my feet, nudging it with the toe of my espadrilles. Nudging. Nudging. Nudging, until the roots break free and the clump tumbles down, down into the swirling surf.

"*Mais qu'est-ce que vous faites? Venez loin de là!*"

My breath catches in my throat at the unexpected intrusion. I spin around too fast, lose my balance, and nearly tumble backwards off the cliff, when the intruder clasps his hands around my waist and roughly pulls me to him. My cheek is pressed against his bronzed, muscular chest. I feel the delicious heat of his body, smell the coconut scent of suntan lotion and the tang of sea salt, hear the steady, soothing thud of his heartbeat, and wonder if I plunged to my death and am now in heaven. Maybe this man is a bare-chested angel.

"*Putain!*" he swears, his breath ruffling my bangs. "*Tu dois être fou.*"

So not in heaven. Angels don't drop the F-bomb.

I pull out of his grasp and crane my neck to look up at him. Sweet Lawd, but he is tall.

"Excuse me?"

"I said you are crazy."

"I am not crazy!"

"You are American." His upper lip curls slightly.

"Yes."

"Same thing."

I snort because I can't think of a response. I am, frankly, too offended by his arrogant manner and too awestruck by his strong, whiskered jaw, chiseled cheekbones, piercing blue gaze, and thick crop of wavy dark hair. He's a walking Dolce & Gabbana advert, all cool sophistication and cultivated European good looks.

And it hits me.

He *must* be an actor. It would explain the movie-star good looks and the cosmically huge arrogance. He is probably some French actor, in Cannes because his film was nominated for the Palme d'Or.

He crosses his muscular arms over his chest and regards me beneath raised brow. "Were you trying to kill yourself? Is that it then?"

"What?" My cheeks flush with guilty heat. "No! Don't be ridiculous."

His blue eyes narrow.

I shift my gaze to my dust-covered espadrilles and wait for my heated cheeks to cool. I want to tell him yelling at a potentially suicidal woman standing on the edge of a cliff is *extrêmement stupide* and there isn't a suicide prevention handbook in print that recommends calling a distraught person a fool. But I don't. If only I had Tara's confidence or Emma Lee's charm; then I would know precisely what to say to this handsome, arrogant Frenchman.

Instead, I start to cry. Tears slide down my cheeks and plop onto the toes of my espadrilles. I am sniffling like some sad, overwrought starlet who has been told her nose is too big/breasts are too small/hair is too frizzy/eyes are too crossed.

"Come"—he fastens his hand around my forearm—"you need to get out of the sun."

"It's not the sun." I sniffle.

"Don't be silly. Of course it is the sun. The heat can be particularly draining in this part of France, especially this time of day."

I don't argue, nor do I fight him as he leads me down the hill. I am too tired, too emotionally spent to muster enough feeling to argue. I follow him to a narrow scenic pull-off and a sleek convertible Jaguar parked close to the guard rail.

"What is your name?"

"Manderley," I mumble. "Manderley Maxwell. My friends call me Mandy, though."

"I will drive you back to your hotel, Manderley."

He pronounces my name with a heavy French accent so that it sounds like Mon-de-lee instead of Manderley.

"I am fine," I say, taking a step away. "Really."

"Are you always this contrary?" He opens the passenger door. "Get in."

"Honestly, I took a bus to get here; I can take the bus back to the hotel."

He scowls. "Why would you ever do that?"

He gestures for me to get in and I obey. Because that is what I do. And because it feels good to have someone take care of me for once.

He walks around the front of the car, moving with the grace of a predatory beast, all sinewy muscles and barely controlled power, and my breath catches in my throat. Am I being reckless? Cannes might be the pleasure ground of Saudi princes, European heiresses, and film stars, but it also attracts the finest criminals in the world. Pickpockets, jewel thieves, human traffickers, prostitutes. I read in a reputable travel magazine that gypsy bosses and gangsters moor their yachts in the bay. What if this man runs an organized crime ring? What if he kidnaps me and sells me to an Eastern European human trafficker?

He jumps in the car. "*Excusez-moi.*"

He reaches over me to open the glove compartment, his chiseled forearm brushing against my bare knees. My heart skips a beat and I silently pray he isn't going to pull out a Taser or gun. He removes a T-shirt from the compartment and pulls it over his head. I catch a whiff of expensive-smelling, citrusy cologne.

"My name is Xavier," he says, slanting a look at me.

I swallow hard. "Nice to meet you, Xavier."

"Tell me something, Manderley. What are you doing out here? This park is off the beaten tourist track."

"That was rather the point."

"I see." He frowns. "So you wanted to be alone?"

"Yes."

"Because you wanted to . . ." He clears his throat.

"Kill myself?" I laugh, but in the quiet of the car it sounds false, maybe even a little manic. "I wasn't going to kill myself. I wanted to escape the crowds, and the concierge said this was a nice place to come to be alone in nature. There aren't many places like this where I am staying."

He fastens his seat belt and pushes a shiny red start button. The engine roars to life and we are off. Xavier maneuvers the powerful sports car around each serpentine curve, manipulating the stick shift with the skill of a race-car driver.

"Where *are* you staying?"

"Hôtel Le Majestic."

He looks at me, one eyebrow raised in that distinctive Gallic expression of astonishment and haughty disdain. I once read that eighteenth-century French believed France to be the center of the universe; the farther one traveled from France, the farther one was removed from culture and reason. In my experience, the French still believe they are culturally superior. It doesn't matter if they work as a valet, taxi driver, or waiter. The woman who turns down my sheets at the hotel gives me serious Gallic face every time she fluffs my pillows.

"Are you visiting Cannes with your . . . husband?"

I brush the hair from my eyes and stare at him to see if he is mocking me in my spinsterhood, but his handsome, inscrutable profile gives nothing away.

"I am not married."

"I thought perhaps you were on your honeymoon and a lover's spat drove you to . . ."

"To contemplate throwing myself off a cliff?"

"*Oui.*"

He pulls to a stop at a flashing yellow light and looks at me.

I attempt, in my best college French, to recite a line from one of my favorite novels, *Bonjour Tristesse,* by Françoise Sagan.

"You speak French?"

"*Un peu,*" I say, holding up my fingers to indicate *a little*.

"*Un peu,*" he says, shifting into first and taking off. "And yet you are familiar with Françoise Sagan?"

"I read *Bonjour Tristesse* in college and wished I could be Cécile, living in a villa on the French Riviera and having a summer love affair with a boy named Cyril."

"If I am remembering it correctly, Cyril broke her heart and the story ended with Cécile returning to her sad life." He looks over at me, his blue eyes piercing my soul. "Isn't there a famous line . . . about loving someone to the point of madness?"

"Yes."

"Have you?"

"Excuse me?"

"Loved to the point of madness?"

I laugh sadly because I haven't ever loved, not deeply, madly, truly loved. Not as Cécile loved Cyril. Pangs of longing echo in my heart. I am almost certain Xavier can hear them.

"No," I finally say, my voice wavering.

"Why not?"

The bold question knocks me off balance.

"I don't have time for romance," I say, honestly. "I am too busy helping everyone else achieve their hearts' desires."

"Go on."

My words come out in a nervous rush, a powerful stream of consciousness and raw emotions I usually keep contained behind a shy smile and nondescript attire. Not that there have been that many people lining up to hear my most inner emotions. People in Hollywood don't do deep. They do air kisses and narcissism-fueled cocktail parties at the Viceroy on Friday nights.

"I work for Olivia Tate," I say, as if that explains everything. "I am her assistant, editor, brainstorm partner."

"Who is Olivia Tate?"

He takes a sharp turn and I have to hold on to the door handle so I don't slide sideways into him.

"Olivia Tate. *Love's Requiem. Postmodern.*"

He shrugs.

"*A Quaint Milieu?*"

I wonder if he is feigning obtuseness or if films made beyond the borders of the center of the universe aren't worthy of note for a French film actor.

"Olivia Tate is a screenwriter. Her screenplay, *A Quaint Milieu*, was nominated for the Palme d'Or."

"I am sorry, but I don't make it to the theater that often."

"Then, you're not an actor?"

"*Non.*" He chuckles, a deep, rich laugh that rumbles in his broad, muscular chest. "What made you think I was an actor?"

Your impossibly large ego. Your breathtaking, leading-man good looks. Your luxury sports car that costs three times the average American's annual income.

I shrug.

"So, you are an assistant to a Palme d'Or–nominated screenwriter. What made you choose that career?" He glances over his shoulder at me, his gaze moving from my high ponytail to my shabby espadrilles. "You don't appear to be the sort of woman attracted to that lifestyle. Do you have dreams of making it big in Hollywood?"

He clenches his jaw and grips the steering wheel so tight his knuckles turn as white as the eyelet lace on the hem of my sundress.

"Olivia Tate is my best friend."

"Really?"

"Yes, really. It surprises you that a famous screenwriter would be friends with someone like me?" *Someone plain. Someone shy. Someone in dirty espadrilles.*

"I am surprised you would mix business and pleasure. I would never employ a friend. Ever."

"Olivia sold her first screenplay to a major studio the week after we graduated from college. Her career took off after that first sale. She needed someone she could rely on, a life preserver in the shark-infested waters of Hollywood."

"And that is what you are . . . a life preserver?"

I think of all of the people who rely upon me and sigh. "Yes, I suppose I am."

"What happens when too many people cling to a life preserver?"

"Disaster," I say, rubbing my hands over my bare arms.

"*Exactement.*" He flicks the turn indicator and steers the Jaguar off the busy Boulevard de la Croisette into the driveway of the Hôtel Le Majestic. "Wouldn't you rather be a shark?"

"Me?" I laugh. "Sadly, I don't have the teeth."

He pulls to a stop and looks at me. "That is not sad."

A valet hurries to open Xavier's door. "*Bienvenue, monsieur,*" the valet says.

Xavier hands over his keys and walks around the car, opening my door and holding out his hand. I step out of the car and am blinded by flashes of light. The paparazzi have been camped outside the hotel since the beginning of the Festival. When they realize I am not an A-lister, they focus their attention on the next car pulling up to the valet stand.

Xavier places his broad hand on the small of my back and leads me through the revolving door and into the opulent lobby. Even though the Festival officially ended last night, the lobby is buzzing with activity. We move through golden halos of light created by the crystal chandeliers hanging overhead, past plush velvet sofas and marble replicas of classical Greek statues, until we arrive at the elevators.

He jabs the up button.

"Thank you for the ride and for seeing me into the hotel, but I will be fine from here."

A wry smile tugs at the corners of his mouth. "I am sure you will be fine, but this is where I am staying."

"Oh."

The elevator doors slide open and we step inside.

"Floor?" he asks.

"Three, please."

He jabs the round number three button and then the number six. Lawd! The sixth floor is where the hotel's most exclusive suites are located. The Christian Dior suite includes a butler, swimming pool, and furniture designed by Nathalie Ryan, interior decorator at House of Dior.

The elevator dings, announcing our arrival on the third floor, and the doors slide open.

I don't want Xavier to remember me as a hopeless case, even if we never meet again. It's not because he drives a Jaguar F-Type convertible and stays in the Christian Dior suite at Le Majestic. I can't explain why, but I have an inexplicable need to leave him with something more than the memory of me weeping and sniveling about my problems.

"Thank you for driving me back to the hotel and for listening to my problems," I say, turning around, my back to the hall. "It was very kind of you."

"It was nothing."

I look up into his eyes and forget what I had been about to say. The doors start to close and he sticks his hand between them to keep me from being crushed. I catch another whiff of his citrusy cologne as his arm brushes my shoulder and my breath catches in my throat.

"*Au revoir*, Life Preserver, don't let the sharks drag you down."

"I'll try," I murmur.

I turn and step out of the elevator. Xavier pulls his hand back and the doors slide shut.

Chapter Two

"Are you seriously telling me a Leo rescued you from falling off a cliff and gave you a ride back to the hotel in a car straight off the set of a James Bond movie and you didn't get his phone number?" Olivia takes a sip of her Grande Dame, one of Le Majestic's signature cocktails, made with verbena-infused water, gin, and champagne, and looks at me through her false eyelashes. "And he had serious designer stubble?"

"Yes."

In Olivia vernacular, a "Leo" is a man who possesses enough charisma and good looks to play the leading man in almost any film. As in, Leonardo DiCaprio. "Designer stubble" is closely-cropped facial hair intended to give the actor a majorly macho appearance. Jake Gyllenhaal, Colin Farrell, and George Clooney are famous for their designer stubble. Harrison Ford worked the stubble in *Raiders of the Lost Ark* and Leonardo DiCaprio in *Blood Diamond*. Olivia can deliver a lengthy monologue on the history and success of designer stubble. To her, male supermodel David Gandy is the poster boy for designer stubble, while Brad Pitt and Joaquin Phoenix are quintessential examples of chin bush gone bad.

We are sitting in Le Majestic's Bar Galerie du Fouquet's, a sumptuous Art Deco cocktail lounge decorated with black velvet armchairs and gilded fixtures, while we wait for a reporter from *Variety* to arrive to interview Olivia.

"You should have asked him to join you for cocktails tonight."

"I couldn't have done that."

"Why not?" She grins, her full, red-lacquered lips curling up. "The Festival is over, which means we have a month of men, Moët, and Monte."

Olivia loves the film *To Catch a Thief,* starring Cary Grant and Grace Kelly, and wants to visit Monte Carlo so she can find her own debonair jewel thief. She probably will, too. Olivia is a force. Hurricane Olivia doesn't let anything—or anyone—stand in her way of following the path to happiness. It's one of the things I admire, and envy, in her.

"I am not as bold as you, Olivia."

"Bold, schmold," she says, dismissively waving her manicured hand. "Not all men desire a bold woman, Mandy. You are pretty, loyal, and damned clever. Monsieur X would have probably jumped at the invite."

"I doubt it."

"Why?"

An image of Xavier behind the wheel of his convertible flashes in my mind. The strong, leading-man profile, the designer stubble shadowing his jaw, the wind ruffling his dark hair.

"You didn't see him, Olivia. If this were *Gone with the Wind*, he would be Rhett Butler and I would be pale-faced, mealy-mouthed Melanie Hamilton."

The waiter appears bearing a silver tray laden with two Grande Dames. He places one in front of Olivia and the other in front of me.

"There must be some mistake," I say, sliding the heavy crystal glass away from me. "I didn't order a drink."

"C'est bon," Olivia says, sliding the glass back.

The waiter bows and backs away.

"I don't drink when I am working."

"Fiddle-dee-dee, Miss Mellie," Olivia simpers. "Step out of those stiff petticoats and have a good time. We are in Cannes, for Scarlett's sake!"

She glares at me until I take a sip of my drink. My daddy was a gin drinker. Hayman's 1850 Reserve and a splash of tonic every night after dinner. I shudder as the alcohol burns a path down my throat. When it comes to gin, I am not my daddy's girl. I would rather gargle sea water.

Olivia smiles at me over the rim of her cocktail glass. "Do you know what I think?"

"No, but I have a feeling you are going to tell me."

"I think you work awfully hard at being plain and un-memorable, but deep down you have an inner sex-kitten, clawing to get out."

I snort.

"Me-ow," Olivia purrs, raising her hands like claws. "Let it out, Mandy. Let your inner sex-kitten out."

I push my glasses up my nose and snort again. "I do

not have an inner sex-kitten. I have a fat, boring, depend-able calico that hides under furniture because it is fright-ened of its shadow."

"Bullshit!" Olivia hisses. "If I were in Monte, I would place all my chips on the bet that you have a fierce, feral, inner sex-kitten. The right catnip will lure it out."

My cheeks flush with heat.

"Maybe you need a dose of French catnip!"

She laughs and the heat spreads from my cheeks down my neck, fanning out over my chest. I reach for my cock-tail, and that's when I see Xavier striding through the bar, dressed in an impeccably tailored black suit and crisp white shirt, open at the neck to reveal a tantalizing V of tanned skin. My hand bumps my glass, tipping it over. The cocktail spills onto the table, my lap, and the floor.

"Mandy? Are you . . ." Olivia follows my gaze and gasps. "Yowza! That wouldn't happen to be your—"

Xavier stops at our table and pulls a monogrammed hankie from his pocket.

"Mademoiselle Maxwell," he says, handing me the hankie. "I believe Emanuele intended for you to drink his cocktails, not bathe in them."

"Emanuele?"

"Emanuele Balestra. Le Majestic's *Chef Barman.*"

"Oh, yes. Of course."

Of course he would know the *Chef Barman*.

I use the hankie to dab gin from my skirt and hand it back to Xavier.

"Keep it," he says, smiling. "It would appear you have more need of it today."

He bows slightly, nods his head at Olivia, and strides away, joining an older, paunchy man in a private booth at the back of the bar.

"Well done, Mandy!" Olivia stares at me through wide eyes. "I think you found your catnip."

I am spared from responding as a waifish blonde holding a slender notebook, an iPhone, and a small pocket recorder, approaches our table. I recognize her as the *Variety* reporter.

"Good Evening, Miss Tate," she says, thrusting her hand at Olivia. "I believe we have an interview. I am Lana Legend with *Variety*."

"That is *not* your name!"

The reporter frowns and looks at me. I properly vetted Lana Legend before approaching Olivia with the interview request. I read her clips to make sure she hadn't penned any hack pieces.

"This is definitely Lana Legend," I say.

"What a fab name!" Olivia claps her hands. "Is it your real name or a pen name?"

"Real."

The reporter takes a seat in the empty armchair between us. Olivia introduces me as her best friend and assistant extraordinaire, orders another round of Grande Dames, and the interview gets underway.

I listen to the first few questions—softballs about Olivia's childhood—but am too acutely aware of Xavier's presence in the bar, and his hankie lying in my lap, to focus on anything as mundane as a Hollywood interview. I try not to stare, but my gaze keeps drifting from Lana Legend to Xavier.

About an hour into the interview, Xavier stands and shakes hands with his companion. I watch him leave the bar out of the corner of my eye.

"This might be a good place for us to stop," Lana says. "Our photographer is waiting on the upper deck so he can get a few pictures of you for the piece. You don't have to worry about a thing though, we have a stylist and a makeup artist."

"Just give me a minute," Olivia says. "I will be up after I have a word with Manderley."

"Sure," Lana says, gathering her notebook and recorder. "Take your time."

Lana hurries out of the bar.

"You don't have to stick around for the photo shoot if you don't want to," Olivia says.

"Are you sure?"

"Yes. I know how much you hate photo shoots. I hate them, too."

"No, you don't."

"No, I don't," she says, laughing. "Go, have some fun. I will meet you in the room later. Maybe we can go for a swim and plan our adventures in Monte."

Olivia drains the last of her cocktail, swipes a slash of red lipstick over her lips, and blows me an air kiss.

I stand to leave when I notice Reed Harrington headed my way. Several other personal assistants trail behind her. Reed is a personal assistant to three-time Academy Award–winning actor Alec Elkins, star of *A Quaint Mileu*. She gives the impression of being quiet and demure, but don't let her purring fool you. She is a panther. If you cross her, she will rip your heart out with her claws, feast on your carcass, and use your bones as toothpicks. I sit back down, whip out my iPhone, and pretend to be absorbed in a text. If I am lucky, they will walk right by me.

"Manderley!" Reed purrs. "Is that you?"

I guess I am not lucky.

"Yes." I say, standing quickly. "Hello, Reed. How are you?"

"I am fab, just fab. Sit back down," she commands,

claiming the seat beside me. "You're not going any-where."

"I'm not?"

She shakes her head and her long, glossy red hair spills like molten copper over her shoulders and down her back. The other assistants situate themselves around Reed, like sycophants paying court to a monarch.

"I know for a fact that Olivia is having her picture taken by a photog from *Variety*, which means you are free to join us for a drink."

Reed knows everything. She is a major authority on the industry, with contacts stretching from Hollywood to Bollywood. She arrived in Los Angeles when she was sixteen with her best friend, popular teen singer/actress Jessie Lee. When Disney Darling Jessie was caught by the paparazzi snorting cocaine in a club, Reed ditched her BFF and took a job as one of a legion of assistants to a major director of action-adventure flicks. Alec Elkins starred in one of the director's films and was so im-pressed with Reed he lured her away.

Apparently, loyalty isn't Reed's thing.

"What are you drinking?" she asks, gesturing to my cocktail glass.

"Grande Dame," I mumble.

A waiter appears. Reed orders champagne for every-one and introduces me to her friends. There's Josh Har-rell, personal assistant to an A-list actress famous for her toothy grin and long legs; Loren Knight, executive assis-tant to the president of a major production company; Gillian Davis, personal assistant and tour coordinator to a pop diva/actress; Reilly Altmann, personal assistant to a network chairman, and Sköda, a personal assistant who tells me she is "contractually forbidden from mentioning her employer by name."

I sit quietly, listening as Josh talks about his desire to one day direct movies. Gillian shares her ten-year plan for "conquering Hollywood." Loren confesses working as an executive assistant is merely the first rung in her climb up the production company ladder. Reed wants to be an actress—a "serious" actress.

Hollywood should be renamed Wannabe, because it is filled with people who wannabe something more than they are. Waitresses who wannabe actresses. Secondary actors who wannabe leading actors. Celeb husbands who wannabe producers. Second directors who wannabe lead directors. Visual effects editors who wannabe visual effects supervisors. Stunt performers who wannabe stunt coordinators.

Personal assistants? They are the queens and kings of Wannabe. They wannabe close to power players. They wannabe famous. They wannabe rich. They wannabe married to a celeb.

Most people don't know it, but a celebrity's personal assistant wields a lot of power. They are the gatekeepers to the Golden Ones. Nobody gets to Angelina Jolie or Brad Pitt without first speaking to one of their assistants.

Sure, it is an exhausting, oftentimes demeaning job. Hollywood personal assistants must be willing to sacrifice their personal lives because they are required to be available 24/7. George Clooney's assistant even lives in a house on his property! They spend their days catering to the whims of A-listers and power players. They charge cell phones, make Starbucks runs, administer enemas (true story), arrange childcare, book meetings, deal with bat-shit crazy agents, hustle to get tables at the hottest new restaurants, procure prostitutes . . . the list is endless.

But every once in a while, a PA gets a big payoff. Scooter Braun, the music mogul who discovered Justin

Bieber and Carly Rae Jepsen, promoted his assistant to a supervisory role within his record company. Sarah Jessica Parker gave her assistant an associate producer credit on *Sex and the City*. Jessica Simpson's assistant, CaCee Cobb, became a popular Hollywood party girl before settling down with an actor.

After listening to Reed talk (and talk), it is obvious she believes her big payoff is imminent.

"Don't tell anyone," she says, raising her voice an octave. "But, last week I read for a part in the new Stephane Goldberg movie."

"The World War II picture?" Loren asks.

Reed nods her head.

"I heard Tom Cruise is the lead," Josh says.

"It's definitely not Tom Cruise"—she smiles smugly—"but the lead star is major!"

She pronounces it *may-jah*.

"Did you read with him?"

Reed nods her head. "Halfway through my third callback, I suddenly realized I was living most of the world's wish fulfillment. It was surreal—even by Hollywood standards. I know he has a reputation for being douchetastic, but—"

"If it is who I think it is, he has unprecedented levels of douchebaggery," Josh interrupts. "I've heard he has a fifteen-page rider that includes things like Cuban cigars, special bath oil made in the Yucatán Peninsula, and a separate trailer for his bullmastiff."

"I've heard he insists that everyone working in craft service must wear a uniform made of natural fibers," Loren adds. "He hates manmade fibers."

"I've heard he has a thing for bald-headed, toothless male prostitutes," Reilly adds.

"Me too," Gillian agrees.

Sköda remains tight-lipped.

The conversation turns to Cannes nightlife.

"Bâoli is *the* spot," Reed sniffs. "A-listers and Saudi princes hang out there—people with enough money to afford magnums of Krug Private Cuvée and Moët et Chandon Dom Pérignon."

"I went to Le For You last night," Loren says. "Gigi was there and she looked fierce. She had on Gucci leather leggings and thigh-high suede boots. That girl can dance."

Josh sniffs. "I prefer Gotha, at the Cap de la Croisette. The DJs are next level. Naked dancers writhe around on pink velvet chaise lounges and muscular waiters carry flaming bottles of champagne. And, their VIP rooms are the best in Cannes."

When Reed launches into another high-octane, narcissism-fueled conversation—it's all about Reed, Reed, Reed—I suddenly feel as if the walls are closing in around me, pressing against my back and chest, squeezing the air from my lungs. I can't breathe. My neck feels prickly hot, the kind of prickly hot that comes from a rash.

I look down at my iPhone and pretend I have received an important text.

"I have to go," I mumble, grabbing my purse. "Sorry."

I practically run out of the bar and I keep running out of the hotel, across the Boulevard de la Croisette, until I am standing on the beach, staring out at the sea. I kick off my shoes, wiggle my toes in the warm sand, close my eyes, and take several deep breaths. When the claustrophobic feeling subsides, I slip my feet back into my shoes and climb the stairs leading to the Promenade de la Croisette, a wide, paved walkway that hugs the coastline from one end of Cannes to the other.

During the Festival, the Promenade was crowded with

gawkers, paparazzi, and members of the press, separated from the celebrities by crush barriers. Tonight, it is deserted.

I let my purse dangle from my wrist and stroll the promenade, away from the hotels and luxury shops, in the direction of the marina.

I am leaning against a low stone wall, watching the yachts bobbing in the harbor, their silvery lights reflecting on the water like a thousand diamonds, when someone tries to yank my purse from my wrist. I clutch the strap and turn around. My attacker is a tall, skinny teenager with broken teeth and eyes as black as his long hair. He is bare chested and reeks of urine.

"Let go," he growls, violently tugging the purse strap from my hand. *"Salope."*

I scream.

With his free hand, he shoves me hard right between my breasts, knocking the air from my lungs. I almost fall back over the stone wall and into the water, but another hand grabs my arm and holds me steady.

I hear the teen curse again in French and realize he is now engaged in a tug of war over my purse with the person holding my arm. The strap breaks. The thief curses and runs away. Only then do I have the opportunity to look at my rescuer.

"Xavier!"

"Are you hurt?"

His deep voice wraps around me like a cashmere blanket and I shiver.

I shake my head.

"Are you certain?"

"Yes."

"Thank God. I am afraid the same cannot be said of your purse."

He hands me my purse and I wrap the strap around my wrist and tuck it under my arm.

"What are you doing out here, alone, you silly fool? Don't you know the marina is prime hunting grounds for pickpockets?"

"I am a fool," I say, my voice wavering. "The valet warned me to be careful around the marina, but . . ."

"But, you have a death wish. Is that it?"

"No." Heat flushes my cheeks as I realize the picture I must make, an American woman, strolling alone, at night, in an unlit section of the marina. "I wanted to be alone."

To my humiliation, my legs begin to tremble.

He sighs and runs his hand through his hair. "I understand your desire to be alone," he says, softening his tone. "Truly, I do. But you have to know you could have been robbed or . . . worse. Much worse."

Tears spill down my cheeks. He is going to think I am an overwrought woman prone to weeping, but I can't stop the emotions surging through my body.

"Come along then," he says, protectively placing his arm around my shoulders. "I will see you safely to the hotel."

We leave the marina and follow the promenade back to the hotel. We step through the revolving door and into the dimly lit lobby, pausing at the stairs leading to the elevators.

"This is the third time you have come to my rescue, monsieur."

"Xavier."

"Xavier," I say, smiling shyly. "How will I ever thank you?"

"Don't be ridiculous."

I remember Olivia's admonition and pluck up the courage to invite him for a drink.

"Can I at least buy you a drink?"

He looks over at a beautiful brunette in towering red-soled heels who has just walked into the lobby and nods his head at her. She narrows her gaze, like a cat eyeing a mouse she plans to eviscerate.

"Perhaps another time," he says.

"Of course." I jab the elevator button so he can't see the color rising in my cheeks. "You have more important things to do than go for drinks with a foolish American. How silly of me."

His expression alters to something shadowy and unreadable. Anger. Disgust. Boredom. Pity. I cannot tell. He stares into my eyes as if my expression is equally unreadable. The elevator dings and the doors slide open. I hurry inside.

"Another time, then."

And for the second time in the space of a few hours, elevator doors close, separating me from the most handsome, intriguing, and frightening man I have ever met, leaving me alone with my humiliation and longing.

Chapter Three

Text from Emma Lee Maxwell:
  You'll never guess what I woke to this morning. Flashing lights and an annoying back-up beeper. The dealership sent a tow truck to repossess my Lexus. Did you know Daddy leased my car? He BOUGHT Tara's car. Why would he lease mine? What am I going to do? How will I get around? Oh the humanity!

Text from Tara Maxwell:
  I need your help thinking of a birthday gift for Callie. Her birthday is next week. What is the perfect gift for the world's best friend?

"Would you be a love and ask housekeeping to send up more of that Fragonard body wash? It's to die." Olivia pops her toweled head through the door connecting her terrace suite to my room, squinting against the bright morning light streaming in through the open curtains. "Then, call room service and order a Bloody Mary with three shots of Tabasco and the greasiest breakfast on the menu. And would you pop down to the gift shop and buy a bottle of ibuprofen and box of Alka-Seltzer?"

"Absolutely."

"Have you had breakfast yet?"

"I was waiting for you. You asked me to make brunch reservations at La Plage, remember?"

"Did I? When?"

"Last night, when you woke me up."

"Oh, well," she says, pressing her fingers against her temple, "I have a crushing hangover. You can order something from room service, if you like, or go to La Plage by yourself."

"Are you sure?"

"Go," she says, stumbling into my room and collapsing on my bed. "I am suffering with the Grande Dame flu. Acute chills, headache, and nausea from overexposure to champagne and gin."

I walk into my bathroom, grab a fresh washcloth from the counter, turn on the cold water, and hold the cloth under the stream. Wringing out the cloth, I walk back to the bed and press it to Olivia's clammy forehead.

"Ugh!" She groans. "Etienne should be shot."

"Who?"

"Etienne," she repeats. "The hotel's drink wizard. The one who created the Grande Dame. Wasn't that what your Monsieur X called him? "

"Emanuele," I correct. "And he is not *my* Monsieur X."

"So you say." She cracks open an eye and looks at me from beneath the edge of the washcloth, her lips curling in a teasing smile. "Yet, when I came looking for you last night, you were nowhere to be found. *Scandaleux.*"

"Scan-dah-lou?"

"Scandalous *en français.*"

"When did you look for me?"

"After the photo shoot." She closes her eye. "Lana invited me to a club and I came up to see if you wanted to join us."

"Oh."

"Oh, indeed! So, where were you?"

"I must have been in the bar. After you left, I ran into Reed Harrington."

"Try again."

"What?"

"I went to the bar first. I saw Reed. She said you got a mysterious text and hurried off." She pulls the washcloth down over her eyes and moans. "You dirty, dirty girl. Did the French catnip do the trick? Has your inner sex-kitty been unleashed?"

Heat flushes my cheeks. I jump up and hurry over to a basket of fruit sitting on my dresser. I take a banana out of the basket, remove half of the peel, and walk back to the bed.

"Here," I say, handing the banana to Olivia. "Lie on your right side and eat this."

Olivia throws the washcloth on the floor and rolls onto her right side, squinting up at me.

"Your daddy's hangover cure?"

I nod my head.

She grabs the banana and takes a bite. "You're the best," she says. "I don't deserve you. You know I love you more than Michael Fassbender, right?"

"What about Bradley Cooper?"

"Definitely."

"But not more than Cary Grant?"

"Never."

We laugh. This has been our routine since college. Back then, it was Josh Hartnett and Zac Efron.

Olivia reaches out and grabs my hand. "Say it."

"Say what?"

"Say you love me back."

"Lawd, you are so needy."

Olivia squeezes my hand. "Pleeease?"

"Fine." I sigh. "I love you."

"More than Jon Hamm?"

"Absolutely."

"More than Jake Gyllenhaal?"

"Usually."

She finishes the banana and hands me the peel, grinning, and I know what she is about to say.

"More than Monsieur X?"

I knew it! I knew she was going to mention Xavier. I grab the banana peel and toss it into the waste can on my way out the door. "I am going to get your ibuprofen and Alka-Seltzer."

"Wait!"

I turn around. "What?"

"Do you love me more than Monsieur X?"

"Never."

She bursts out laughing and then grabs her head, moaning in pain. I close the door with a soft click.

When I return fifteen minutes later, Olivia has crawled back into her own bed and is snoring softly. I tiptoe into her room and deposit the pills, a large bottle of water, and a silk eye mask on her nightstand. I tiptoe out of the room and into the hallway to wait for room service. It arrives seconds later. I sign the bill and carry the tray into Olivia's room, arranging the Bloody Mary and fluffy omelet with strips of greasy bacon on the table in the sitting room. I tiptoe over to my friend.

"Olivia?" I whisper. "I have your medicine."

Olivia wakes with a start. "Has room service arrived?"

"Yes. It is in the sitting room."

"Thank God."

She throws the covers back and carefully climbs out of bed. We are walking into the sitting room when someone knocks loudly on the suite door. Olivia grabs her head and moans.

Knock. Knock. Knock.

"Make it stop. For the love of George Clooney, make it stop!"

I hurry across the room and open the door.

A valet is holding a large, glossy, white Dior shopping bag with triangles of silvery white tissue paper protruding from the top.

"Bonjour, madame," he says, thrusting the bag at me. "The concierge instructed me to deliver this to you."

"Merci," I say, taking the bag and closing the door.

"What is it?" Olivia calls.

I carry the bag by its silky white rope handles over to the table and hand it to her. "You received a package."

"Ooo!" Olivia says, clapping her hands. "You know how I love prezzies! I wonder who sent it."

She tears the tissue out of the bag and throws it in the air, a cyclone of silvery paper swirling around us. A thick white gift card falls at my feet with the tissue paper. I pick the card up and hand it to Olivia. She turns the card over. Her eyes widen and she looks at me with her mouth open.

"What?"

"Here," she says, handing me the card. "It's for you."

I take the card and stare at my name scrawled across the front of the envelope in bold, loopy handwriting. My heart thuds wildly and I press a hand to my chest.

Manderley Maxwell. It definitely says Manderley Maxwell. Sliding my finger inside the back of the envelope, I tear through the thick paper and remove the card.

You came to the South of France with so many wonderful dreams, didn't you, Cécile? I hope what happened last night hasn't spoiled them. If it did, I hope this gift will restore your faith in the beauty of my country and the generosity of my people.

X.

P.S. I selected this color because it reminded me of your eyes. If you don't like it, please visit the Dior boutique beside the hotel and they will make sure you get something you like.

"Well, don't keep me in suspense!" Olivia cries. "What does the card say? Who sent it? Was it Monsieur X?"

I hand Olivia the card. Her eyes dart back and forth as she reads Xavier's words. She finishes reading, looks at me, and reads the card again.

"Who is Cécile? What happened last night?"

"I was mugged."

"What? Where?"

"Near the marina."

"Oh my God, Mandy!" Olivia says. "You could have been raped or murdered and it would have been all my fault."

"Your fault? Why?"

She rests her elbows on the table and cradles her forehead in her hands, pushing her palms against her closed eyes.

"I am a crap best friend."

"No, you're not."

"Yes, I am." She sniffles. "I have been so caught up in writing and preparing for the Festival, I have turned into a CC Bloom."

CC Bloom is the lead character in *Beaches,* the movie we watch when we need a good ugly cry. In the movie,

CC Bloom and Hillary Whitney meet when they are young girls. Despite their different backgrounds, they become best friends . . . until CC's ego pushes them apart. Olivia mimics one of CC's most hilarious, egotistical scenes.

I laugh softly, because I do not want to hurt Olivia's feelings, but the truth is, she has been demanding and just a little self-absorbed.

"You haven't been *that* bad."

"Yes, I have! You almost died last night. You could have been shanked and tossed in the bay. Your body would have washed up on the shore and the *gendarmes* would have called me down to identify you." She is crying now. *"Yes, Officer, that is my best friend, Manderley Maxwell. She was in Cannes because I am a selfish, narcissistic twatwaffle, and if I hadn't been letting some photographer stroke my ego, I would have been there to save her from the shanking."*

"Ew! That is a disgusting word."

She looks up, sniffling. "Which word? Shanking?"

I tilt my head and narrow my gaze, giving her my best *seriously* look.

"Twatwaffle?"

"Olivia!"

"Too graphic?"

"Too revolting."

"It is rather revolting, isn't it?" She laughs, brushing the tears from her cheeks. "I heard Alec Elkins use it on set when he was talking about his ex-wife. If he wasn't such a brilliant actor, I think he would have been thrown out of Hollywood years ago for being a volatile, egotistical, misanthropic ass. Still, I rather like that word—"

"Please don't say it again!"

She laughs. "I am glad you weren't hurt last night,"

she says, sobering. "I don't know what I would do without you. Who else could put up with CC but Hillary?"

I reach for her hand across the table, squeezing it. "You're being too hard on yourself, Olivia."

"No, I am not," she says. "You have been so busy helping me launch my writing career, you've barely had time to launch your own, let alone deal with the grief of losing your father and aunt. I am sorry, truly. I want you to be happy."

"What makes you think I am not happy?"

"Puh-leez," she says, absentmindedly stirring her Bloody Mary with the stalk of celery protruding from the glass. "I am your best friend."

I remain silent because I don't want to plaster a false smile on my face and lie to my best friend. I am not happy. I haven't been happy for years, even before my father's death. I yearn for something I can't even name. Freedom. Independence. Adventure. Romance. I don't know. Something bigger, more rewarding, than administering homeopathic hangover cures and editing someone else's writing. Even if that someone else is my best friend. I can't say these things to Olivia, though, not without hurting her feelings. Several seconds pass with Olivia staring glumly at the pulpy red liquid swirling in her glass.

"I promise to be a better friend. I will support you in your writing the way you have supported me. If you want to quit and finish your novel, I will find another assistant. When you finish your book, I will help you find an agent or an editor. I swear."

"Thank you, Olivia. That means a lot."

She stops swirling and smiles. "Now," she says, pushing the Dior bag across the table, "let's see what you got."

It takes me a moment to understand what she is saying.

I look at the large white bag with the Dior name embossed in gray, a sheer white and gray bow attached to the handle, and my heart skips a beat.

I reach into the bag and remove a lambskin purse the color of leaden skies over a foggy sea, an indefinable, mutable color that is not blue, nor is it gray. A large, iconic silver Dior charm logo is attached to one handle.

"Ooo!" Olivia coos. "That's the Lady Dior bag in *hiver bleu-gris*. Jealous."

Hiver bleu-gris. Winter blue-gray.

I place the purse back in the bag.

"What are you doing?"

"I can't keep it."

"What?" Olivia snatches the purse back out of the bag and holds it to her chest as if cradling an infant. "Why not?"

"It's too lavish."

"Darling," she says, thrusting the purse back into my arms, "a gift given from the heart can never be too lavish."

"So you think I should accept a four-thousand-dollar—"

"Five," she excitedly interjects. "The Lady Dior medium in lambskin with *cannage* topstitching is five thousand four hundred dollars!"

"I can't accept a five-thousand-dollar gift from a stranger," I say, putting the purse back in the bag again.

Olivia came from a poor family, while I grew up the daughter of an extremely wealthy man and the recipient of a generous trust fund from my momma. I have had designer bags and clothes. They don't mean as much to me as they do to Olivia. I would trade all of my worldly possessions to spend one more day with my momma and daddy.

"There are two gifts you never return: diamonds and designer handbags, darling."

I roll my eyes, because I know this is part of Olivia's urbane-LA-woman shtick.

"You're killing me here, Manderley. Kill-ing." She lifts her glass and drains half of her Bloody Mary in a single swallow, wipes her mouth with a napkin, and fixes me with a determined gaze. "Did Scarlett return the hat Rhett bought her in Paris?

"No."

"Did Vivian return the designer clothes Edward bought her in *Pretty Woman*?"

"She was a prostitute, Olivia!"

Olivia dismisses my objection with a wave of her manicured hand. "Did Holly Golightly refuse the gifts her many beaus gave her in *Breakfast at Tiffany's*?"

"Again, call girl."

Olivia sighs and rubs her temple with two fingers. "Last time I checked, you are not a call girl, so I don't think your Monsieur X is using a Dior purse to lure you into an immoral arrangement."

"You don't?" I bat my eyelashes and make duck lips with my mouth.

"Be serious, Mandy. You don't look anything like the high-priced call girls that service the rich and famous here in the South of France."

"How do you know what high-priced French call girls look like?"

"I saw *Priceless*!"

"That was a movie, Olivia. Not real life."

"Movies often mimic real life."

"Okay," I say, speaking to her as I would my slightly vapid younger sister, Emma Lee. "But the high-priced call girl in that movie was played by Audrey Tautou, who is stunning. I doubt there are any call girls that beautiful."

"Exactly!"

I shake my head to clear the cobwebs of confusion spun by Olivia's ridiculous logic. We have always had vastly different approaches to love and life, but Olivia's unorthodox approach is one of the reasons she is so precious to me. She challenges me to peek outside of my rigid box. While I come from a place of *maybe, if*, Olivia comes from a place of *yes!*

"So you are saying I should model my behavior after two fictional call girls and keep this expensive purse?"

"I'm saying, little Miss Literal"—she points her celery stick at me—"you are searching for a hidden, nefarious motive behind this gift when there might not be one, which, I think, says more about *you* than him."

"Meaning?"

"You don't think you are worthy of extravagant kindnesses, Manderley. Maybe it was losing your mother at a young age or growing up the eldest of three girls, but somewhere down the line you decided you needed to put your wishes last."

Olivia is right. I do put my wishes last, because that is what my mother did, and all I have ever wanted to be is a strong, silent, pleasing Southern woman. Like my momma.

"There is something else to consider," Olivia says.

"What's that?"

"Maybe Xavier is a good guy." She finishes her Bloody Mary before speaking again. "Maybe your chance encounter on the cliff the other day was the beginning of your happily-ever-after; maybe it was your meet cute."

My meet cute. Leave it to Olivia to see a potential screenplay in a meaningless encounter. I can hear the trailer voice-over. *Sometimes, when you're standing on the edge of a cliff, you might need Fate to give you a little push. Manderley Maxwell, Xavier No Last Name, in . . .* Falling for You.

My stomach growls and I press my hand to my abdomen.

"Was that your stomach or your inner sex-kitten letting out a satisfied meow?" Olivia wiggles her eyebrows.

"My stomach. I am starving."

"Go to La Plage, have brunch. You will see things more clearly after you eat something."

"Do you want to join me?"

She pops a piece of bacon in her mouth before stumbling back to her bed. She climbs beneath the covers and snatches the eye mask off the nightstand. "No," she says, pulling the mask over her head. "I need more time to recover from the Grande Dames."

"If you're sure."

"I'm sure."

I gather the gift card, Dior bag, and purse, and tiptoe across the suite into my room. I am about to close the connecting door when Olivia's voice follows me.

"Diamonds and designer handbags, darling."

Chapter Four

La Plage Barrière Majestic is one of the restaurants attached to the hotel's private beach club, a posh place with sweeping views of the Mediterranean, a VIP area, a nautical center with watercraft, and hundreds of sun loungers and parasols artfully situated on the narrow swath of sand. Billowy white curtains and potted paradise palms act as a partition, sectioning the restaurant from the rest of the club. Black-and-white photographs of movie stars decorate the walls over banquettes strewn with plump pillows and sleek white Scandinavian tables.

The maître d' greets me with a closemouthed smile. *"Bonjour, mademoiselle."*

"Bonjour," I say. "Manderley Maxwell. I have a reservation."

He taps the home button on the iPad in his hands and slides his finger down the screen. "Had."

"I beg your pardon?"

"Your reservation was for 11:45, not 12:02," he says, shrugging. "I am sorry, mademoiselle, but when you didn't arrive, we offered your table to another party."

"Manderley?"

I turn at the sound of my name. Reed and two of the wannabes are crowded around a small table set for two.

My table.

Reed waggles her long, manicured fingers in a Hollywood wave, a smarmy smile curling her heavily painted lips. I apologize to the maître d' and walk over to Reed.

"Good Morning, Reed."

"Manderley! Do you have a reservation? We were lucky enough to snag this table after the loser who booked it was a no-show. Score, right? So, what are *you* doing here?"

The wannabes, and several guests lounging on nearby tanning beds, focus their attention on me. Scorching heat spreads from my cheeks to my sandaled feet, an effect not caused by the Mediterranean sun.

"I was going to have brunch"—I ignore the pitying stares of the beautiful lounging people and focus my gaze on Reed—"but it appears I missed my reservation and there's not a table available."

"Bum-mer! I would invite you join us, but there isn't enough room. Sorry." She draws the last word out, placing special emphasis on the ending *ee* sound, so it sounds like *SOR-eeee*. "Buh-bye!"

The wannabes snigger.

My fight-or-flight response kicks in—actually it is only my flight response—and I turn around so fast I collide with a waiter carrying a tray of mimosas. The champagne glasses tip over, spilling their orange liquid down the front of the waiter's white shirt.

Reed snickers. The wannabes giggle. I want to let the sun melt me so I can slide down to the ground and between the cracks in the patio. I am about to run away when I feel the warm pressure of a hand on the small of my back.

"There you are," Xavier murmurs in my ear. "I hoped to see you this morning. Come. You will join me, won't you?"

"I wouldn't want to impose."

"Nonsense."

His hand still on the small of my back, he leads me over to his table, but not before I catch Reed's open mouth and wide eyes. He pulls a chair out for me and I sit on the edge of the seat, my back stiff, my hands clutched nervously in my lap.

"Thank you," I say, once he is seated across from me. "You didn't need to do that, you know?"

"Do what?" His flinty gaze remains focused on my face and I realize he is being gallant, pretending as if he didn't hear Reed humiliate me. "Don't you want to have breakfast with me?"

"Of course I do!"

He smiles and I realize how eager, how naïve I must appear to this urbane Frenchman.

A waiter appears. I order scrambled eggs and a pot of tea. While Xavier orders a cappuccino and toast, I look at his angular face, broad shoulders, and strong, tanned forearms. He is wearing only a T-shirt and a pair of Dolce & Gabbana boat shorts, but he holds himself with such dignity and self-assurance you would think he was posing for a high-fashion magazine shoot. When the waiter finishes taking his order and bows away, Xavier turns his full attention on me.

"Your friends," he says, nodding his head to indicate Reed and the wannabes, "they don't look like the sort of people you would associate with."

I steal a quick glance over my shoulder at Reed, her glossy, Alex Polillo–styled, honey-blond hair hanging down her back, and self-consciously smooth my side-swept bangs.

"They aren't my friends."

"Why not?"

"Because I don't care to spend my evenings getting drunk on expensive champagne at Bâoli in the hope I will meet someone who can advance my career," I say, my shyness momentarily replaced by my indignation. "And because I believe a person's worth should be measured by their morality, not by the amount of plastic surgery they've had or the number of designer dresses hanging in their closet."

"You're awfully young to be so jaded."

"Living in Los Angeles can do that to a person."

"A person of quality," he says, smiling so that dimples appear on each of his stubbly cheeks. "I am glad you don't want to spend your nights at Bâoli."

"You are?"

"Very. I have formed a picture of you and I shouldn't like it ruined by learning you dance on top of tables to EDM."

I am suddenly and painfully aware of my simple cotton sundress and my mother's conservative pearl studs at my ears and imagine the composite he has mentally drawn of me to be drab, boring. A bookish sort of girl in tortoiseshell glasses. The sort you sip tea with, not guzzle champagne with and dance until dawn. Self-conscious, I focus my attention on the napkin lying across my lap, twisting one corner around my pointer finger.

"I meant that as a compliment."

"You did?" I look up and am surprised to discover him staring at me earnestly, a gentle, almost compassionate smile curving his lips.

"Of course."

"Thank you."

"You're welcome."

His unexpected compliment has the same effect on me as when I stepped out of the air-conditioned hotel lobby into the warm, sultry sunshine. I want to stretch and bask in it, prolong the wonderful sensation. "There is something I must thank you for."

"What is that?"

"Your gift. The purse."

"You like it, then?"

"It is lovely."

"And yet, you are not carrying it." He fixes me with an unreadable, unnervingly direct gaze. "Perhaps you think it too generous a gift?"

"Well, yes."

"It would only be too generous if I couldn't afford it, but I can. Besides, you looked sad last night and I thought a gift might cheer you up." His gaze alters, his eyes darken and his lips press together in a thin line. "It has been my experience that, no matter how low they may be, a woman's sagging spirits can be lifted with a gift."

The air leaves my lungs in a rush. That statement says as much about Xavier as it does about the women he has known. "Perhaps that is true of some women, but . . ."

"But?"

"But I am not like most women. I know it probably sounds old-fashioned and hopelessly lame, but I am like Marianne Dashwood from Jane Austen's *Sense and Sensibility*. I would much prefer a man to read me poetry than buy me hot-house flowers."

He leans back in his chair and chuckles as if I said something humorous. The sound nettles me and makes me sad all at once. What a bleak view he has of women . . . *of me*.

"You gave me something far more valuable than a designer handbag, monsieur," I whisper, my cheeks flushing with heat. "You gave me your compassion and security. For that, I will forever be in your debt."

He stares at me for several uncomfortable seconds and when he speaks again, the hard edge to his voice has dulled. "No, I don't think you are like other women, Manderley Maxwell. Not at all."

A new wave of heat floods my cheeks. I look down at the napkin I am clutching in my hands. My palms are sweaty and my knuckles white. I release my hold on the napkin, spread it on my lap, and smooth the wrinkles away.

"Stop fidgeting," Xavier commands. "There is no reason for you to be nervous. And, please, stop calling me *monsieur*."

"What should I call you?"

"Why, Xavier, of course."

The waiter arrives with our food.

"Ah, here is our breakfast."

I busy myself with pouring tea from a small silver pot into my cup and adding two packets of sugar.

"You take your tea sweet?"

I look up. His expression has altered again, rapidly, unexpectedly, like the weather along the Côte d'Azur. The dark clouds behind his gaze have drifted away, leaving bright blue.

"Guilty," I say, smiling. "You can take the girl out of the South, but you can never take the South out of the girl."

"You're from the South? I wouldn't have guessed. You don't have an accent."

"I lost it while I was in New York."

"What were you doing in New York?"

"Attending college. I graduated with a degree in literature from Columbia University."

He looks up from his cappuccino and smiles enigmatically. "You are a dark horse, aren't you?"

"What do you mean?"

"Never mind." He takes a sip of his cappuccino. "Go on now, eat your scrambled eggs before they grow cold."

When I have finished my eggs and Xavier his toast, we sip our drinks quietly, staring out at the sea. It's not one of those awkward silences often present when strangers are becoming acquainted.

Xavier pushes his empty cappuccino cup away and leans back in his chair, staring at me as if I am a puzzle he wants desperately to solve.

"How do you spend your time—that is, when you are not acting as Olivia Tate's life preserver?"

It takes me a few seconds to answer, not because I am lacking in interests, but because I have spent the last four years living in a narcissistic bubble called Los Angeles, a bubble inflated with the hot air produced by people talking about themselves. Nobody asks me what I like, what I think, what I feel.

"I like to read, watch old movies, and write. I also take photographs."

"You're a photographer? Are you any good?"

"Moderately." My cheeks flush with heat.

Xavier chuckles. "Are you always this refreshingly honest?"

"Of course."

He rests his elbows on the arms of his chair, steeples his fingers, and regards me with open, undisguised curiosity, as if he is not accustomed to conversing with an honest person.

"What about you?" I say, smiling. "What do you like to do?"

"*Pfff!* You don't want to hear about me. I live a relatively boring existence."

"I can't believe that."

"Why not?" he snaps, narrowing his gaze. "Have you heard something?"

What an odd question. "No," I say, clutching my napkin. "What could I have heard?"

"It doesn't matter." He reaches for the leather bill presenter the waiter left on our table and scrawls his name across the bottom of the check.

"Please, won't you let me pay for breakfast?" I say, reaching for my wallet. "It's the least I could do."

"Don't be absurd." He stands suddenly, circling around the table and pulling my chair out. "Shall we?"

We walk back toward the hotel together, crossing through the park. A gilded carousel with painted horses stands in the center. I must have rushed through this square at least two dozen times throughout the Festival— on my way to screenings at the Palais des Festivals et des Congrès—but I never paused to appreciate the festive mood.

I stop walking and watch the carousel spin around and around, feeling wistful for my youth and grateful finally to have a few moments to stop, breathe, and enjoy the moment.

Xavier stops walking, too. "Is something the matter?"

"No."

"Then come along," he says, cupping my elbow.

"Not yet," I say, smiling up at him. "Please."

He releases his hold on my elbow and we stand side by side, watching the blinking lights and listening to the bubbling Wurlitzer music.

"Have you ever ridden on this carousel?"

"Non."

"Would you like to?"

He frowns slightly. "How old are you?"

The note of accusation in his question makes me feel like a foolish, wide-eyed child. I start to walk again, but he grabs my elbow again.

"I am twenty-seven," I say. "How old are *you*?"

"Thirty-six."

"Thirty-six? So old?"

"Ancient as Lascaux," he says, chuckling. "Go ahead, ask me the significance of the famous shaft scene."

Most people outside of France probably haven't heard of Lascaux, the complex labyrinth of caves located in southwestern France famous for their Paleolithic cave drawings. I, however, read *The Cave Painters: Probing the Mysteries of the World's First Artists* by Gregory Curtis, so I know the shaft scene is the most famous of the drawings.

I laugh.

"Come on then," he says, grabbing my hand and pulling me toward the carousel. "If mademoiselle wishes to take a ride, it would be my pleasure to give her one."

My cheeks flush with heat even as I tell myself his declaration is not a double entendre.

"That's okay." I resist. "Really."

"Would you let me leave Cannes without knowing the thrill of riding a carousel?"

"Of course not. Only . . ."

"Only?"

"Are you leaving Cannes soon?"

"Why? Would you be upset if I were?"

Truthfully, I feel a strange melancholy at the thought of Xavier leaving Cannes and disappearing from my life. The heat spreads from my cheeks to the tips of my ears. I shift my gaze to my feet, to the slender straps on my sandals.

He chuckles again, as if he read my thoughts, and raises my hand to his lips.

We wait for the carousel to stop spinning and the riders to disembark. Xavier hands the carousel operator the fee. We step onto the carousel. I choose a white horse with a brightly painted saddle. Xavier lends me his hand and I climb on the horse, sitting sidesaddle. Xavier leans against the horse beside mine, crossing his arms and observing me with solemnity.

"Aren't you going to ride a horse?"

He raises an eyebrow. "I am not sure my arthritic bones could handle the excitement."

"Oh, Xavier," I say, pressing a hand to my heated cheeks. "I am sorry for calling you old. I was terribly rude."

"So you don't think I am a Neanderthal?"

I look at his thick wavy hair devoid of gray, his sparkling blue eyes framed with laugh lines, and his broad, muscular shoulders visible beneath his thin navy tee. I detect an electrifying vitality beneath his urbane, self-contained exterior, a vitality more powerful than that of men half his age.

"No, Xavier," I whisper. "You are definitely not a Neanderthal."

A smile tugs at one corner of his mouth. "Have you always enjoyed riding carousels?"

"I don't know. This is the first time I have ridden one, but I suspect I will enjoy myself. There are so few things in this world that allow one to recapture the fleeting, wondrous days of innocence. Wouldn't you agree?"

He fixes me with an inscrutable stare, and I wonder, not for the first time, what he thinks when he looks at me.

The carousel begins spinning slowly, picking up speed to match the energetic organ music blaring from the speakers. I grip the golden bar and try to avoid Xavier's intense gaze. We go around and around, until I am dizzy with the motion and with my happiness.

When the ride slows, Xavier reaches up, places his hands on my waist, and lifts me off the horse, as casually as if he had done it a hundred times before.

For a few breath-stealing seconds, we are standing so close I can feel the heat from his skin, smell the warm, spicy scent of his cologne, see the flecks of silver in his dark blue eyes. A shiver of pleasure spreads through my body.

"Did you enjoy the ride?"

His lips curl in a teasing smile and I experience that thrilling, frightening sensation one feels when they are at the top of a rollercoaster, waiting to plunge down, down, down.

"I did."

"Bon."

We step off the carousel and follow the path leading to the hotel.

"This is such a pretty square, but I wonder who Reynaldo Hahn was and why it is named after him."

"He was a composer who specialized in Mozart. He was also a decorated World War I soldier and a close friend of the French writer Guy de Maupassant," Xavier explains.

"I love Guy de Maupassant."

Xavier looks at me. "Do you? I do, too."

We cross the street and make our way to the hotel entrance. Xavier motions for me to walk first through the revolving door and then follows me.

"What are you doing now?"

"Olivia is not feeling well, so I am free for the next few hours. I thought I would stroll along the Croisette."

"How utterly pedestrian," he says, grabbing my elbow. "Come along then, we will go for a drive."

"A drive. Where?"

"Does it matter?"

"Not really, only . . ."

"Only what? Are you frightened I will ravish you?"

My cheeks flush with guilty heat.

"You are blushing. How marvelous."

"I was going to say that I need to be back before Olivia wakes up, in case she needs anything."

"Olivia is a big girl. She can fend for herself for an afternoon," he says, steering me toward the elevators. "Go on now, run upstairs and get whatever you need. I will wait for you out front."

It occurs to me, as I am standing in the elevator, humming the tune from the carousel, that Xavier's manner is, at times, old Hollywood: *Go on now. There's a good girl.*

As a modern woman living in the most progressive feminist age, I should balk at his patriarchal attitude. After all, I am not Joan Crawford and he is not Clark Gable. We are not filming a scene from *Forsaking All Others*, where I sass him and he grabs me by the waist, tosses me over his knees, and gives me a good spanking.

And yet . . .

If I am being entirely honest, deep down, I like being ordered about by Xavier.

Chapter Five

Text from Winter V. Hastings, Esquire:
Wonderful news, Manderley. Since your aunt was, indeed, a citizen of Ireland, and the property she bequeathed you is not situated in the United States, you will not have to pay gift taxes for the yacht.

"All set?"

I adjust the lap belt snugly against my abdomen and click the seat belt buckle into place. "I believe so," I say, clutching my camera lying in my lap.

Xavier smiles, wraps his long, lean fingers around the leather steering wheel, and we take off, windows down, wind whipping through my unbound hair. Xavier maneuvers the sports car through the congested streets until we arrive at the entrance to the D6185. He revs the engine and the Jaguar flies up the on-ramp. It takes only a few minutes before we are high in the hills overlooking Cannes. Xavier shifts gears and maneuvers into the fast lane.

"Manderley Maxwell."

"Yes?"

He looks over at me and I clutch my camera strap tighter. A shaft of afternoon sunlight slanting through the windshield illuminates his eyes, leaving the rest of his face hidden in menacing shadows.

"Tell me, are you always so trusting of strangers?"

My palms begin to sweat. "I . . . I don't know?"

I stare into his eyes, falling into their unfathomable depths, like a person plunging off the side of a cliff, spiraling helplessly, too paralyzed with fright to scream. He returns his gaze to the road and I relax my hold on my camera strap, wiping my damp palms on my skirt.

There is something strange about Xavier. I can't put my finger on it—just a vague feeling that he is like the cypress swamps surrounding my daddy's plantation. It is a place of beauty, with dark, still waters, magnificent trees, and leafy ferns as intricate as Belgian lace, a place of beauty filled with creatures lurking beneath the water and in the foliage. Bobcats. Coyotes. Cottonmouth snakes. Wetland gators. Fiddleback spiders.

What lurks beneath Xavier's dark, beautiful surface? Is it threatening? Or am I seeing serpents when there are only shadows? I am not usually one to let my imagination run wild. My daddy used to tell me to go with my gut.

Of course, he also used to say if commonsense were lard, my sisters wouldn't have enough between them to grease a skillet.

"What are you thinking?"

Xavier's deep voice in the quiet car startles me. I hold my camera strap, balling it up in my closed fist. "Nothing."

He looks at me.

"N . . . nothing important."

He narrows his gaze and I am reminded of that vulnerable, exposed feeling I get each time I step into the full body scanner at LAX. Guilty heat flushes my cheeks and I shift my gaze to a distant place out the front window.

"I don't believe you."

"Y . . . you don't?"

"Non." He changes lanes, races around a slow-moving Citroën SUV, and then looks back at me, reaching out and rubbing the spot between my brows with his thumb. "Now, what is causing those unsightly little lines? What worries you, *ma bichette*?"

Ma bichette. My little deer. "I am thinking how much I like the way you pronounce my name."

He smiles and, again, I feel as if I have stepped into the full body scanner. I pull the summer sweater draped over my shoulders closer together.

"I like the sound of your name: Manderley Maxwell."

My breath catches in my throat.

"Mon-de-lee," he says again, drawling it out in his slow, gravelly accent. "It's unusual. Is it a family name?"

I shake my head because the breath is stuck in my throat. One of the benefits of working as a Hollywood assistant is the opportunity to meet fantasy-worthy actors, men gorgeous without Photoshop or soft-focus filters. In the beginning, I was goggle-eyed and tongue-tied. Spend enough time around luminaries and you become impervious to their glow. Their toothy grins and smoldering gazes lose their dazzling effect.

It's different with Xavier. He thrills and terrifies me like no man has. I think I could spend the next sixty years staring at him and still feel breathless and sweaty-palmed.

"My mother loved classic novels," I whisper, my voice barely audible over the Jaguar's purring engine. "Daphne du Maurier's *Rebecca* was her favorite. Have you read it?"

"Non."

"Oh, but you must! It is a brilliant novel, truly. Maxim de Winter, the moody, mysterious protagonist, lives in a Gothic manor named Manderley."

"Your mother named you after a fictitious home?"

"Yes . . . well, you see, the opening line of the novel is famous. The narrator says she dreamt about visiting Manderley again, the hero's haunting, Gothic estate on the coast of Cornwall." I close my eyes and conjure the wispy, ghostly image of my mother, curled up beside me on my bed, reading from her dog-eared copy of *Rebecca*. "My mother had difficulty conceiving and had almost given up hope when she fell asleep watching *Rebecca*, the film adaptation starring Laurence Olivier and Joan Fontaine. Anyway, she dreamt she was walking through the gardens at Manderley, lost in the fog and sad, terribly sad. Maxim de Winter suddenly appeared out of the fog. He told her to cheer up, that she would soon be the mother of a beautiful baby girl. The next day, my mother learned she was carrying me. So, she decided to name me Manderley."

I open my eyes and blink against the bright sunlight, my mother's ghost vanishing from my mind's eye, her voice fading away like the fog.

"What a charming story."

"Yes. My mother was a charming woman."

"Was?"

"She died many years ago, when I was a child."

"I am sorry to hear that, Manderley," he says, reaching over and squeezing my hand, a fleeting touch as powerful and warming as a jolt of electricity.

"Thank you."

"Do you have any siblings?"

"Two sisters."

"And are they also named after fictitious places?"

Out of the corner of my eye I see his lips twitch in a playful, teasing smile and a satisfied warmth spreads through my body. "Tara is named after Scarlet O'Hara's cotton plantation in *Gone with the Wind*, but Emma Lee is named after Jane Austen's *Emma*."

"Your mother was fond of novels and old movies and now you work as an assistant to a woman who writes stories for movies. Interesting, the effect a parent has on a child's subconscious, especially an absent parent."

"I had never thought of that before, actually."

He glances over at me. "Hadn't you?"

I shake my head.

He smiles and looks back at the road. "My father fell ill while I was in La Royale."

"La Royale?"

"The French navy."

"You were in the navy?"

He nods. "My father's illness put an end to my dreams of being a career naval officer. I had to go home to help run the family business."

I have a difficult time imagining the polished, sophisticated Frenchman sitting beside me in anything but tailored business suits and expensive wristwatches. I am about to ask him about his family's business when he abruptly changes the subject.

"Tell me about your life in Los Angeles. Do you socialize with movie stars?"

I chuckle softly. "The Invisibles do not socialize with movie stars."

"The Invisibles?"

"The people of little consequence—anyone who isn't *someone* or married to *someone*. Actors. Directors. Producers. Agents. Writers. To them I am of little consequence, easily overlooked or dismissed, invisible. I am not wildly rich or stunningly beautiful. By Hollywood standards, I have nothing of substance. Sometimes . . ."

"Sometimes, what?"

"Nothing. It's silly."

"You don't strike me as a silly girl. Go on, then. What were you going to say?"

"Sometimes I wish I had more substance."

He looks at me, his eyes as dark and hard as obsidian stones. "You mean money?"

A trickle of unease travels down my spine.

"I do not care about money," I say, rubbing the goose-flesh that suddenly developed on my arms.

I wish I hadn't said anything. If he keeps pressing me, what will I say? That I sometimes wish I were a bold, buxom blonde with a black book full of hot guys and an over-scheduled social calendar? I wish I had more confidence than common sense.

"People of 'substance' are often the hollowest, most superficial people, incapable of giving love and without *fidélité*." Even though he is responding to something I said, I have the strange feeling he is talking to someone else. "You are a lovely and unusual person, Manderley. Do not ever let someone make you feel invisible."

"Thank you."

"You don't need to thank me!"

We drive in silence, Xavier concentrating on the traffic, while I, I replay his compliment in my head. *You are lovely and unusual, Manderley. You are lovely and unusual . . .*

"Do you attend movie premiers?"

"I beg your pardon," I say, blinking.

"I asked if you attend many movie premiers." His tone is softer, his expression less haunted, than it was moments before.

"Only Olivia's."

"But you like movies."

"Old ones, yes."

He looks at me and smiles. "Just like your *mère*."

"Yes, like my mom."

Xavier follows the signs for the D9 to Grasse.

"Why do you prefer old movies?"

"They are cleverer than today's big budget films. *Casablanca. Citizen Kane. Laura. Suspicion* with Cary Grant." I sigh. "Alfred Hitchcock conveyed more drama with his lighting than any of the modern directors do with their massive explosions or car chases. I would love to travel back in time and live in the 1940s or '50s."

"Really? Why is that?"

"It was a quieter, more elegant time."

"You prefer quiet?"

"Absolutely."

"Yet, you work in Hollywood."

"I don't plan on living there forever."

My mind flies from the bright lights and congested highways of Los Angeles to the palmetto-lined streets and pastel-colored houses of Charleston. How many times have I dreamt of packing my bags and leaving LA's smog-choked skies behind, of returning to my home-town, walking barefoot on Folly Beach while breathing in the fresh, salty air? More times than I could count.

"You mentioned you like to write. Why aren't you writing?"

"Excuse me?"

"You said you wanted to be a writer, yet you work as a writer's assistant. Why is a Columbia graduate working as a writer's assistant and not a writer?"

"Actually," I say, looking at his chiseled profile, "I wanted to be a book editor, not a writer."

"But you said you enjoy writing. Why not do it professionally?"

"I believe it was Hemingway who once said, 'There is nothing to be a writer. All you do is sit down at a typewriter and bleed.' I do not have it in me to bleed for mass consumption. I can't be that . . ."

"Yes?"

"Tough. I do not have the resilience to withstand the many agonies and ecstasies associated with professional writing."

"Perhaps you underestimate yourself."

I think of everything that has happened in the last year—the freak boating accident that claimed the lives of my father and beloved aunt, the IRS investigating and seizing my father's assets—and hot, salty tears scald my eyes. Truthfully, I don't have enough energy to juggle another ball.

"No, I am not underestimating myself," I say, my voice trembling. "I am not as tough as Olivia or as buoyant as my sisters."

"Yet you described yourself as a life preserver, an object which is, by nature, durable and buoyant."

He maneuvers the car across three lanes of traffic, weaving around vehicles, and takes the exit ramp.

"So," he says, stopping at a traffic light. "You work as an assistant, helping someone else achieve their dreams instead of achieving your own."

"Olivia is my dearest friend. She needed me."

"Are you always so eager to sacrifice your happiness for those you love?"

I frown. "I am not sure I would put it that way."

"How would you put it?" he snaps.

"Helping those I love brings me happiness. Is that such a bad thing?"

He turns to look at me and his hard expression softens slightly—so slightly I wonder if I imagined it. Then, he does something completely unexpected. He reaches out and puts his wide hand on my face, staring into my eyes. I can't look away. I am like a deer mesmerized, yet terrified, by the lights of an oncoming car.

"Non, ma bichette." He strokes my cheek with his thumb. "There is nothing wrong with being generous of spirit and heart. The world needs more selfless people. I hope you remain this way forever, even when you are an ancient, thirty-six-year-old Neanderthal."

The driver in the car behind us beeps his horn, but Xavier continues to stare at me. He removes his hand from my face, presses his fingertips to his lips, and touches the kiss to my forehead. It is the sweetest, most tender gesture a man has ever made to me.

Xavier starts driving again, but I don't hear the rev of the engine, the whine of passing traffic. I hear a romantic symphony of harps and violins playing in my head. It's silly, I know, but I am becoming dangerously infatuated with Xavier.

"Hollywood. Cannes. They aren't the most Zen-like settings, are they? Have you always longed for a quiet life or is it a consequence of your career choice?"

"I grew up with two outgoing, boisterous sisters who surrounded themselves with a giggling, squealing, chatty coterie. Believe me, I have always longed for quiet and solitude."

"What about your father? Is he sociable like your sisters, or quiet, like you?"

A lance of pain spears my heart and I inhale sharply. "I lost my father in a boating accident fifty-nine days ago." I haven't been able to talk about my father's death with anyone other than Olivia and my sisters, but I feel unusually compelled to share my grief with Xavier. He makes me feel safe. "It seems like a horrid nightmare, like maybe I will wake and discover I am sitting on the veranda with him watching the sun dip below the marsh, listening to the breeze rattle the magnolia leaves."

He takes his eyes off the road for a split second, just long enough to fix me with a breathtakingly sympathetic gaze.

"Je suis désolé, ma bichette."

His gentle voice wraps around me like a cashmere sweater and I want to pull it close, let it thaw the chill that invaded my heart upon hearing of the accident.

"You were thinking about your father the day we met on the cliff, weren't you?"

I nod. "I cannot bring myself to the realization that my father is really gone. I get up each morning, move through the day as if in a fog, and climb back into bed. It is only then, as I am lying in bed, the fog lifts a little and I am able to see my world clearly, my new world without my father." I draw in a jagged breath. "Some nights, I worry I will forget him. I lie awake recalling as many details as I can, cataloguing them in my memory. How the aroma of his cigars would fill the house at night, the cocoa- and espresso-scented cloud would drift from the sitting room up to my room. The way he insisted on wearing a bow tie and blazer even with chinos. How he went to an old barbershop off King Street twice a week for an old-fashioned blade shave. The way his face always lit up when he talked about my mother. His daily ritual of reading the Faith and Values section in the *Post and Courier* while eating biscuits and jam . . ."

I smile at the last memory. Daddy loved his biscuits and peach jam. Well, he loved Beulah's biscuits and peach jam. Beulah was our cook. Daddy used to say she could burn a bowl of cold cereal, but she made the most delicious peach jam and the fluffiest biscuits in the Carolinas. *She's keeping me as fat as a tick with jam and bread!*

Poor old Beulah. When the IRS seized Daddy's assets, including our home, Beulah was tossed out on the street with a suitcase of aprons and peach jam. I tracked her to her niece's house on Kiawah Island and promised to help her find a new employer, but she said she was sick of making biscuits and jam. *I've been busier than a moth in a mitten for as long as I can recall. I am ready to rest my tired old bones.*

"Go on, then," Xavier says, placing his hand on my knee. "You have suffered a terrible loss, *ma bichette*, and it will take you time to find your way through the grief, but talking about your father will help you keep his memory alive."

A wave of shame washes over me. I am a Southern woman, by birth and behavior. Southern women keep conversations interesting and light. They do not share personal problems with strangers or burden others with their problems.

"Do not worry about me," I say, crossing my legs so Xavier is forced to remove his hand. "I will be fine. I worry about my sisters, though."

Xavier respects my conversational barrier. He doesn't try to crawl under it or push through it the way others might, and it makes me like him even more.

"Tell me about your sisters. Are they older or younger than you?"

"Tara is twenty-five and Emma Lee is twenty-three. Tara works for a news station in Charleston, filming segments about local restaurants and recipes. She loves to cook and talk, so it is the perfect job for her. She makes friends easily and thrives on her connections. She is relaxed and easygoing. She is the peacemaker, the people-pleaser. She is also extremely sensitive. I worry that she cares what others think too much."

"And Emma Lee?"

"Emma Lee," I say, sighing. "How do I begin to explain the marvelous, maddening Emma Lee Maxwell? She's the baby. Our mother died shortly after Emma Lee's birth and my father compensated by coddling and spoiling her. She learned early on how to manipulate people to get what she wants and she can be extremely self-centered."

A memory of Emma Lee curling her bottom lip and batting her long blond eyelashes at our father pops into my brain. *But Daddy, Annabelle Ashland's momma is letting her go to New York to pick out a dress for the debutante ball. If I had a momma, she would be helping me choose a gown. Please, Daddy, please let me go to New York with Annabelle.*

"It sounds as if you don't care for your sister much."

"What?" I blink and the memory disappears. "Does it? I am sorry then. I didn't mean to paint her with such an unflattering brush, truly. I love Emma Lee. She's is a whirlwind of fun and energy. She is charming, confident, outgoing, and audacious. Everything I am not."

"You are not audacious?"

"Me?" I snort and push my glasses up my nose. "I do not have an audacious bone in my body. I am too anxious and responsible to take bold risks, though I admire people who do."

"What is the most audacious thing you have ever done?"

I frown. What is the most audacious thing I have *ever* done? Think. Think.

Xavier turns off the paved road onto a narrow dirt track lined with tall plane trees, their leaves uniting to create a beautiful green canopy.

"I used to wait until everyone was in bed and then sneak down to the kitchen to steal cookies from the cookie jar. I kept a library book once. Just didn't return it and then fibbed and said I thought I had. Oh, and when the maid wasn't looking yesterday, I took *two* bottles of the Majestic's divine scented bath wash from her cart." I sound pathetic. "Goodness, those stories make me sound dreadfully boring, don't they?"

Xavier chuckles. "I wouldn't say that. They do hint at a predilection for larceny, though."

I laugh.

My text tone chimes. Once. Twice. Three times. Four times. I reach into my purse and remove my phone.

"Do you mind?" I ask. "It might be Olivia."

"Not at all."

I open my text app. Four texts and all of them are from Emma Lee. Right on cue.

Text from Emma Lee Maxwell:
Did you get my text about the dealership repossessing my car? What am I going to do, Mandy?

Text from Emma Lee Maxwell:
Hello?

Text from Emma Lee Maxwell:
I hope you are having a fab time in Cannes, rubbing elbows with sexy celebs, going to VIP clubs, riding in limousines. Meanwhile, your baby sister is stranded in Charleston. Mobility challenged. On the brink of being

evicted. Destined to spend her nights sleeping on a park bench in White Point Garden.

An image of Emma Lee curled up on a bench using her bright pink leather Esteban Cortázar jacket as a blanket and her Balenciaga city bag as a pillow flickers in my brain and have to stifle a laugh. Why Emma Lee has never entertained a theatrical career is beyond me.

Text from Emma Lee Maxwell:
Why aren't you answering my texts?

I open my Notes app and enter a reminder to talk to my sister about pursuing a career on the stage or in front of the camera.

Text to Emma Lee Maxwell:
You won't ever be homeless, Em. Why don't you come and stay with me in Los Angeles? I will help you find a job and cosign a loan for a leased car.

Exhaling, I slip my phone back into my purse. Emma Lee might be the baby, but it is high time she grew up. The only job she has ever had was social chair for her sorority—and that was a volunteer position.

"Another person clinging to you?"

"Afraid so."

"Anything I can do to help?"

"No, but thank you for offering."

Xavier pulls to a stop. "We're here."

I look out the window at a grand rustic stone house with a terracotta roof and faded French gray shutters. Fields of gray bushes with small white flowers stretch as far as I can see.

"Where exactly is here?"

"The essential oil used to manufacture some of the world's most exclusive scents—Chanel No. 5, Roja Dove, Guerlain Le Bouquet de la Mariée—is manufactured here, in Grasse, using the flowers growing in these fields." He reaches over me to pull an envelope out of the glove compartment, his hand brushing my bare knee. "I needed to drop off some paperwork for Thierry Lambert, the owner of this farm, and thought you might like to take some photographs of the fields."

"Are you in the perfume business, then?"

"What?" He chuckles. "No, I am most definitely not in the perfume business."

Sliding the envelope into his inside jacket pocket, he climbs out of the car and closes the door. A moment later, he opens my door and holds out his hand. The sultry afternoon air is heavy with the sweet, heady scent of tuberoses. I accept Xavier's hand and climb out of the car, inhaling deeply, trying to steady the wild *thump-thump-thump* of my heart.

"Thank you."

"Please excuse me," he says, smiling. "I will be back as soon as I drop these papers off and then we can take a stroll through the fields, if you would like."

"Of course."

He disappears into the stone building. I take my glasses off and slip on a pair of prescription Oliver Goldsmith "Grace" sunglasses. The cat-eye shaped sunglasses are modeled after a pair Grace Kelly wore while filming *To Catch a Thief*. Olivia bought us each a pair as a pre-Cannes "prezzie." *We are going to Cannes, which means we need to channel Grace, darling*.

Walking around the car, I lift my camera to my face, focus on the tree-lined drive, and snap a picture of golden sunlight filtering through the leaves. I wander over to the side of the building, to a row of shiny pink rain boots lined up beside a scarred wooden door, and snap another picture. I am focusing my lens on a pile of faded wicker baskets when Xavier returns with an older, silver-haired gentleman wearing a slightly rumpled summer suit and a slouchy beret.

"Thierry Lambert," Xavier says, "allow me to introduce Mademoiselle Maxwell."

"It's a pleasure to meet you, Monsieur Lambert," I say, holding out my hand.

He lifts my hand to his lips, pressing a kiss on the back and murmuring, *"Enchanté, mademoiselle."*

The sparkling eyes, infectious grin, and red scarf knotted at his neck remind me of Maurice Chevalier's character in *Gigi* and I half expect him to burst into the French rendition of "Thank Heaven for Little Girls."

"I hope you don't mind, but when Xavier told me he was accompanied today by a pretty American girl"—he holds out his arms and shrugs in an unapologetic, yet charming gesture—*"pfft* . . . every man has his . . ." He looks at Xavier and frowns. *"Comment dit-on 'la faiblesse' en anglais?"*

"Weakness," Xavier offers.

"La! Mais bien sûr! Sometimes my old brain struggles to recall the simplest of words." He sighs heavily and then returns his gaze to me, watery gray eyes twinkling. "Every man has his weakness, *ma chérie*, and mine, much to the dismay of Madame Lambert, is pretty American girls."

I doubt Xavier described me as pretty—plain, passable, perhaps—but not pretty. Monsieur Lambert is being kind. Still, I thank him for the compliment and try to ignore the tingling sensation moving up the back of my neck and across my cheeks.

Monsieur Lambert chuckles. "Your face is as pink as the roses climbing up the side of my barn. My, but you are *charmante*."

I fiddle with my camera strap, adjusting the buckle even though it doesn't need adjusting. Monsieur Lambert chuckles again. My palms suddenly feel slick with perspiration. I can feel Xavier's gaze on the back of my neck.

"Do you have time for a tour?"

"Yes," Xavier answers.

Monsieur Lambert heads for the field to the right of where we are standing.

"Stop fidgeting," Xavier whispers, taking my elbow. "It was only a compliment."

I stop fiddling with my camera strap and follow along. We walk between two rows of green bushes with tight white buds not yet blossomed. Monsieur Lambert stops walking and faces us, lifting his arms and opening them wide.

"These fields have been in my family for fourteen generations," Monsieur Lambert says, lowering his arms. "My ancestor, Guillaume Baptiste Lambert, an enterprising young man, began cultivating flowers in these fields during the reign of the Sun King. He developed a revolutionary method for extracting essential oils and partnered with a local tradesman. Together, they began selling perfumed leather gloves. It wasn't long before they expanded their line to include perfumed sweet bags, which were essentially small, embroidered square purses carried by ladies of substance, pomanders, casks of scented water, and even bibles with perfumed leather covers."

While Monsieur Lambert shares the history of his land, I quietly snap his portrait. With his hands pressed together solemnly, hooked, aquiline nose, and thick, bushy eyebrows below the wool brim of his beret, he is the quintessential Frenchman. I continue taking photographs of the fields and the unfurled buds.

Monsieur Lambert bends down, groaning a little. He plucks a bud off a bush and gently rolls it between his fingers.

"What do you smell?" he asks, holding his hand out.

I close my eyes and inhale the hauntingly familiar scent of jasmine and am transported back to my birthplace, back to South Carolina. To a place where Spanish moss hangs like a pirate's beard from the branches of ancient trees and the tea is so sweet it makes your teeth ache. When I open my eyes, both Monsieur Lambert and Xavier are staring at me. I blink several times to clear the haze of nostalgia before my eyes.

"Jasmine," I whisper, my eyes prickling with tears.

"Brava!" Monsieur Lambert claps his hands. "How do you feel when you smell jasmine?"

Xavier narrows his gaze—giving me that full-body-scan stare—and my spine seems to melt inside my body. My shoulders roll forward. "Melancholy."

Monsieur Lambert raises a bushy brow.

"I am from South Carolina. The yellow jasmine is our state flower. The aroma reminds me of home and how much I miss it." I blink back tears. "It's funny how a scent can do that, isn't it? Transport you to another time and place, evoke emotions hidden somewhere deep down."

I catch Xavier studying me and quickly look away, embarrassed for him to see my vulnerabilities and raw emotion displayed so openly—again. He must think me a silly, overwrought American girl, weeping with every floral-scented breeze and mention of home.

Monsieur Lambert smiles and pats my shoulder.

"That is the Proust phenomenon, *ma chérie*."

"As in Marcel Proust?"

"*Oui!* You are familiar with Marcel Proust?"

"Mademoiselle Maxwell is a writer," Xavier says, his voice as warm as the sun heating my cheeks and bare shoulders.

"Is that so?" Monsieur Lambert clucks. "*Merveilleux!* The French revere writers, you know, far more than the Americans or the Brits."

He spits the last word.

I consider telling him that I am not a writer, that I am the assistant to a screenwriter, but don't want to sound churlish. Xavier was being encouraging.

"The Proust phenomenon?" I say, prodding our guide back onto a more comfortable conversational path.

"*Oui!*" He begins walking again and we follow. "In Proust's novel, *In Search of Lost Time*, the narrator dips a madeleine into a cup of tea and suddenly a flood of forgotten childhood memories washes over him. Now, when an aroma evokes a memory, it is attributed to the Proust phenomenon."

Monsieur Lambert leads us through his fields and factory, explaining each step of the process of distillation— from bud to bottle. He tells us the harvest is from August until October and that each blossom is handpicked by a female harvester, because women are more precise and take greater care with the blooms. We end our tour where we began, in front of the factory.

"I wish I could invite you to stay for dinner, but I regret I have a previous engagement," Monsieur Lambert says, looking at his watch.

"You've already been terribly generous. This has been an unexpected, lovely afternoon. Now, when I smell the scent of jasmine in bloom, I won't only think of my home. I will think of this day and your kindness." Standing on my tiptoes, I press a kiss to his whiskered cheek. *"Merci, monsieur."*

"Je vous en prie, ma chérie. It has been my pleasure."

Xavier opens my door and I climb in.

Monsieur Lambert and Xavier shake hands. Xavier says something in French, the words muffled through the glass. The old man nods his head and disappears into the stone house. He returns moments later and presses something into Xavier's hand. Xavier slips it inside his jacket pocket. He climbs into the car, pushes the engine button, and we are off, racing down the tree-lined driveway, leaving a cloud of dust in our wake.

Do you remember Monsieur Lambert said every man has his weakness? Well, my weakness is the kind that kills the cat. I am the curious sort. Right now, I have a mighty powerful curiosity to know what Monsieur Lambert gave Xavier, but my Southern manners are keeping me from asking him.

I hope it isn't drugs. It sounds ridiculous, but I read an article about the French drug scene before my trip. Unlike some places in the United States, cannabis is illegal in France. The article stated hippies started growing marijuana illegally in communes in the Pyrenees in the '70s, but since then there has been a growing demand for marijuana, which has increased the profitability and cultivation. Even though there are "grow shops"—places where people can go to purchase supplies and seeds to grow cannabis in their homes—professionally cultivated cannabis is a major business in the South of France.

Is it possible Monsieur Lambert is growing more than jasmine and roses in his fields? Is Xavier a cannabis distributor, one of France's drug kingpins?

Chapter Six

I look at the expensive whip-stitching on the leather passenger seat and wonder what Xavier does professionally that allows him to drive a top-of-the-line luxury vehicle—and stay in the Christian Dior suite. He laughed when I asked him if he was in the perfume business. In fact, he has been evasive every time I have asked him a question about himself.

Maybe he *is* a cannabis kingpin.

"Monsieur Lambert is your associate?"

"Client."

"Client?"

Maybe Xavier sells cannabis seeds to growers on the down-low. Please don't let this tall, dark, handsome stranger be a drug lord. Please.

Oh, Sweet Jesus! He gave me a Dior purse. I look down at my buttery-soft satchel and wonder if it is ill-gotten gains.

You are being ridiculous, Mandy, my common sense side argues. *You know what Daddy used to say: Mandy, darlin', letting your imagination run wild is like trying to wrestle an alligator. Only a fool would wrestle a gator, because it will grab you, spin you around, drag you down the bottom of the swamp, and feast on your good parts.*

Daddy thought a body's common sense was their best part. Logic over fancy. Reason over passion. The only thing Daddy loathed more than a "featherbrained flibber-tigibbet" was a busybody. So, even though I am burning with curiosity, I will not quench it by asking intrusive questions.

"*Oui*, client." Xavier turns off the dirt track onto the paved road. "Did you get some good photographs?"

"What?" I am still staring at my Dior and wondering how many ziplock baggies of marijuana had to be sold to earn the money to buy such a pricey purse. "Oh, yes. Thank you."

Xavier pulls into a service station.

"I need to fill up. Be right back."

While he is pumping gas, I grab my iPhone out of my purse, turn off airplane mode, and do a quick google search using the words: *Xavier*, *French*, *drug*, *dealer*. The search returns over three hundred thousand hits, including an article about a $56 million cocaine bust at a Coca-Cola plant in Marseilles by a detective named Xavier Dubois. I scroll down, but don't see anything of note.

Xavier climbs back into the car and starts the engine. I slip my phone back into my purse.

"Would you like to stop for something to drink?" he asks, turning onto the highway. "I know a little place with a spectacular view of the sea."

"Yes. Thank you."

He drives to an outdoor café perched on the edge of cliff, with striped awnings and a terrace overlooking the sea. We choose a table for two in the sun. The table is covered with a starched white tablecloth and the chairs are painted a bright, happy Mediterranean blue.

"Do you know what you would like to drink?" Xavier asks as he pulls out my chair.

I thank him and take a seat. "A *citronnade*, please."

"Mademoiselle voudrait un verre de citronnade, s'il vous plaît," Xavier says to the waiter. *"Et je vais prendre un café . . ."*

I lean my elbow on the table and rest my chin on my hand, watching Xavier from behind the obscurity of my big sunglasses. Sigh. Listening to a handsome Frenchman with serious designer stubble speak in his native tongue makes me want to do a foot pop. You know in old movies, when the romantic pair kiss and the actress bends one leg at the knee, lifting her foot behind her? That movie trope started in the 1930s, as a silent protest to one of the stipulations specified in the Hays Code (a set of rules governing filmmaking), which specified that actresses filming love scenes must keep one foot on the ground at all times.

The waiter gives us a little bow before disappearing inside the café.

"Citronnade?" he asks with a wry smile.

I sit back and cross my hands in my lap, embarrassed to have been caught gawking at Xavier as if he were Cary Grant and I a lovesick, starry-eyed Shirley Temple. *The Bachelor and the Bobby-Soxer.* One of Cary's best.

"I have always wanted to visit the South of France and I have always wanted to order a *citronnade*. The heroine of *Rebecca* drinks a glass of *citronnade* the first time she is alone with the hero, Maximillian de Winter."

"Is that what I am to you? A romantic hero?"

My cheeks suddenly flame with intense heat, like the

strike of a match. He notices my discomfort and laughs, though not unkindly. He is breathtaking when he laughs. His eyes shine, dimples appear on either side of his mouth, and the severe, dark expression that usually clouds his face disappears. I don't even mind that he is laughing at me.

"I am no hero, *ma bichette*."

My phone chimes and I use the text as an excuse to busy myself, distract myself from Xavier's disconcerting stare and statement.

"Excuse me."

"Olivia calls."

I want to say *How do you know it is Olivia texting me? Maybe I have a secret lover who is sending me sexts*. But I am not that brazen. I look at the screen and suppress a disappointed groan. It's from Olivia. Of course.

Text from Olivia Tate:

Ugh! The entire cast of Stomp is practicing in my head. I am not leaving my bed until the pounding-pounding-pounding stops. Tell the Grande Dame we are on a break . . . for now. Go do something wicked—preferably with Monsieur X. See you in the morning for tennis, k?

I smile and slip my phone back into my purse. Olivia doesn't drink that often, but when she does, she suffers the worst hangover followed by the surliest mood. That she has chosen isolation over socialization is a good thing, a very good thing.

"Good news?"

"Olivia has given me the evening off."

"Good news, indeed. How will you spend your free time?"

I shrug because the answer that comes to mind sounds

tragically boring. *I thought I would have a bowl of onion soup and then grab a book and curl up in bed.* Snooze.

The waiter arrives with our drinks. Xavier waits until I have taken a sip of my zesty lemonade before repeating his question.

"So, what will you do this evening?"

"Nothing exciting. How do you plan to spend the evening?"

He smiles. "I regret I have a work function at the marina. A boring black-tie affair hosted by a stuffed shirt with more money than sense. One of those people of 'substance' you spoke of earlier."

"How would you prefer to spend the evening?"

Though he doesn't alter his countenance, the intensity of his gaze increases, like smoldering embers that suddenly burst into flames, combusting and consuming everything in their path. Beads of perspiration break out all over my body. It is a look intended to convey words unspoken.

Is Xavier flirting with me? I believe he is!

I wish I had more experience flirting. I feel like such a child. A naïve, blushing schoolgirl bungling her first kiss.

I lift the long, slender spoon inside my glass and stir my *citronnade*, watching as the bits of pulp and zest whirl around, and force myself to take deep, steady breaths. When I find the courage to look at Xavier again, I discover a small, seductive smile curling his lips, and have the terrifying, thrilling realization that he was, indeed, flirting with me. He is a self-actualized man, adept at wielding his sex appeal like a weapon and fully aware of his potent effect on everyone around him.

"What I would prefer to do and what I would do depend entirely on who I was with, *ma bichette*." He winks and I stir my *citronnade* again. "Assuming I was alone, I would go for a swim in the sea or watch *le football* on *L'Équipe*. Then, I would probably answer business emails and fall asleep reading a book."

The image of Xavier lying in bed, his muscular arms behind his head, his broad, tanned chest bare, and a sheet covering his . . . *little Elvis* . . . pops into my head and my pulse quickens. A lot. If I were living in the Old South, I would flick open my fan and wave it rapidly near my face. I might even mutter *I do declare, I have the vapors!*

Xavier winks again, and I know, I know, he used his strange, x-ray vision to read my dirty thoughts.

"Drink your *citronnade* before the ice melts. I can't imagine pressed lemons and sugar would taste good warm."

I obey, swallowing half of my *citronnade* in one un-Southern-ladylike gulp. To my chagrin, Xavier's lips are still curled in a teasing smile as he casually sips his café au lait.

The sun is hanging low in the sky, a blazing orange beach ball about to fall into the sea. I lift my camera off the table and snap several shots of the terrace awash in the amber glow of sunset, the rows of empty tables and prettily painted chairs, the Mediterranean stretching like a blue carpet from Cannes to Antibes and beyond.

"It's beautiful, isn't it?"

"Breathtaking."

"Would you consider giving me a copy of one of the photographs you took—whichever you think most captures this moment?"

"Of course!"

"Merci."

"No," I say, smiling. "Thank *you* for a lovely day. I won't ever forget it."

"*De rien*, Manderley." He reaches into his pocket,

pulls out a small cut-crystal bottle, and stands it on the table. "For you," he says, nodding his head at the bottle. "A little gift to help you remember this day, something you can carry with you wherever you go to remind you of . . . home."

"What is it?"

I lift the bottle and hold it up to the light, looking at the thick, yellowish liquid inside.

"Jasmine Absolute, an essential oil made from the flowers grown on Monsieur Lambert's farm. It is the same oil used to make Chanel perfumes."

"You bought this for me?"

"Oui."

Silly, foolish, schoolgirl tears fill my eyes and I blink to clear my vision. "Thank you, Xavier. I will cherish it, always."

I unscrew the silver top and inhale. The sweet, familiar floral aroma fills my senses. I am back in the fields with Xavier, walking among the jasmine bushes, the Mediterranean sun burning my exposed skin. I close my eyes and savor the scent, relive the new memory. When I open them, I find Xavier staring at me with a furrowed brow.

"A little bottle of oil means that much to you?"

"Yes." I sniffle, frustrated with my weepiness. My emotions have been just below the surface since the death of my father. "It is the most thoughtful gift I have ever received."

I remember the tall, beautiful brunette who met Xavier in the hotel lobby a few nights ago. I am sure she is accustomed to receiving lavish and sentimental gifts from handsome men. Black satin gowns and pearls. Sable stoles and luxurious perfumes in pretty little bottles.

"Men don't give lavish gifts to women like me," I say, letting my shoulders roll forward.

"Then you have been dating the wrong men, *ma bichette*."

A spark of excitement ignites inside me. Is that what we are doing, I wonder, dating? Is Xavier courting me? I hear Olivia's laughter in my head. *Nobody under seventy uses the word* courting. *It's hooking up. Cuffing. Tindering. Conscious coupling.*

"You've been terribly kind to me. I don't know how I will ever thank you."

He brushes my gratitude away as if it were a pesky fly circling his café au lait. "I have never known a woman to show so much emotion over such a small gesture."

"Then you have been dating the wrong women, Xavier."

His smile fades and the light behind his eyes extinguishes, like the sputtering wick in a lantern when the kerosene has suddenly run out. Although he is still looking at me, I have the distinct impression he does not see me, that he is looking through me at a distant, ghostly place existing only in his imagination.

I look down at my hands in my lap, still clutching the beautiful perfume bottle. Even though I meant them in jest, I wish I could take back my words. But, like my daddy always said, *Once the buckshot is outta the shotgun, you can't suck it back in.*

I force myself to lift my shoulders and my gaze and am surprised to discover light flickering in Xavier's eyes once more and a polite smile upon his lips.

"Tell me, Manderley Maxwell," he says, casually leaning back in his chair and draping his arm over the back of the chair beside him. "How do you like your *citronnade*?"

"It's delicious."

"And what about the French Riviera? Is it everything you dreamt it would be?"

"More!" I take a deep breath of the salt-stained sea air and exhale slowly, smiling. "I understand why Zelda and F. Scott Fitzgerald, Hemingway, Picasso, W. Somerset Maugham spent part of each year here. Such beauty is stimulating. Did you know F. Scott's *Tender Is the Night* was inspired by the years he spent living in a villa in Cap d'Antibes? After it was published, Americans associated the Riviera with glamour and excess."

"Do you find it excessive?"

"A little."

"So you have not allowed the Riviera to seduce you with her world-class hotels, exclusive casinos, and luxury boutiques?"

"I am not seduced by glitz or glamour."

He smiles as I imagine the wolf smiled before he devoured Little Red Riding Hood's poor old granny, a wickedly charming, wickedly dangerous smile that does funny things to my lady region.

"You aren't?"

I swallow hard and shake my head.

"Well, what are you seduced by?"

Are we still talking about the French Riviera? I am not so sure, but I decide to answer as if we are.

"The food."

"You enjoy French cuisine?"

"Yes," I say, smiling. "Grilled sardines sprinkled with sea salt, crusty bread that melts in your mouth like butter, and those potatoes soaked in wine and covered in bacon fat and cheese."

"*Tartiflette.*"

"*Tartiflette?* Is that what it is called?"

"*Oui.* My grandmother used to serve it for Christmas."

"The taste of heaven," I say, licking my lips.

Too late I realize Xavier is watching my mouth, his gaze following the path my tongue makes as it circles around my lips. Heat flushes my cheeks. "Mussels and fries!"

Xavier smiles. *"Moules et frites?"*

"That is my favorite thing to eat in Cannes."

"Mine, too."

"Really?"

"Oui."

We smile at each other and my shyness disappears, chased away by the discovery that we have something in common.

"Is that all that you like about the Riviera? The food?"

"Of course not." I laugh. "I am not a glutton. Though I might become one if I continued to take all of my meals at the Majestic." He laughs and the warm sound washes over me like the waters of the Mediterranean. "The South of France reminds me of home."

"How?"

"The slow and easy pace, the cobalt skies that fade into the sea, waking to the sound of gulls crying and palm fronds rattling, the taste of salt on my tongue, and the sultry breezes blowing over my skin."

"Brava, ma bichette. You have described the Côte d'Azur as only a writer could."

"Thank you," I say, flushing. "What about you? Do you vacation in Cannes often?"

"My grandmother lived in Aigues-Mortes. I spent every summer of my childhood splashing through her marshes, chasing wild herons, fishing off the shore."

"Funny."

"What?"

"We had similar childhoods. My family's home was

surrounded by swamps and marshes and I also spent summers at my grandmother's house near the sea, fishing and swimming."

"You fish?"

"I couldn't be the daughter of Malcolm Maxwell and not know how to bait a hook and cast a line. My daddy threatened us with no dessert for a month if we didn't catch something big enough to fry each time we went fishing with him." I sigh. "Of course, he never made good on his threat. Daddy was a marshmallow when it came to his girls, sweet and pliable."

"My father was the same way with my sister."

"*You* have a sister?"

Xavier chuckles. "Is that so difficult to believe?"

"No." My cheeks flush with heat again. "I didn't mean . . . or, rather . . . I don't know why, but I imagined you came from a family of boys. I am sorry . . ."

"Don't be. I like knowing you spend your time thinking about me." He shifts positions and his leg brushes against mine, a brief, gentle touch. "Tell me, what else do you imagine?"

Lawd have mercy! Is it me or did the temperature suddenly climb several degrees? I take a sip of my *citronnade* and look at him over the rim of my sweaty glass.

He chuckles again, a smooth, satisfied chuckle, and I imagine him in a fencing ring, foil in hand, skillfully parrying and thrusting, a veritable master at sexual banter.

I sip my drink, glad for the cool glass against my heated hand, and try to appear unaffected by his flirting.

"Did you enjoy it?"

My hand trembles and some of the *citronnade* spills out of my glass, splashes onto my lap.

"I beg your pardon?" I ask, putting the glass on the

table and dabbing the stain with my napkin. "Are you asking if I enjoyed imagining you as a child?"

He throws his head back and laughs. It's the happiest sound I have heard in months, and even though I suspect it is being provoked by my naïveté, I don't want it to stop. My lips twitch and soon I am laughing, too.

"You are utterly charming, Manderley Maxwell. Innocent and utterly charming."

"Thank you," I say, neatly folding my napkin and placing it in my lap.

"I wanted to know if you enjoyed fishing with your father."

"You know what?" I push my glasses on top of my head and lean my elbows on the table, more relaxed now that he has steered the conversation out of dangerous waters. "I did enjoy fishing. It was calming. The steady sway of the boat and the quiet that comes when you're out at sea—just the water lapping the sides and the wind flapping the sails . . ."

A sharp pang of longing reverberates through my soul and I need to take a moment so I don't burst into tears over my loss. This is how the last fifty-nine days and eleven hours have been for me. Sudden, excruciating pangs of longing, triggered by the most benign things. From happy to sad in the space of a breath.

"You are thinking about your father, aren't you?"

I nod.

He reaches for my hand. "If you want to talk about him"—he rubs the back of my hand with his thumb, a gentle, intimate gesture that ignites a longing in me, the same inexplicable longing I felt when I spoke about Cécile and Cyril's love affair—"I would be happy to listen."

"Thank you," I say, pulling my hand away and then instantly mourning the loss of his warm touch. "I would rather not, though."

He sits back again. "Because I am a stranger?"

"Because"—I swallow the thick lump of emotion forming in my throat—"for the last two months, I have been dwelling in a pit of despair. It's as if I have been lost in darkness, unable to find the light no matter how wide I open my eyes. Spending time with you reminds me I am still a member of the land of the living. Tonight, after we part ways, I will slip back into that pit. So, for now, I want to enjoy the light."

The waiter approaches our table, but Xavier discreetly waves him away.

"That is the kindest thing anyone has ever said to me, *ma bichette*." He reaches for my hand again and lifts it to his lips, kissing the place where his thumb had brushed. "I am honored, truly."

My pulse races faster than the engine of his shiny sports car, thump-thumping in my throat. Can he hear the blood humming in my veins? Does he know what his attentions—what his kisses—do to me?

He lets go of my hand and I snatch it away, cradling it in my other hand as if it had been scalded.

"Finish your *citronnade* now and I will drive you back to the hotel."

"Yes, Xavier."

Obeying, I take another sip of my drink.

My sister Emma Lee would say *You're so thirsty, Mandy, like a withered old maid desperate for a drop of affection* and she wouldn't be talking about the way I am gulping my *citronnade*, either. Emma Lee likes to pepper her vernacular with slang, and *thirsty*, as in desperate for sex and/or affection, is one of the more vulgar words in her lexicon. Maybe Emma Lee is right, though. Maybe I am thirsty. Maybe my thirst for affection is the cause of all those pangs of longing I have been suffering.

The sun is making a last valiant gasp, its orange rays stretching like long, slender fingers grasping to hold on to the remains of the day. I feel the same way—reluctant to bid adieu to this magical day.

Xavier pays the bill and pushes his chair back to stand. "Shall we?"

"Wait!" I grab my camera off the table. "Before we go, would you let me take your picture?"

"Me?"

I nod my head.

"I can't imagine why you would want to take my picture." He brushes an invisible speck of lint from his immaculate trousers. "Surely, the view holds more interest for you."

The view pales in comparison to you, Xavier. "I want to remember . . . everything."

He frowns. "Am I forgettable?"

"Forgettable?" Heat rises up my body from my toes to the tips of my ears. "Of course not! How rude of me. I am sorry . . . I didn't mean . . ."

"Relax, *ma bichette*. I was only teasing." He laughs. "Go on then, take your picture."

Xavier leans back in his chair, away from the light and my lens, like a sleek jungle cat sinking into the shadows. His dark shirt and black hair blend into the background, making it difficult for me to get a good focus. I hold my breath and wait for the reflection off the water to shimmer on his face and illuminate just enough for me to photograph. The hairs on the back of my neck rise, like a big game hunter who suddenly realizes he has become the prey. The light ripples over part of his face. I push the shutter button and exhale.

I look at the LCD display and my heart misses a beat. Xavier, a dark, ominously immortalized version of Xavier, is staring up at me from the small screen. The light hit him in such a strange, fragmented way that only part of his face and neck are visible. One narrowed eye, the sharp plane of his cheekbone, the tip of his nose, the corner of his mouth, the curve of his stubbly jaw. His lips are pressed together in a serious line, neither smiling nor frowning, a brooding expression that transforms his handsome face into something almost sinister.

"Well?"

I startle at the sound of his voice.

"Got it." I turn off the display and replace the lens cap. "Thanks."

"Are you going to let me see it?"

I am silently debating whether it would be rude to refuse to allow him to look at his own photograph, when he stretches his hand across the table. I turn the display back on and hold the camera up so he can see the image.

He looks at the display and his lip pulls up in a snarl.

"Is that the way you see me?" The words roll around in his throat before coming out of his mouth so it sounds as if he is growling instead of speaking. "Am I really that forbidding?"

"I . . . I think it is a lovely p . . . portrait."

"Do you?"

I nod my head.

He stares at me for several long seconds as if searching for signs of my duplicity, so I fight the urge to bow my head or look away. I did not lie. It is a beautiful portrait—a disconcerting, beautiful portrait that captures the unusual duality of his nature. The beauty that shimmers on his surface and the darkness—the mysteries unsolved—I sense lurking somewhere below. Despite my powerful attraction to the man, he remains an enigma, a charming, handsome, thoughtful, thrilling, disconcerting enigma.

"Yes, well, from now on perhaps you should focus on the view. It is more worthy of your talent."

During the drive back to the hotel, Xavier tells me about Château de Maloret, his ancestral home in Brittany, describing it as a lovely pile of stones precariously perched on the edge of a cliff, overlooking the ocean.

"We are one gale away from losing the west tower."

"That's tragic. Isn't there anything that can be done to save it?"

"I am trying to raise the capital, but such projects take infinite time and resources." He removes his hand from the steering wheel just long enough to rub his temple. "The château has been in my family since the seventeenth century. It has endured two fires, countless storms, and a revolution. The weight of responsibility for preserving a historic home is . . . exhausting, but I must endure. It is my duty and my honor."

The worry in his voice touches my heart. I felt the same sense of duty to preserve my daddy's home after he died. I was devastated when I learned it was being seized by the IRS. My six times great-grandfather built that home before the Civil War and now it's sitting empty, waiting for some bottom-line motivated developer to snatch it up and turn it into a high-class B & B.

"Château de Maloret. It's such a lovely name. What does it mean?"

"That depends on who you ask."

Xavier pulls to a stop in front of the valet stand, opens his door, hands the keys to the waiting valet, and circles around the back of the car to open my door.

"Allow me," he says, taking my heavy camera from my hands.

He rests his hand lightly on the small of my back and we walk across the parking lot toward the hotel. He keeps his hand there even as we step through the revolving door and into the lobby, a protective, proprietary gesture that is so old-school Hollywood, so Laurence Olivier-esque, it makes me want to sigh. I wish all men would treat women with such deference, such decorum.

We ride the elevator to my floor. This time, instead of bidding me goodnight from inside the elevator, Xavier follows me down the dimly lit corridor. He is going to ask me to invite him in for a nightcap and then he is going to pick me up, throw me on the bed, tear the clothes from my body, and make violent love to me.

Lawd have mercy! Emma Lee is right. I am thirsty!

I fumble around inside my purse, searching for my room key. When I finally find it, I slide it in the slot with the magnetic strip facing the wrong way. The little light above the lock flashes red. My hand begins to sweat. I pull the key card out, turn it around, and slide it back in. The light flashes red again. *Damn!*

Xavier takes the key and slides it into the slot. The light flashes green. The door clicks open.

"Relax." A slow smile spreads across his face. "I am not going to push my way into your room and make violent love to you . . . unless, that is, you want me to make violent love to you."

The air leaves my lungs in a sudden rush, the sound unnaturally loud in the quiet hallway.

Violent love? Did he just ask if I want him to make *vi-*

olent love to me? Sweet baby Jesus in heaven! I thought those same words only seconds ago. Is he a mind reader or is my thirstiness that apparent?

"W . . . what did you . . ."

He bends down and brushes his lips against my shoulder, his beard grazing my bare skin, and my words become a moan in the back of my throat. The door clicks shut behind me.

"You want me to make love to you," he whispers, kissing a path to my neck. "Don't you, *ma bichette*?"

I stand with my arms hanging limply at my sides, my purse dangling from one clenched fist, and nod my head. The feel of his warm lips and stubbly chin against my naked skin is sending tremors through my body, mounting shockwaves of pleasure. I can't speak. I can't move. It's like I have sleep paralysis. Terrifying, thrilling sleep paralysis.

When he takes my earlobe into his warm mouth, my brain sends a message to my limbs, telling them to move, to act before it is too late. I drop my purse and clutch the front of his shirt, pulling him to me. He murmurs something in French and groans low in his throat, wrapping his arm around my waist and kissing me on the mouth. I am vaguely aware of the spicy scent of cologne and the chocolatey taste of coffee before I am plummeting, tumbling head over sandals, clutching Xavier's shirt as if it will keep me from falling in love, profoundly, perilously in love with him. And I am only vaguely aware when he stops kissing me. I feel the cool air on my moist lips, hear his jagged breathing, and I open my eyes.

"Why did you kiss me?"

"Because you looked as if you wanted to be kissed . . . and because I wanted to kiss you." He leans down and brushes his lips over mine again, lightly. "You deserve to be kissed, *ma bichette,* and you deserve someone who will shower you with thoughtful gifts."

"I don't know about that," I say, laughing nervously.

"I do." He bends over, picks my purse up from the floor, and hands it to me. "There is nothing I would like more than to spend the evening with you, but . . ."

He brushes another light kiss over my lips.

"I understand. You have a prior commitment."

"I must go now." He brushes my hair from my forehead and kisses it. "*Bonne nuit*, Manderley. Sweet dreams."

Chapter Seven

After spending an hour soaking in a lavender-scented bath and three hours twisting myself up in 1800-thread-count sheets, I realize Xavier's wish, that I should have sweet dreams this night, is not going to come true. How am I supposed to dream when I am too disconcerted to fall asleep? Disconcerted. Disturbed, as in one's composure or self-possession. Distracted. Flustered. Agitated. Unsettled. Discomfited. Some people count sheep to fall asleep, I count synonyms. Xavier's kiss has me thinking of synonyms for *disconcerted*. Rattled. Ruffled.

I remember the taste of his lips on mine, the pleasure-pain sensation of his beard scratching against my shoulder and neck. Maybe *disconcerted* isn't the right word. Maybe *astonished* is the right word. I am astonished anyone as beautiful as Xavier would want to make love to me.

Befuddled. Bemused. Beguiled.

Soon, I will be singing the 1940s Broadway hit, "Bewitched, Bothered and Bewildered." I have become a simpering child because a Frenchman has bewitched, bothered . . . Great! Xavier's kisses and promises of lovemaking have me singing saccharine-sweet show tunes in my head.

. . . I feel restless, like I drank a tea made from poison ivy leaves and I am all itchy inside.

I click on the bedside lamp, throw off the covers, and climb out of bed, padding over to the minibar and flicking the switch on the electric tea kettle.

A minute later, I am lounging on the balcony, the hotel's plush robe wrapped around my shoulders, a cup of hot tea in my hands, watching moonlight spill like mercury down the hills and into the sea. The sultry night breeze on my skin and hot chamomile tea in my belly work their magic, soothing my itchy nerves. My lids feel heavy and I am about to go back inside to climb into bed when I notice Xavier striding across the Boulevard de la Croisette. I sit up so quickly the robe slips off my shoulders.

He is dressed in a tuxedo. The moonlight shining off his slicked-back black hair makes it appear as if it is glowing blue, an entirely strange, haunting effect. He steps onto the cement island in the middle of the crosswalk and waits for the traffic going in the other direction to clear. It gives me a chance to secretly study him, to memorize every gorgeous detail about this man who has bothered and bewitched me. Like the way his perfectly tailored tuxedo jacket fits over his broad shoulders, or the crisp white line of his collar against his tanned skin, or the way he is standing, with one of his hands casually thrust inside his pants pocket, his chin lifted to a confident angle. How I wish I had my camera in my hands instead of an empty teacup; though, I am confident I won't need a photograph to recall how handsome Xavier looks at this moment, how the unexpected sight of him makes me feel breathless and dizzy. I haven't felt this girlishly

giddy since Drew Landon let me wear his letter jacket—
and that was my sophomore year in high school.

The light changes and Xavier finishes crossing the
boulevard. I scoot down the lounger until I am close
enough to the railing to peek between the wrought-iron
bars, keeping Xavier in sight as he strides along the side-
walk leading to the hotel. I can almost hear the heels of
his shiny oxfords striking the pavement. He is nearly to
the hotel entrance, nearly out of my sight, when a tall,
slender woman in a slinky gold cocktail gown emerges
from a parked car and calls to him, her lilting, accented
voice carried to me on the breeze.

"Xavier."

He stops walking and turns around. She raises her
hand, waggling her fingers. He takes a step back. Perhaps
it is a trick of the moonlight, but the relaxed, confident
man I watched stride across the Boulevard de la Croisette
moments ago now seems transformed into someone unrecognizable, a tense, almost sinister shadow of Xavier.

Undaunted, the woman hurries over to him. She
moves as if she intends to kiss his cheeks, hesitates, and
steps back, leaving an arm's-length between them.

"Laisse-moi tranquille," I hear Xavier say. *Leave me
alone.*

And then the woman speaks, her full, red lips moving
rapidly. Her words do not carry to me. I turn my head,
pressing my ear between the rails, but still I cannot hear
what she is saying. This muted conversation continues
for another minute before Xavier turns to leave.

"Xavier, wait!" she cries, her voice louder now.

She reaches for his sleeve, but he knocks her hand
away. She recoils from the slap, stepping back, her foot
slipping off the curb. Her ankle turns and she lets out a
pained cry.

I expect Xavier to hurry back to her, to offer his assistance, but he has already disappeared through the revolving door, leaving the woman alone in the dark, and leaving me to wonder if he is the debonair, tuxedo-clad hero who rescued me from a purse snatcher; or the sinister, hand-slapping shadow.

Chapter Eight

I am standing on the deck of a magnificent sailboat staring at a sky as black as satin and stars as bright as pearls. The boat rocks gently, like the reassuring sway of a newborn's bassinet, and the breeze hums a nocturnal lullaby in my ears. I feel at peace.

Calm. Quiet. Safe.

My cares and concerns are a distant speck on the horizon, a barely visible blemish on the face of this wondrous beauty.

I watch as the strand of stars in the sky snaps and a cascade of orbs fall around me—giant, glowing pearls dropping into the sea, bouncing on the deck, leaving a trail of brilliant light. It's mesmerizing.

I reach my hand out, hoping to capture one of the pearls of light in my palm, but the light alters, transforms into a shimmering, shadowy, humanlike form. I wrap one hand around the railing and lean far out over the water, stretching, grasping for the form. My fingertips finally reach the light. It ripples and then an angry voice says, "Laisse-moi."

The shape becomes Xavier. He grabs my wrist and jerks me from the deck. I open my mouth to scream, but no sound comes out. I flail blindly, reaching into the nothingness for something solid. I feel the wind between my fingers and realize with sickening horror that I am falling . . . falling into a bottomless, black sea . . .

Chapter Nine

To: **Manderley Maxwell**
From: **Emma Lee Maxwell**
Subj: **Find a job! Find a job!**

Tara is driving me crazier than Miley Cyrus on a wrecking ball. She's normally so chill, but she has turned into a magpie with her endless chirping. "Find a job." "Find a job." "Find a job." Make her stop. Please.

To: **Manderley Maxwell**
From: **Tara Maxwell**
Subj: **One-Way Ticket to Waverly Hills**

Remember how Daddy used to say, "You don't need to hang from a tree to be a nut?" Emma Lee is living proof Daddy was right!

When the dealer repossessed her car, I swear, something snapped in her brain. She spends all day on the sofa watching *Married at First Sight* and reruns of *Millionaire Matchmaker*.

Yesterday, I found her watching a British show called *Naked Attraction*. It's like *The Bachelor* . . . except the contestants are naked! I am here to tell you, darlin', Khloé Kardashian is wrong: Strong doesn't always look better naked.

When I ask her why she isn't out looking for a job, do you know what she says? "I am seriously considering becoming a matrimonial broker. Watching these shows is like taking a master class in matchmaking and courtship."

Lord knows I am a patient woman, but she is working my last nerve with a handsaw. If you don't talk to her, I am going to pack my bags and move to . . .

"Is Tara threatening to run away from home again?"

The sound of Olivia's voice startles me and I bang my knee on the table. My teacup rattles against its saucer. Tea splashes out of the cup and onto the pristine white tablecloth. Needles of heat prick the back of my neck. I don't have to turn around to know my clumsiness was witnessed by the A-list couple eating their breakfast at the table behind me.

"I'm sorry." Olivia slides onto the chair across from me. She whips her napkin off the table and drops it onto her lap. "I didn't mean to startle you."

Dressed in a short, pleated tennis skirt and sleeveless top, her high cheekbones brushed with bronzer, her edgy black bob styled to face-framing perfection, Olivia appears fully recovered from her Grande Dame drinking binge.

"You were serious"—I dab the tea stains with my napkin—"about wanting to play tennis this morning?"

"Uh, yeah. Have you seen the tennis pro? He makes me want to work on my stroke, if you know what I mean," she says, waggling her eyebrows. "If I am lucky, he will offer to be my ball boy."

"Olivia!"

"Don't *Olivia* me! You would say the same thing if you saw him."

The waiter arrives. Olivia orders her usual breakfast— an egg white omelet, two slices of multigrain toast, and a black coffee.

"So," she says, looking at me from beneath an arched brow. "How dire was this morning's email? Did Emma Lee write to say she broke a fingernail and would like you to fly home and file it for her?"

I laugh. "As far as I know, Emma Lee's nails are intact. Tara did say that Em is spending an alarming amount time watching reality television, though."

"And Tara is at her wit's end?"

"Naturally."

"And threatening to run away from home?"

"Of course."

We laugh, because Tara has been threatening to run away from home ever since she learned how to put one tiny foot in front of the other. I don't know why. Maybe it's because she's consumed by a fierce restlessness, a desire to find her unique place in this world, a place where she isn't Manderley Maxwell's less ambitious little sister or Emma Lee Maxwell's less beautiful older sister. Maybe it is because she is the middle child and grew up feeling *not*. Not Daddy's favorite and not Daddy's baby.

"Where is she threatening to run away to this time?"

"Tásúildun."

"Where?"

"Tásúildun." I take a sip of my tea. "The castle she inherited from our aunt."

"She inherited a castle and all you got was a leaky old sailboat? Robbed! What did Emma Lee inherit, a palace?"

"No," I say, laughing. "Emma Lee inherited Wood House."

"Wood House?"

"My aunt's cottage in England."

"A boat. A castle." Olivia holds out her hands, moving them up and down as if they were scales. "A boat. A cottage. I guess we know who Aunt Pattycake loved best."

I laugh to be polite, but my thoughts drift away on a current of time, back to the day my Aunt Patricia's solicitor read me the letter she attached to her will, the letter in which she explained her reason for leaving me her cherished yacht.

> *You have always been a sensible girl, Manderley. I am confident your common sense will continue to serve you well and you will be a successful woman, a woman your mother, my dear sister, would have looked upon with abundant pride. You are so much like her. Sensible. Selfless. Shy. Satisfied, but still yearning. In her absence, you have become the rock, my dear girl, the rock to which your father and sisters cling. Be careful there, for even rocks can be worn away over time. At the risk of being officious, please allow an old woman to impart these last words of advice: Take time out for yourself to do the things that fill your soul. If you don't, you will find one day that you have nothing left to pour into others. I know your passion for the sea—a passion we share—and for that reason I am bequeathing you the Constante Sur—*

"Hello!" Olivia snaps her fingers in front of my face. "Earth to Manderley."

I blink and the spell that took me back in time is broken.

"I am sorry," I whisper, a little sad to discover I have returned to a café in the South of France instead of to a place in time when my aunt still walked amongst the living. "I was remembering the day my aunt's solicitor told me I had inherited the *Constante Sur*." I take a shuddering breath. "Memories can be like sandspurs, can't they? Treacherous, sharp little things that poke into your most tender spots and make you feel foolish for not remembering to be more careful."

Olivia smiles sadly and grabs my hand, gently squeezing. "Memories can also be like sand, soft and warm and inviting, beckoning you to sit and appreciate. Right now, your memories are as spiny as sandspurs, but that won't always be the case, I promise."

"Thank you, Olivia."

"Always," she says, squeezing my hand before letting go. "Maybe sharing your memories will help lessen the sting of the spine."

"Maybe."

"Well"—she smiles encouragingly—"you won't know unless you try."

I take a deep breath, hold it, and release it slowly. "Before she died, Aunt Patricia wrote me a letter. She wrote letters for Tara and Emma Lee, too. Her solicitor gave them to us on the same day he read her will." I close my eyes and visualize the wood-paneled conference room of Winter V. Hastings III, Attorney-at-Law, the gilt-embossed law books lined up along the shelves, the dust motes dancing in the air heedless of our grief. I open my eyes again. "Aunt Patricia said she wanted me to have her yacht to remind me life doesn't always need to be a scrupulously charted journey. She said the most spectacular adventures happen when we just set sail and let the wind take us where it wishes. She said I needed to get out of my head and let my heart lead me. Passion over duty, or something like that."

"I love Aunt Pattycake. She's one smart broad."

"Was. She *was* one smart broad."

Olivia frowns and color stains her cheeks. "Of course. Was. Sorry."

"It's okay," I say, smiling sadly. "I don't think any of us have accepted the fact that a woman as vibrant as Patricia MacCumascaigh has faded away."

The waiter arrives with Olivia's breakfast. He places the omelet before her with a flourish (he presented my scrambled eggs sans flourish). For as long as I have known her, Olivia has had this effect on men. Waiters, professors, studio execs. They break a sweat trying to please her.

"Would mademoiselle care for more coffee?" the waiter asks Olivia.

"No, thank you."

The waiter backs away, keeping his gaze fondly fixed on Olivia and her coffee cup.

"Passion over duty," Olivia says, removing the lid from the silver saltcellar and sprinkling several grains of coarse sea salt over her omelet. "You were saying?"

"Do you think I am too sensible?"

"There's nothing wrong with being sensible, Mandy."

"But am I too sensible?"

"Too sensible?" She rolls her eyes. "That's like saying someone is too rich or too beautiful. One can never have too much sense, money, or beauty."

"I suppose you're right," I sigh. "Still . . ."

"What?"

"I wish I were more like Emma Lee."

"What do you mean? You wish you were sleeping on Tara's couch and watching crap television instead of partying like a rock star in the South of France with your best friend?"

"No! That's not what I meant."

"Well"—she cuts a small piece of omelet and forks it into her mouth—"what do you mean?"

"I wish I were more impulsive and uninhibited."

"Okay, your fairy godmother suddenly appears and"—she waves her fork in the air as if it is a wand—"*poof!* You're suddenly impulsive and wild. What would you do differently?"

"What do you mean?"

"Stop stalling, Manderley Maxwell. You know precisely what I mean. How would your life change?"

I shrug. "I don't know."

"I think you do."

She busies herself with spreading jam on her toast.

She's right. I know how my life would change, but what's the point in entertaining Cinderella dreams? My fairy godmother isn't going to magically materialize and sing "Bibbidi-Bobbidi-Boo." She's not going to change my tennis shoes into glass slippers. Life is not a fairy tale.

If it were . . .

I exhale.

. . . if life were as dreamy as a fairy tale, I would have long, flowing platinum hair, wide blue eyes, and pink, bow-shaped lips. People would notice me when I walked into a room in my blue ball gown and matching satin gloves. I would have the courage to pursue my dreams . . . and my Prince Charming.

Instead, I have dirty-dishwater blond hair and drab gray eyes. People usually ignore me and the closest thing I own to a blue ball gown is a hideous periwinkle bridesmaid dress I wore to a friend's wedding.

I don't know what my dreams are anymore. At one time, I thought I wanted to be a journalist and work on hard-hitting, investigative pieces. Then, I imagined myself as a novelist, living in a coastal home on stilts, pounding away on an old manual Smith Corona as the surf swirled below me. Now . . . I am not even certain I have a talent for writing. Perhaps my creative muscle atrophied while I was busy helping Olivia flex hers. (And I don't mean that to sound as bitter as it might, because helping Olivia has been *my* choice. Nobody forced me to become her assistant. I volunteered.)

The waiter suddenly appears, pours a few drops of steaming black coffee into Olivia's cup, and backs silently away, a vassal pleased to have successfully completed his duties. For her part, Olivia has perfected Monarch Face— that blank expression that says *If there are little people out there toiling to prepare my food and keep my goblet filled with wine, I do not know. I see nothing except the dazzling reflection of my greatness in the cutlery.*

As far as Prince Charming . . .

. . . I think of Xavier, dressed in a tuxedo, leaning casually against the hood of his sports car, and my heart sinks. I am employing fairy-tale thinking if I imagine Xavier as my Prince Charming. I don't know if he is married. He could be someone else's Prince Charming. Maybe the woman in the slinky dress is his Cinderella. After all, I know little about him.

"I don't even know his last name."

Olivia looks up from her toast. "Who?"

"Xavier."

"And knowing his last name is vital if you are to continue allowing him to rescue you from peril and shower you with beautiful designer handbags?" Olivia brushes bread crumbs from her fingers and leans forward. "He is single and seriously interested in you. Isn't that enough for now?"

Let's say he is single *and* seriously interested in me. He is French. I am American. We live half a world apart. How could we possibly make a relationship work? Courting via text? Holidays spent somewhere halfway in between, like Kuujjuaq, Canada, or Ashtabula, Ohio? Forty percent of couples in long-distance relationships break up, so the odds aren't great.

There I go again. Sensible Manderley. Throwing a big bucket of icy logic on my kindling passion. Why can't I do as my aunt suggested and let my heart lead me, even if it takes me somewhere my head thinks I should not go?

Olivia sighs. "If I were able to tell you his last name, would that be enough for you? Would you release your inner sex-kitten long enough to have a little vacay prowl?" She sits up in her chair, craning her neck to look around me. She smiles, raises her hand a little, and wiggles her fingers.

"What are you doing?"

"You'll see."

The waiter appears at our table. "*Oui, mademoiselle.* Is there something you desire?"

"Absolutely," Olivia purrs, batting her long, fiber-mascara-enhanced lashes at him. "I desire some information and I believe you are just the man to provide it."

The waiter straightens, lifting his chin. "Of course, mademoiselle—"

"Olivia. Please, call me Olivia."

"How may I assist, Mademoiselle Olivia?"

"It's my friend here."

The waiter reluctantly redirects his gaze from Olivia to me. His shoulders sag a little. His smile falters. I push my glasses farther up my nose and smile apologetically, embarrassed for him.

"This is Manderley," Olivia says, nodding her head at me. "She is my best friend, and I would do anything in the world to make her happy. I'll bet you feel the same way about your best friend, don't you—" Olivia gasps and slaps her hand to her cheek. "How rude of me! I didn't even ask your name."

"The name is Robert, mademoiselle."

"Robert. What a wonderful name. So strong and masculine."

Robert grins.

"The thing is, Robert, Manderley was accosted by a pickpocket just outside the hotel."

"*Mon dieu!* I should alert hotel security immediately. Perhaps there is still time to apprehend—"

He turns to leave, but Olivia grabs his sleeve. "I am afraid it's too late, Robert." She lets go of his sleeve. "Manderley was attacked two nights ago. The thief is probably long gone. I am sorry. I should have said that from the beginning."

"Would you like me to call hotel security anyway?"

"No, thank you." Olivia lowers her voice. "Fortunately, my friend was rescued from serious harm thanks to the intervention of another hotel guest. Perhaps you know him? He is staying in the Dior Suite."

"I am sorry, but we are not permitted—"

Olivia leans over the table, giving Robert an unobstructed view of the deep valley between her breasts. "Robert, we know his first name is Xavier, but we don't know his last name. Manderley would like to send him a thank-you gift. Please won't you be *my* hero and tell me his last name?" She bats her eyelashes again. "Pretty please?"

Robert looks around nervously before answering. "Monsieur de Maloret," he whispers. "The guest staying in the Dior Suite is Monsieur de Maloret."

"Mallory? With a y?"

"Non." Robert shakes his head. "M-a-l-o-r-e-t."

"Brilliant!" Olivia leans back, smiling broadly at Robert. "I knew you were my hero. *Merci*, Robert."

"Is there anything else? Some more coffee, perhaps?"

"What?" Olivia looks at her coffee cup and then back at Robert. "No, I am perfectly content. You have taken wonderful care with my coffee cup, Robert."

Robert is beaming as he bows and walks away.

"There you have it!" Olivia snaps her fingers. "Monsieur X has a name. Xavier de Maloret."

"You didn't need to do that, you know."

"Pshaw," she says, waving her hands. "It was nothing."

I have to laugh. Charming a staff member at an exclusive hotel known for their discretion into divulging personal information about one of their guests is child's play for a master like Olivia.

"It was nothing for you. You're Olivia Tate."

"The name's Bond." Her lips quirk in a slight smile. "Olivia Bond." She grabs her iPhone off the table. "And now, Miss Honey Ryder, why don't we see what we can uncover about your mysterious Monsieur de Maloret?"

"No!" I reach across the table and grab the phone from her hand. "And why am I Honey Ryder? I would rather be Vesper Lynd. She was clever."

Olivia sighs. "Vesper Lynd was cold. You are not cold, Manderley."

"But Honey Ryder was merely boobs in a bikini."

"Honey Ryder was more than boobs in a bikini!" Olivia cries. "She was a beautiful, mysterious, sexually liberated woman."

"Vesper was smart and a double agent."

"You look more like Honey Ryder."

"Still"—I sniff and hand her back her phone—"I would rather be Vesper Lynd."

"Fine! But you know how it ended between Vesper and Bond. She betrayed him and then died, prompting him to speak one of the cruelest lines ever uttered, 'The bitch is dead.'"

She takes her phone and pushes the home button. "Search the web for Xavier de Maloret."

A second later, Siri's disembodied voice says, *"Here's what I found on the web for Xavier the Malaria."*

A distinguished elderly gentleman who has taken a seat at the table beside us glances over, his bushy gray eyebrow rising in disapproval. I can almost hear him thinking, *In France, dinner companions are to be seen and not heard,* ma cher mademoiselle!

"Olivia, stop!" I hiss.

Olivia pushes the button again, raising her voice. "Xavier de Maloret!"

"I am sorry, Olivia the Brilliant, I couldn't find anything on the web for Savored the mallory."

"Xavier de Maloret!"

"Okay, here's what I found for David and Valerie."

Before I can grab the phone out of her hands, Olivia growls and jabs the button again. She speaks slowly this time, enunciating each word.

"What . . . do . . . you . . . know . . . about . . . Xavier . . . de . . . Maloret?"

The shadow of a man, a tall, broad-shouldered man, falls over our table.

"A bit, actually. What would you like to know?"

Olivia looks up from her phone and gasps.

Chapter Ten

"Xavier!"

Xavier steps out from behind my chair and it is my turn to gasp. He's wearing abdomen-hugging black-and-white swim trunks in a houndstooth pattern and a black cotton tee. Dark sunglasses hide his gaze.

"*Bonjour*, Manderley." He nods at me. "How did you sleep? I trust you had sweet dreams?"

Guilty heat flushes my cheeks. *No, I did not have sweet dreams. I had a nightmare about you that left me as disturbed and disquieted as your kisses.* There is an awkward silence as I try to mentally sort through the jumbled images from last night. Xavier kissing me in the hallway. Stars dropping from the heavens and bouncing like pearls on the deck of a beautiful sailboat. Xavier yanking me off the boat and into the sea. Xavier wishing me sweet dreams.

"Hello there," Olivia says, thrusting her hand out. "I am Olivia. Olivia Tate. Manderley's best friend. You must be . . ."

"Xavier." His smile is tight as he shakes her hand. "But, please, call me Xavier the Malaria."

Olivia chuckles, either oblivious or intentionally ignoring the tension crackling in the air between her and Xavier like tiny bolts of static electricity.

"Funny." Olivia laughs. "You don't look like a killer."

Xavier stops smiling. "I beg your pardon?"

"Malaria." Olivia laughs again, inelegantly. "A life-threatening blood disease caused by parasites."

He smiles politely but does not laugh. Amazingly, he appears immune to Olivia's dazzling wit and trademark charm.

"It's a pleasure to meet you, Mademoiselle Tate. Manderley has told me much about you."

"She has told me a lot about you, too."

"Evidently, not enough."

Olivia laughs. "Oh, well, you know. A woman can never be too cautious when her best friend is flitting off to Monte with a tall, dark, handsome stranger. Information is like champagne, one can never have too much. Wouldn't you agree?"

"I have always held to the adage that too much information can be as troublesome as too little."

I wonder what he is thinking. If only he would remove his dark sunglasses and let me look into his eyes. Would those deep blue pools reflect irony or annoyance?

"I see you are to play tennis. Don't let me keep you. The weather can be so unpredictable here in the South of France. One moment, you are basking in the sunshine"—he turns his head to look at me and I feel sick with regret—"and the next moment your joy is obliterated by meddlesome clouds."

He nods at me and strides away.

"What a rude man!"

"You were shouting his name into your phone, wanting Siri to search the internet for juicy gossip about him, and then you called him a parasitic disease. How was he supposed to behave?"

"It's the twenty-first century, Manderley! Googling a guy is what you do before you . . . you know . . . google him! It's one of the steps in modern-day courtship."

"I hate the twenty-first century," I say, tossing my napkin on the table in frustration. "There's no mystery, no romance. Frankly, I don't want to google a man before our first date. I would rather learn things about him organically, over time. I wish we could go back to the—"

"Stone ages?"

"The 1940s."

Olivia rolls her eyes. "Same thing! The men living in the 1940s were patronizing sexists who thought women were only good for making meatloaf and mixing martinis. You've watched the movies from that decade. They said things like, *Be a good girl and bring my slippers*."

"They treated women as creatures who were delicate and worthy of their respect and protection."

"They treated women as inferiors."

"Well," I say, pushing my glasses up my nose, "technically, women are inferior to men."

"Good God and Gloria Steinem!" she cries. "Please tell me you are joking."

"No, I am not. Biologically speaking, men produce more testosterone. For centuries, societies have prized behavior associated with testosterone production: strength, dominance, competitiveness, sexuality, protectiveness. So, from a male perspective, they are the stronger, more dominant, sexual, protective, and competitive gender. Ergo, they are superior."

Olivia groans and slaps her forehead. "Next you will

quote Darwin by saying feminism is just unchecked female militancy that will eventually lead to a disturbance
in the races and divert the orderly process of evolution."

"From a statistical standpoint, that is a possible even-
tuality. After all, there is a direct correlation to lower fertility rates in countries with greater gender equality."

"Because the women in those countries are educated!"

"So, education equals independence which results in
lower fertility. Right?"

"Yes, smart women know that fewer children means
higher status." Olivia crosses her arms and repeatedly
taps her foot against the leg of the table. "What does that
have to do with you thinking women are inferior creatures?"

"I don't think women are inferior! I was merely sharing the popular theory that women are inferior because
they produce less testosterone, and, therefore, typically
demonstrate fewer testosterone-associated and culturally
revered behaviors."

She growls. "What does that even mean, Manderley?
To you. You say you wished you could live in the '40s.
Does that mean you are looking for a man who will call
you Dollface as he orders you about? Do you want to be
treated as an inferior and . . ." She stops talking and holds
her breath, her lips forming a slash across her face.

"Of course not. I believe women deserve to be treated
as equals, but I think we have lost something in our pur-
suit for equality."

She exhales. "Thank God!"

"I say I want to go back to the 1940s because it seemed
to be a more genteel decade, when men treated women
with courtesy and care. That's what we have lost: men
treating us with courtesy and care. The last date I went on
was—"

"—in the '40s?"

"Funny! It wasn't that long ago."

"Are you sure? Have you been on another date since I set you up with"—she grimaces, snapping her fingers as if the gesture is somehow linked to her memory— "what's his name? The cute ginger literary agent who works for Nathan Allenberg?"

"Samuel Sampson."

"Sam! That's his name." She crosses her arms and looks at me from beneath an accusatory, raised brow. "You haven't been on a date since Sam, have you? And don't say Xavier the Malaria, he doesn't count."

"Don't call him that!"

"Sorry. Primacy effect."

"And he does count."

"I didn't mean it that way. Of course he counts."

I pick my iPhone up, flip it over, and press the home button. "Gee! Look at the time. We better hurry or we will be late for our court reservation."

"Nope," she says, leaning back in her chair, closing her eyes, and raising her face to the sun. "I am going to stay right here until the Restylane evaporates from my lips and they look like two wrinkled up, withered balloons on my chin."

I sigh. Olivia had lip augmentation shortly after we arrived in Los Angeles, because, she said, *I look like the Joker when I wear lipstick.* I argued that plenty of beautiful women have thinner lips, like Heidi Klum, Kate Hudson, and Kirsten Dunst, but she said getting lip fillers was her little "prezzie" to herself for selling her screenplay. The first thing she said after Dr. Yaseef finished the injections was, *When the Restylane wears off, are my lips going to look like an old woman's breasts, all deflated and crinkly?* Even though Dr. Yaseef assured Olivia her lips would look as they did before the injections, my slightly neurotic friend continues to believe she is going to end up on *Botched*—that television show where plastic surgeons attempt to fix botched cosmetic procedures.

"You know Doctor Yaseef told you that your lips would not look wrinkled or withered."

"Really?" She lifts her head and opens one eye. "Do you want to test that theory?"

I laugh. Olivia always makes me laugh, even when she's being annoying. Her audacity and humor are two of the things I truly love about her.

"No." I laugh again. "I do not want your withered lips on my conscience. What do you want me to know?"

She licks her lips and then lifts her water glass to her mouth. Pretending to take a sip, she lets the remaining slivers of ice floating in her glass rest against her lips. When she is satisfied she has sufficiently cooled her heated Restylane enough to avoid a cosmetic surgery emergency, she stops "drinking" and puts the glass back on the table.

"Have you gone on any other dates in Los Angeles?"

"Yes."

"When?"

"Three months ago."

"With who?"

"A professor."

"Which professor?" She looks skeptical. "How did you meet him?"

"He taught the advanced digital photography and Photoshop class I took this winter. The one offered through the UCLA adult extension program."

"Ooo!" Olivia rubs her hands together. "Now you're talking! Hot for teacher. You dirty, dirty girl. How *Children of a Lesser God*. How *Wonder Boys*! Was he a sexy

prof like Harrison Ford in *Raiders of the Lost Ark*? Did
you write love messages on your eyelids so he could see
them when you blinked? Why didn't you tell me? Are
you going to see him again?"

"Which question would you like me to answer? In the
interest of brevity, I will answer one."

"Was he scholarly hot?"

I open my mouth to answer.

"Wait!" she cries, holding up her hand to stop me from
answering. "Are you going to see him again?"

"Is that your final question?"

"Yes. No!" She props her chin on her fist and I can almost see the dozens of questions popping up in her brain,
like thought bubbles over a comic-book character. "If you
wanted to see him again, you wouldn't have gone out
with Xavier the—"

I clear my throat.

"—you wouldn't have gone out with the Frenchman,
even if he is *très*, *très* hot." She taps her lips and thinks
for a few more seconds. "Why aren't you dating the professor?"

"He was twenty-five minutes late for our date."

She crinkles her nose. "Seriously?"

"Punctuality matters. It's a way of showing someone
you respect them."

She rolls her eyes.

"That's not all," I say. "He asked me to go to dinner
and a movie."

"Ick," she says, wrinkling her nose. "Basic. No wonder you dropped him."

I laugh. "It was an uninspired choice for a first date,
but I wouldn't have minded if he had put some effort into
it, a little planning. Instead, he waited until we were in his
car and then he said, *Where do you want to eat?*"

"Maybe he was being considerate. Maybe he didn't want to pick a seafood place only to discover you were allergic to shellfish."

"Couldn't he have just googled it? I am sure my allergies are listed somewhere on the internet, maybe gathered after I took some *BuzzFeed* quiz."

"How Obsessed with Food Are You?"

I laugh. "Which Ryan Gosling Character Is Your Soul Mate?"

We look at each other and we both say, "Noah!"

Olivia and I might not agree on which decade produced the finest gentlemen, but we have always agreed that Noah, Ryan Gosling's character from *The Notebook*, is the superlative romantic lead.

Olivia signs the check. We grab our racquets and make our way across the terrace, in the direction of the pool and tennis courts.

"You realize *The Notebook* was set in the 1940s, right?" I say. "Noah was a '40s man."

"He was a fictionalized man. Honestly, Manderley, I think you are idealizing that time. Men might have appeared more chivalrous, but they were still men. Take Spencer Tracy, for instance. He was an actor known for playing honest, righteous men, but off screen he carried on a not-so-secret affair with Katherine Hepburn. Can you imagine how humiliating and frustrating it must have been to be his wife? Did you know she was an actress before they met and she gave up her career to support him? Pig!"

"Olivia! Spencer Tracy wasn't a pig."

"If the snout fits. That's all I am saying."

We follow a path covered by a red canvas awning.

"So the professor was more of a dud than a stud. All I am saying"—she twirls her racquet in her hand—"is you better get your groove back, Stella, or it's gonna be lost forever."

"What does that mean, lose my groove?"

"It means I don't want you to become a spinster." She opens an iron gate and waits for me to go through. "Edith Wharton. Jane Austen. Edna St. Vincent Millay. Emily Dickinson. Louisa May Alcott. Do you know what they have in common?

"They were brilliant authors?"

"They were spinsters! Unmarried, often unhappy, spinsters. Do you want to be like them?"

"Hmm, do I want to support myself by writing literature that stands the test of time? Was that a rhetorical question?"

"Stop pretending to be obtuse. You know what I—" She stops walking and grabs my arm. "Good God!"

I follow her gaze and gasp. Xavier is reclining on a nearby lounge chair, one arm behind his head. He isn't wearing a shirt and his tanned, muscular chest is glistening with sunscreen.

He lifts his head and opens his eyes, piercing us with that unnerving blue-eyed stare. He notices my expression and his lips curve in an enigmatic smile.

"See ya," Olivia says, releasing her grip on my arm.

"Wait! Where are you going?"

"Go talk to him! Do it for Edith and Jane."

"I thought we were going to play tennis."

"We are," she says, pushing my shoulder. "Right after you practice getting your groove back a little. Go talk to him. I will meet you at the court."

She hurries off, leaving me standing by myself in the crowded pool area, withering beneath Xavier's scorching gaze.

Chapter Eleven

Xavier stands and walks over to me. "Please," he says, gesturing to the empty lounge chair beside his. "Won't you join me? I have something to say. I won't keep you but a minute. I know you are expected on the courts."

"Of course."

I follow him around the pool and sit on the edge of the empty lounger, clutching the handle of my tennis racquet in my sweaty hands. Xavier sits on his chair and faces me. His sun-warmed knees press against my knees. He puts his hand over mine, gently prying my fingers from around the leather grip.

"I am sorry for my boorish behavior." His voice is low and gravelly. "It's just, you see, I am rather a private person, and, well, I have these old-fashioned notions about courtship. If there is something you wish to know about me, I would prefer you to ask me. Less confusion that way, don't you think?"

It's nearly impossible to think clearly when he is stroking my hand with his thumb and pressing his knees against mine. I want to move closer to him, close my eyes and sink into the heat of him. I imagine it would be like taking a nap on the beach, losing yourself to the feel of the soft sand, the heat warming you clear down to your bones . . .

"You weren't boorish," I say, looking down at the strings of my racquet. "I would have been mortified if the tables had been turned and I happened by as someone was shouting my name into their phone. I feel the same way about my privacy. And, Olivia is always teasing me about my old-fashioned notions about c—" I look up. "Wait a minute. You did say courtship, didn't you?"

"Yes."

"That means dating."

He laughs. "Yes, it does."

"Are we dating?"

"Unless there is someone else?" He continues to make slow, nonchalant circles on my hand with his thumb, but there is a new intensity to his gaze. Our knees are still touching, and yet, I feel as if he has moved away from me. "Is there someone else, Manderley? Do you have a boyfriend waiting for you back in California?"

"Of course not! I wouldn't be here with you if I had someone waiting for me back home."

He smiles. The clouds move away and the sun returns, the fleeting darkness I sensed about him has vanished.

"*Bon*. I know you are leaving for Monte Carlo soon. Until then, let's enjoy our time together and get to know each other better."

The memory of last night creeps out of the dark, quiet recesses of my subconscious into my active consciousness, like a brash uninvited guest crashing a party. Loud, disturbing memories as difficult to ignore as a slinky gold dress moving through a dimly lit parking lot at night. Does Xavier have someone waiting for him at home or, perhaps, upstairs? I want to ask him, but I am afraid to confess I was spying on him.

"What is it, *ma bichette*?" He raises my hand to his lips and kisses the spot where his thumb had just been. "Something is bothering you."

For once, I wish I had the confidence to respond like a silver-screen ingénue. Lauren Bacall. Bette Davis. They would look into his eyes and say something dismissive, like *Don't be ridiculous, darling. What could possibly be bothering me?*

I am not a sultry, sharp-eyed, knows-what-she-wants kind of woman like Lauren Bacall. I don't have Bette Davis's brashness and talent for clever dissimulation.

"It's only . . ."

"Only what?"

"I saw you."

"When?"

"Last night."

He narrows his gaze and two deep creases appear between his eyebrows. "Last night, when?" he asks, letting go of my hand.

"When you were returning from your engagement."

He leans back slowly and lowers his chin, studying me through the veil of his thick lashes. "Did you follow me?"

"What?" My legs begin to tremble and I have to push my thighs together to keep my knees from knocking. "Why would I follow you?"

"Why would you google me?"

"I didn't! Olivia did."

He glares at me and the trembling spreads throughout my body. Did you know Lauren Bacall came up with her sultry camera "look" by accident because she was so nervous the first time she acted in a film she pressed her chin to her chest and looked up at the camera? She said the position helped calm her. I want to channel Lauren now, but am afraid I would only end up making her sultry look psychotic. Instead, I take a deep breath and hold it for several seconds before exhaling.

"I had insomnia last night," I say. "I was sitting on my balcony, drinking a cup of tea, when I saw you walk up to the hotel." He nods his head, silently commanding me to finish my story. "I was about to go back to bed when I saw a beautiful woman—the same woman you met in the lobby the other night—get out of a car and approach you. I don't know what was said, but I could tell it wasn't a pleasant exchange."

"You are correct. It was not a pleasant exchange."

"Is she your . . . someone?"

He clenches his jaw and a muscle beneath his cheek contracts. "Definitely not."

"But she was, once?"

"What?" He scoffs. "Jacqueline has never been, nor will she ever be, my someone. I always want to be honest with you, Manderley, but I would prefer not to talk about Jacqueline. All you need to know, for now anyway, is she played an insignificant role in my life once, a part of my life I am trying hard to forget."

"I understand, Xavier."

"Do you?" He exhales heavily and rubs his forehead. "I don't think you do, but you're kind to say so."

"I want to understand."

"I know you do, and I thank you for it." He leans forward again. "So, you haven't said if you will go out with me tonight."

"You haven't asked me out."

"I haven't, have I?" He chuckles.

I shake my head.

"Very well." He grabs his shirt and pulls it over his

head, then he takes my hand and holds it, absently stroking his thumb over my knuckles. "Manderley Maxwell, would you like to have dinner with me tonight? We could go dancing afterward at a lovely rooftop bar with sweeping views of the sea."

My heart misses a beat. Spending the evening with Xavier is exactly what I want, but I wish he hadn't asked me to go dancing. I am not a good dancer and I have never been into the club scene. Someone as athletic and sophisticated as Xavier probably dances beautifully and visits the most exclusive clubs.

I remember Olivia's words about losing my groove and realize I have never had a groove—and if I keep living for my work and everyone else, I won't ever develop one.

"I would love to go out with you tonight."

"Would you? *Bon!* It's settled then." He stands and pulls me to my feet. "Now, why don't I walk you to the courts so you can play your tennis game?"

He grabs his towel, tosses it over his shoulder, and rests his hand on the small of my back—a gesture that is fast becoming familiar to me, one I will forever associate with Xavier, like the way he furrows his brow when he is listening intently, or the way his thumb feels when he traces circles on my skin. Other men I have dated held my hand or put their arm around my shoulder when we were walking in public. Xavier is the first to touch me in this chivalrous way, and it excites and pleases me more than any touch ever has.

We arrive at the courts—two magnificently maintained clay courts bordered by tall Italian cypress trees—and find Olivia locked in a fierce match with a handsome man in tennis whites. We stand in the shade of a cypress, Xavier's hand still on the small of my back, my pulse racing faster than Olivia chasing her opponent's rapid volleys.

"She's good," Xavier says.

"Olivia is brilliant at everything she does."

"You admire her, don't you?"

"Absolutely." I turn to face him, tilting my chin up so I can look into his eyes. "What kind of woman would I be if I didn't admire my best friend? Mutual admiration, a desire to encourage each other to reach new heights, these are the foundation stones of all of my deep relationships."

He leans down and presses his lips to mine, kissing me in the shade of the cypress tree, with the fierce *thud-thud-thud* of my pulse pounding in my ears.

"We've only known each other a few days and already I feel admiration for you. Admiration, and a deep desire—"

"There you are!"

Olivia notices us standing on the other side of the fence and walks across the court, her hips doing a sexy Marilyn Monroe sway. She sticks her finger between one of the chain links and crooks it. I step closer.

"It's Gaspard!" she breathlessly whispers. "He's free this afternoon and asked if I might like a lesson. You know? Improve my stroke." She winks saucily and my cheeks flush with heat. "Do you mind?"

"No."

"You're sure?"

"Absolutely. Have fun."

She looks around me, raises her hand, and waves at Xavier. I look over my shoulder in time to see him return her wave.

"Are you kidding me?" she says, raising her voice. "I am going to spend the afternoon getting hot and sweaty with a gorgeous Frenchman. I can't think of a better way to spend the day, can you?"

"Olivia!"

"By-ee." She giggles before hurrying back to Gaspard.

"So," Xavier says, taking my racquet from me. "Are you going to follow your best friend's advice?"

"Excuse me?"

"Do you want to spend your afternoon getting hot and sweaty with a Frenchman?"

Sweet Lawd in heaven! My pits and palms are moist, my lady parts are damp. I am already hot and sweaty because of a Frenchman!

He notices my wide-eyed expression and laughs.

"Relax, *ma bichette*. I was only suggesting we spend the afternoon at the beach, perhaps swim and relax, catch up on some reading. Though, if you would prefer to go back to my room and make mad, sweaty love, I would be happy to—"

"The beach sounds lovely. I will just pop up to my room to change into my suit and meet you in the lobby. Does half an hour sound good?"

. . . Because I am going to need to spend fourteen minutes of it giving myself a major pre-game pep talk. "Great moments are born from great opportunities, Manderley, and that is what is being presented to you now. So, get out there and win-win-win."

"I will reserve two loungers, grab a few things from my room, and meet you in the lobby."

He rests his hand on the small of my back and we walk to the lobby. He pushes the elevator button, the doors slide open, and we step inside. My legs begin to tremble again as adrenaline rushes through my veins. In a few minutes, I will be lounging beside the most virile man I have ever met—and, I will be naked, except for a bit of silky fabric covering my lady parts.

Do you want to sit on the bench with all the other spinsters? Do you want to be a sad, sorry Stella? No? Then stop your whining, suit up, get out there, and get your groove on!

Chapter Twelve

"I need a serious pep talk."

I was dabbing OPI's Breakfast at Tiffany's nail lacquer onto my toenails in a last-minute toenail touch-up when my phone rang. I hobbled out of the bathroom, wads of toilet paper stuck between my toes, to answer the call because I was afraid it might be Xavier ringing to say he wanted to cancel. I didn't remember until after I heard my sister's breathless voice on the other end of the line that I hadn't given him my personal number.

"Good afternoon, Tara. I am fine, thank you for asking. Cannes is even lovelier than Aunt Patricia's postcards. How are you?"

"I'm sorry, Daphne," Tara says. "I want to hear all about Cannes, but first, I need your help with Emma Lee."

My father used to call me Daphne after the Greek mythological water nymph, because of my love of the sea. He said Daphne was so beautiful she brought Apollo to his knees. I think he was being ironic with the last part.

"What has Emma Lee done this time?"

"It's not what she has done, but what she says she is

going to do. She met some old British woman at B. Crav's turn-up last night, who told her she would make a 'veddy splendid marriage broker' and now she is talking about moving to England and becoming a matchmaker."

Beauregard Cravath III—B. Crav to his friends—is a member of Charleston's ancient elite. The Cravaths are an influential political family with roots going back as far as the seventeenth century. In fact, B. Crav's ancestor was a relative of one of the Lords Proprietors, overseers appointed by King Charles to tame and colonize Charleston. B. Crav is an enthusiastic polo player. His Whitney Turn Up is *the* social event of the polo season, drawing bluebloods from all over the world. He's also a philandering playboy who has tried to wed and/or bed Tara *and* Emma Lee.

"I am confused," I say, chuckling. "Are you worried she will make good on her promise to move to England, or are you afraid it's just more of Emma Lee's magical, fairy-dust, wishful thinking, and she will spend the rest of her life watching reality television on your couch?"

"It's not funny!"

"Of course it isn't." I stop laughing. "Emma Lee—a girl whose only serious relationship has been with the man who highlights her hair—thinks she is going to click her ruby slippers and magically travel to a fabled land where she is a wizard of matchmaking. To embark on such a fantastic journey, she would first need to leave your couch. I don't see her giving up the comforts of home for Oz, do you?"

Tara whistles. "I always knew you were more practical than emotional, but when did you become so jaded and biting?"

"I am not jaded. Am I?"

"That sounded a little jaded."

I look down at my shiny, freshly lacquered toes and sigh. Living in the land of prenups and paternity suits has definitely made me skeptical that I will ever be one half of a soul-mates-forever love, but I didn't think I had become jaded about others finding love, or about people having the courage to pursue their passions. Of course, I can't tell Tara this because she expects me to be the brilliant big sister, the one with a nifty bag full of answers and hope.

"I am sorry, Tara."

"Are you okay?" she asks, a new, slightly frantic note of worry in her voice. "You don't sound like yourself."

"Don't worry about me," I say, upping the perk in my tone. "I am just tired. Nothing a few days lounging on the beach won't cure."

"Phew! I don't know what I would do if you started foundering." She lets out a half laugh, half cry. "After all, you're Steady-On Manderley."

Steady-On Manderley, who is terrified at the prospect of spending an afternoon on the beach with a handsome man, surrounded by long-legged blondes in Balmain bikinis who will take one look at her and find her sadly wanting. Steady-On Manderley, who secretly yearns to be as rash and outrageous as her little sister Emma Lee. Steady-On Manderley is foundering, foundering beneath the weight of her unfulfilled dreams.

"Emma Lee will be fine, Tara. She is a charming risk-taker who takes wild, daring leaps and always ends up on her pretty little feet."

"Of course Emma Lee is a risk taker, because she has always had us running after her with a net. I would be a risk taker, too, if I knew someone would be there to catch me if I fell."

"Is that what this is about?"

"What?"

"Are you envious of Emma Lee?"

"No!" Tara sighs. "Maybe. Yes, a little. I envy her courage to boldly chase after whatever shiny thing captures her interest. She sees something she wants and she just goes after it."

"Tara, darlin', if there is a shiny thing you want to chase after, a bold leap you wish to make, do it knowing I will be there to catch you, too. I always have been there and I always will be."

She sniffles and I realize she is crying. "Steady-On Manderley. What would we do without you?"

"Snatch each other bald?"

She does another half laugh, half cry at my reference to a childhood hair-pulling fight she had with Emma Lee, resulting in both of them losing clumps of hair.

"If Emma Lee's heart is telling her feet to head to England to be a matchmaker, or India to be a Bollywood star, let her go. All you can do is let her go and be ready to cheer her on with loud applause when she succeeds, or welcome her home with open arms when she fails."

"Even if we think she is making a big mistake?"

"It's her mistake to make, Tara. Ultimately, we are the only ones who can decide which way we will go in life, and we are the only ones who can say whether our choice to take one path over the other was a mistake or our destiny."

Chapter Thirteen

Even though my heart is palpitating and my stomach is roiling with sour orange juice at the thought of walking down the Majestic's jetty in my department store bikini, I think of Emma Lee's audacity and confidence and keep my head held high as Xavier and I walk from the lobby to the beach.

During the Festival, photo-calls were held on the jetty. Maggie Gyllenhaal. Russell Crowe. Ryan Gosling. Emily Blunt. Charlize Theron. They've all attended photo-calls on the Majestic's famous jetty. Beautiful, glamorous people smiling, pouting, sulking for the camera.

Today, I don't see Ryan or Charlize, only long-legged blondes in Balmain monokinis eyeing my romper cover-up behind their oversized Jackie O–inspired Chanel sunglasses.

Xavier booked us the front row, which means we will have an unobstructed view of the Mediterranean and the Lérins Islands in the distance. It also means we have to walk past a dozen scantily clad beauties lounging beneath pristine white parasols.

I don't need a hand mirror to know that a prickly hot rash is spreading down my neck and over my chest. I frequently break out in a rash when I am anxious.

I want to feel glamorous, like Deborah Kerr in *From Here to Eternity*, a movie with the most erotic beach love scene ever filmed, but I am more like Jack Lemmon in *Some Like It Hot*. Jack was in drag, frolicking on the beach in a large one-piece and wig, when Marilyn Monroe declared him flat-chested.

I feel like a flat-chested man in drag. The black-and-white bathing suit I thought was so Rita Hayworth pinup, with the sweetheart neckline and boy-shorts bottoms, isn't doing me any favors either. Why, why didn't I remember Rita was a C-cup?

"Here we are," Xavier says, when we arrive at the two lounge chairs positioned at the end of the jetty. "Would you care for something to drink?"

"Bottled water would be lovely, thank you."

Xavier leaves me and walks back down the jetty to the bar. I remove my cover-up and perch on the edge of one lounger. I am squirting sunscreen onto my hand when Xavier returns with the bottled water. He looks at my chest and pulls off his sunglasses.

"Manderley?" he says, sitting down on the lounger opposite me. "Are you unwell?"

A Balmain blonde in the row across from ours glances over her shoulder, a bland, bored expression on her face, until she notices Xavier's broad shoulders and muscular back. Her lips quirk.

"I'm fine," I whisper.

"You are not fine," he argues. "You have a rash, *ma bichette*, all over your neck and chest. It looks like an allergic reaction, to something you ate, perhaps?"

The Balmain blonde rolls her eyes dramatically. Heat

flushes my cheeks. I look down at my toenails and notice a tiny piece of toilet paper stuck to the Breakfast at Tiffany's lacquer on my big toe. My humiliation is complete.

"Ah, I see."

Xavier stands and walks back down the jetty, leaving me alone, a rash-covered embarrassment of a woman with toilet paper stuck to her blue nail polish. I want to dive in the turquoise water and swim and swim until I reach the Lérins Islands. Instead, I stick my arms in my cover-up and clutch my beach bag to my chest. Xavier speaks to a hotel employee and returns.

"Come, *ma bichette*," Xavier says, reaching for my hand. "We are leaving."

I take his hand and we walk back down the jetty, hand in hand past the Balmain blondes. I have to resist the urge to scratch my neck when one of them winks at Xavier.

"We don't have to leave the beach."

"We're not," he says, leading me down a set of steps and across the beach to a daybed for two, with white canvas drapes. "We are just moving somewhere a little less conspicuous."

We drop our bags on the sand and take our places on the daybed. Xavier pulls the drapes on his side just enough to shield us from the Balmain blondes. I do the same.

"*Merci beaucoup*, Xavier. That was kind of you."

He looks over his bare, tanned shoulder at me and smiles softly, and the rash on my chest feels a little less prickly. "You're welcome, *ma bichette*."

"How did you know?"

"My sister, Amice, suffers from anxiety, though her rash usually starts on her arms and creeps up her neck, and it rarely looks as painful as yours." He leans his head back and looks out at the sea. "Have you always had anxiety?"

I shrug out of my cover-up, lean my head back, and cross my ankles.

"I've never been diagnosed with anxiety, but the nervous rash started in eighth grade English class, when Bobby Brumbacher heckled me for mispronouncing *mellifluously*."

"Just relax, Manderley," he says, reaching over and grabbing my hand. "I will not judge or heckle you if you mispronounce a word. I promise."

We hold hands and listen to the waves gently lapping the shore. Two relative strangers surprisingly content to just be, no urgency to fill the slender space between us with unnecessary words. My limbs feel more relaxed, sinking into the cushion, and my neck and chest don't itch as much as they did when I first sat down.

I close my eyes and let the warmth of relaxation spread throughout my body.

Before coming to Cannes, my view of the French Riviera was formed from watching flickering images projected onto a fifty-foot movie screen or a sixty-inch flat television screen. Winding roads that cling to the sides of precipitous cliffs in *To Catch a Thief*. Moonlight that bewitches and Catalan port towns that charm in *Pandora and the Flying Dutchman*. A smart set living on moored yachts and swimming in a turquoise sea in *The Talented Mr. Ripley*.

To these fantastical, flickering images, add colorful postcards of alabaster buildings covered in bougainvillea sent each summer by Aunt Patricia. Short notes scrawled on the back in her shaky hand describing leisurely days spent swimming off the coast, dining on fried salty *panisse* at the Hôtel du Cap-Eden-Roc, or taking a speedboat to the island of Saint-Honorat to eat fresh grilled lobster and sip chilled rosé.

The French Riviera became, in my mind, the pleasure grounds of the doyens of fashionable European society, an overindulged, idle set who subsisted on sunshine and champagne. Hedonists in Hermès finding their places in the sun. Just like F. Scott and Zelda before them.

I never imagined, while watching those dazzling flickering images or losing myself in the colorful verbiage of my aunt's postcards, that I would one day find myself part of the idle set—even if peripherally. Sure, I occasionally dreamt of what it would be like to be the chic sort of woman others whispered admiringly about. *That's the beautiful Manderley Maxwell, you know.*

What woman, as a child, didn't dream of growing up to be a witty world-traveler with exotic stamps in her passport and a mysterious handsome man close on her designer heels?

"You're awfully quiet."

"I am sorry." I open my eyes and blink against the bright sunlight. "I was just thinking about my aunt."

"I would like to hear about her, if you care to share your thoughts."

I tell him about my aunt's fabulous summers spent yachting on the Mediterranean—from Antibes to Positano—and how she sent me glossy postcards from exotic-sounding places like Saint-Jean-Cap-Ferrat and Castiglione della Pescaia. I tell him I would hang a map in my room and follow my aunt's journey, pushing red pins into each place she mentioned. I tell him about the buttery lobster and the cold rosé on Saint-Honorat.

"Those postcards always made me feel transported. It was as if, by reading her words, I could travel across the sea and be with her, swimming off the coast of Mallorca or eating dinner at Hôtel du Cap-Eden-Roc."

"Have you been to Hôtel du Cap?"

"No."

"What about Saint-Honorat?"

"I planned to, but . . ."

"But . . ." He stares out at the sea. "You are afraid retracing your aunt's footsteps will only remind you that she is further from you than ever before. You worry that you will visit the places she loved only to discover they aren't as magical as they were in your memory, and then you might wonder why you ever thought them magical in the first place. Is that it?"

He looks back at me, but I have the unsettling feeling he does not see me, that, for a moment, he slipped through some invisible portal in time and traveled to a distant place before I existed in his consciousness. Who, then? Who was he thinking of just now? Who was he speaking to?

He continues to stare at me, unseeing, trapped in that world of wakeful dreaming, and I suddenly have a horrifying thought: What if Xavier is in love with someone else? What if I am merely a seat filler, like the non-celebs the Academy Awards employ to fill empty seats at the Oscars ceremony, ordinary sorts who want to make believe they are one of the beautiful people?

My neck begins to itch again. I resist the urge to scratch.

"It's getting warm," I say, uncertain he hears me. "Would you like to go for a swim?"

"*Je suis désolé*, Manderley," he says, blinking. "*J'ai la tête dans les nuages.*"

"You are sorry you harmed your head?"

He laughs and the portal to the past closes. He is with me again, body and spirit, lying on a lounger, laughing in the sunshine.

"I said I was sorry because my head was in the clouds. I became distracted by my own memories and drifted away from you, *ma bichette*." He raises my hand to his lips and kisses my knuckles. "I won't let it happen again, *je te promets*."

I promise.

My heart skips a beat. Calm down, Manderley. He isn't promising to take your hand in marriage or to pull the drapes closed and make mad, violent, noisy love to you.

I'll bet he would close the drapes and make love to me if I asked him to. I'll bet he would peel my boy shorts from my body with the skill of a French lover, wrap my legs around his lithe waist, and . . .

"Manderley!"

"What?"

"Now who has her head in the clouds?" He laughs. "Come on, then. Let's go for a swim. It might be just what we need to keep our heads where they belong."

He pulls his T-shirt over his head and an electric jolt of desire travels through my body from my boy shorts down my legs, so I feel I have to move. I want to kick my legs, curl my toes. It's compulsive, irresistible, this need to move, to disperse the powerful desire flowing through my body like charged particles.

I jump up and toss my sunglasses onto the lounger. The next second, I am moving toward the water's edge, running, eager to feel the Mediterranean on my over-heated skin. Xavier follows me and we stand waist-deep in the clear water.

"Race you to that buoy," I say, pointing to a round buoy bobbing on the sea. "What do you say?"

"That buoy?" he asks, pointing to the yellow float. "All the way out there?"

"Yes."

"Are you sure? That has to be at least three hundred meters."

"I could swim three hundred meters with my eyes closed."

"You might not want to do that, *ma bichette*. A little off course to the west and you will end up in the marina."

"Stop stalling," I say, eager to move my body. "Whoever wins buys dessert tonight. Deal?"

"Deal." He laughs. "But only if you take a head start. After all, I am nearly a foot taller than you, and . . ."

"And?"

"I am a man."

I want to argue with him, but what's the point? He is a six-foot-three, two-hundred-pound man with a chiseled, muscular body, and I am a five-foot-four, one-hundred-and-eleven-pound woman with a slightly toned body. He definitely has an advantage over me. Besides, the point isn't to defeat him in a swimming race; the point is to get moving, expel the powerful sexual energy that began building up inside me the moment I lay down beside him, close enough to smell the coconut sunscreen on his heated skin.

"Fine."

"One . . . two . . . three . . . go!"

I dive into the water, pushing off the sandy bottom, and start swimming, kicking my legs and moving my arms. Soon, I am in the swimmer's zone, that place where everything slows down, where your movements and breathing develop a steady, solid rhythm. Kick, pull, breathe. Kick, pull, breathe. I do this for several more minutes.

The buoy is closer now.

I keep my rhythm going, kicking my legs, pulling my body through the water, and raising my head to take a breath. I listen for Xavier splashing behind me, but hear only my pulse in my ears and my steady exhalations. Kick, pull, breath. I tap the yellow float, dive under the water, flip around, and surface in time to see Xavier passing me on his lap back to shore.

Sweet Jesus! Where did he come from?

I change from breaststroke to freestyle, fluttering my legs and attacking the water with my palms flat and fingers extended, rolling back and forth. Kick, kick, pull, pull. Kick, kick, pull, pull. I keep at it until I am even with Xavier.

I look over my shoulder. Xavier smiles and winks. Winks! I am freestyling my boy shorts off and barely keeping up. I kick harder, flutter my legs faster, but instead of shooting through the water past Xavier, I fall behind.

Xavier is standing in waist-deep water, hands on hips, breathing as easily as if he had remained on the lounger, flipping through the pages of *Man of the World* magazine when I finally catch up to him. I stand up, my legs wobbly from exertion, my breaths quick and sharp.

To his credit, he doesn't gloat or grin.

"You didn't tell me you were such a good swimmer, *ma bichette*. I never would have guessed."

"Thank you," I say, gasping. "That's kind of you."

"I am not being kind. You're an excellent swimmer, *un poisson*. I like being challenged, particularly when I least expect it."

"A Fish? Challenged?" I snort.

"I am serious."

"Well, thank you." My breathing is even now. "It was fun, and now we have dessert to look forward to."

"I don't want dessert."

"A deal is a deal."

"I would rather have this—"

He grabs me around the waist and pulls me to him, pressing his lips to my wet, bare shoulder. He laps up the tiny beads of seawater with his warm, rough tongue, and my knees, already wobbly from the long swim, go weak. I wrap my arms around his waist and hold on so I don't slip under the water and float out to sea.

"I've wanted to do that since you removed your cover-up, to taste your skin again, to feel you in my arms."

My breasts are pressed against him and I can feel the vibration of his chest as he speaks. It's somehow more intimate than having his mouth on my shoulder, a reminder that we are standing as lovers stand, skin against skin, heartbeat against heartbeat.

I tip my head back and look up at him, the stubble covering his chiseled jaw, the smooth, tanned skin of his cheeks, the two, deep worry lines between his eyebrows, the thick lashes framing blue eyes shot with silver, and my heart aches with a fierce yearning. I want him to make good on his threat.

"I want you to . . ."

"To what, *ma bichette*?" He stares into my eyes. "What do you want me to do?"

I want you to make violent love to me, Xavier, until my legs tremble from exertion and I have to cling to you so I don't fall down.

". . . kiss me."

"Gladly."

He presses his lips to mine. I close my eyes and let the

waves of desire washing over me take me far away, far from Reed Harrington and her band of wannabes, far from the Balmain blondes and their carnivorous looks, far from the annoying little voice warning me about the risks of getting romantically involved with a stranger who lives a world away.

He tastes of salt and cinnamon mouthwash. A strangely addictive combination. Xavier, salt, cinnamon. Mmm. I open my lips and he pushes his tongue into my mouth, lapping at my tongue the same way he lapped at my skin moments before. The kiss ends sooner than I would like, though on the correct side of propriety since we are within view of nearly everyone on the beach.

"That, *ma bichette*, was far sweeter than dessert."

"Yes, it was," I say, flushing, my hands still pressed against his solid chest.

"Come on," he says, taking my hand. "Let's go back to the daybed and I'll order you a *citronnade*. Would you like that?"

"Yes, Xavier."

I enjoy allowing him to take charge because it means I can relax, let go, stop trying to keep dozens of juggling balls up in the air all at once. I am beginning to think being responsible is highly overrated.

We walk up the beach. Xavier orders my *citronnade* from a handsome waiter in white shorts and black-and-white striped shirt, and we take our places on the daybed.

Stretching my arms over my head and pointing my toes, I take a deep breath, hold it for several seconds, and exhale slowly.

"Happy?" Xavier asks.

"Very."

"I am glad. I do not want you to be anxious when you are with me, only happy and relaxed."

The waiter arrives with my *citronnade*. He attaches a metal shelf to my side of the daybed and places the slender glass upon it. "Would Madame de Maloret care for anything else?"

"Oh, I am not Mad—"

"Perhaps the red tuna tataki? I was told madame enjoyed the Asian salad during her previous stays with us."

I look at Xavier. He is staring at the waiter through narrowed eyes, the two lines between his brows now deep wrinkles marring his handsome face.

"That will be all," he says, his tone cold.

The waiter nods and hurriedly backs away.

"It's okay, Xavier."

"What?

"It's okay if you have brought another woman to this beach." I am trying not to wince at the pain stabbing my heart because I imagine a screen ingénue would mask her jealousy. "I don't mind, really."

"You don't?"

He looks at me and the intensity in his gaze startles me. His eyes, usually as bright and blue as the sea on a sunny day, are a portentous leaden gray, as if a tremendous interstellar cloud moved in front of the sun, plunging the world in darkness, and causing the seas to freeze.

"You are here with me now. What does it matter if you have been here before with a dozen other women? You are handsome and worldly, I expected you to have had other lovers."

"It's not what you think."

"Besides," I say, carrying on as if he hadn't spoken, "we only just met. I make no claims on you. We are two adults enjoying a holiday romance. Perhaps we will meet here again next year, or perhaps you will be with someone else and you will remember our time today fondly, but as a distant memory."

I look away, focusing my gaze on the tiny speck of toilet paper still stuck to the nail polish on my big toenail. I am trying to remove the toilet paper by discreetly rubbing my toenail against the lounger cushion when he grabs my chin and turns my head so I must look at him.

"Is that what you think? I am a playboy?"

"Aren't you?" I attempt a coy Lauren Bacall smile, a desperate attempt to keep up the teasing, carefree charade. "You appear to be a wealthy man spending his time enjoying himself. Zipping around the South of France in a sports car, staying in a luxury suite, seducing women with your charm and generous gifts."

"Woman." He places his hands on either side of my face, his fingers sliding into my hairline. "I am seducing only one woman, *ma bichette*. Only one. I do not have the inclination nor the immorality to behave as an inconstant playboy. Do you believe me?"

"Yes, Xavier."

His fingertips press against my scalp, as if he is imploring me to believe his words. *Believe. Believe*, he seems to be saying. He kisses me, an urgent, bruising kiss that thrills and terrifies me all at once. If kisses were fictional characters, the kiss we shared in the sea would be the repressed, amiable Dr. Jekyll, and this kiss would be the dark, earthy Mr. Hyde. The duality is shocking. Who is this man? The aloof, aristocratic man who rescued me from humiliation that morning at breakfast, or this passionate, powerful lover?

He thrusts his tongue between my lips and I move closer, closer, until I am lying on top of him, melting over his chest. He has this effect on me, this *throw caution to the wind, forget my proper Southern upbringing* effect.

When I tentatively slide my hands up his chest, resting my palms on his pecs, he growls deep in his throat and tightens his grasp on my face.

"You drive me insane," he says against my lips, his voice so gravelly as to be almost unrecognizable. "*Je suis fou de toi.*"

I don't know what he said because my mind is too clouded by the fog of lust to translate the words. When he kisses me like that, I have no situational awareness. I am a hopelessly lost soul, fumbling around with my hands in front of my face, trying to find my way through the miasma of desire to the clear light of rationality.

He removes his hands from my face and puts them on my shoulders, gently pushing me away from him.

"Move back to your side of the daybed and say something sobering."

I blink. "Wh . . . what?"

"Please, *ma chérie*, unless you want me to make love to you right here, right now, you need to stop touching me."

"Oh!" I quickly roll off of him, self-consciously crossing my arms over my chest. "I am sorry."

"Never apologize for arousing and being aroused. You apologize for lying, cheating, stealing, but never for loving, *ma bichette*."

My cheeks flush with heat.

"You are marvelous, Manderley Maxwell," he says, laughing. "You kiss me like a woman and blush like a girl."

To my mortification, my cheeks flush with a more intense heat. *"Merci."*

"De rien." He frowns. "Now, talk to me about something boring, something sobering."

"Sobering?"

"Something that will take my mind off the way your lips taste like Boules de Miel."

"Boules de Miel?"

"Honey drops."

My heart feels as if it is filled with helium and some-one just let go of the string tethering it to my body. Xavier thinks my lips taste like Boules de Miel. Just repeating the words, Boules de Miel, makes me want to cry with happiness, soar like a helium balloon spiraling up, up, up to the heavens.

"You have never told me what it is you do for a living."

"You've never asked." He leans over and pulls a slender book and his sunglasses from his duffel bag. He rests the book on his lap and slides the sunglasses on his face. "What do you think I do?"

"Well, I know you're not an actor."

He chuckles.

"The way you maneuver through traffic and around those hair-raising mountainous roads, are you a race-car driver?"

He laughs. "No."

I study his profile out of the corner of my eye, the proud nose, square jaw, and the tiny hook-shaped scar beneath his right ear, a faint curved white mark just visible through his dark stubble. He looks rakish, like Errol Flynn in *Captain Blood*, and I find myself wondering again if he might be a member of an organized crime ring.

"My family has been making ships for over a century. I am the chief operating officer of Théophilus, the oldest luxury yacht manufacturer in Europe. We are, incidentally, also one of the largest luxury yacht manufacturers in the world."

Is God, or one of his more mischievous angels, playing a cruel trick? First, my father and aunt die in a shipwreck. Then, my aunt leaves me her sailboat. Now, I have fallen in love with a man who makes yachts? Xavier mentioned he had to leave the French navy after his father died, to help run the family business. I just never imagined the business was boat building.

"Théophile?"

"Théophile was my great-great-great grandfather's first name. He was the founder."

"Do you like to sail?"

"I would spend my life at sea, if I could. What about you? Do you like the sea?"

"I respect the sea."

It's true. I do respect the sea, but like all deadly beasts, it should be respected from afar. Watching moonlight dance upon her waves is fine. Swimming close to the shore is also fine. But I don't ever want to go sailing again. Not ever.

Chapter Fourteen

"You bought a Grace Kelly gown!" Olivia coos, reverentially lifting one of the tissue-thin layers comprising the skirt of my new dress. "It's so elegant, so ethereal! It looks like one of the costumes Edith Head created for Grace Kelly in *To Catch a Thief*. I am chartreuse with envy."

I was walking back from the beach this afternoon, glowing all over from sunshine and Xavier's kisses, when I suddenly realized I hadn't packed a suitable dress to wear to dinner with a gorgeous Frenchman. Not a *Gasp! Who is that beautiful creature?* dress. So, I splurged on a little designer gown.

"You went into the Dior boutique dressed in a beach cover-up and purchased this spectacular gown right off the rack?"

"Yes." Okay, so I splurged on a little Dior gown.

"Ooo!" Olivia claps her hands excitedly. "I like Cannes Manderley! So bold. So confident."

I twirl in a circle and the soft, silver-gray chiffon layers float around my legs. The bodice of my dress is body conscious, tight in all the right places, with slender straps that leave my shoulders exposed.

"You really like it?"

"Are you kidding me? The dress is gorgeous. Your makeup is gorgeous. Your hair is gorgeous. Turn away. I am beginning to hate you."

I laugh because we both know she has no reason to be jealous of me. She is standing in my bedroom wearing a La Perla embroidered tulle bodysuit and high heels, a confident Glamazon in expensive lingerie.

"Are you sure you don't want to ask your Monsieur X to make it a double? Gaspard is taking me to a historic absinthe bar in Antibes, where you are expected to wear a silly hat and sing along to piano tunes. Then, we are going to a jazz club he said is the cat's meow. Gaspard said they serve pricey giggle water."

"Giggle water?"

"It's Jazz Age slang for champagne."

"I know what it means. I just didn't realize you had developed such an interest in jazz music."

"Cannes has inspired me, darling!" She walks back into her room, but her voice carries through the open connecting door. "I am thinking of writing a screenplay set in Cannes in the '20s. You know, when it was a haven for artists and writers . . ."

I look in the mirror to inspect my appearance one more time before Xavier arrives. I usually wear my hair up in a messy bun or sleek ponytail because it is more practical, but I styled it down, curled in soft waves, with my long bangs swept to the side, à la Lauren Bacall. Since I usually only bother with tinted moisturizer, a sweep of bronzer, mascara, and a dab of Burt's Bees lip balm, my smoky eyes make me feel as if I am a little girl playing dress-up with her mother's fancy clothes and cosmetics.

My tortoiseshell glasses are tucked neatly into their case beside my bed in favor of contacts.

"So, what do you say?" Olivia walks back into my room, plucked, spritzed, and lacquered to perfection. She is now wearing a silky rose gold–colored jumpsuit and several layered necklaces. She looks like she walked out of the pages of a modern retelling of *Gatsby*.

"What do I say about what?"

She narrows her gaze and her arched brows knit together in irritation. "You weren't listening to me, were you?"

"Guilty."

"When did I lose you?"

"Right after you said 1920s Cannes was a haven for artists and writers."

"I said I want us to write a screenplay set in Cannes during the Jazz Age."

"Us?"

"Yes. Us." She sticks her hand inside the bodice of her jumpsuit and pulls a tube of lipstick from between her breasts. She takes the lid off and dabs the lipstick on the plumpest parts of my lips. "You're a brilliant writer, Manderley. Besides, you're an expert on the 1920s." She stops dabbing my lips and steps back to survey her handiwork. "Spec. Now, rub your lips together."

I obey. "I am not an expert on the 1920s."

"Your college thesis was on literary influences on the shifting cultural perspectives of the 1920s. You wrote about how Zelda Fitzgerald became the unwitting role model for a generation of young women eager to rebel in more ways than bobbing their hair, wearing flapper dresses, and dancing the Charleston."

"How do you even remember that?"

"It's my job to mentally record all of your brilliant,

dazzling moments and then remind you of them when you are forgetting you can shine."

"Am I not shining tonight? Should I brush a little more highlighter on my cheekbones?"

I glance in the mirror and wince when I notice the bold crimson slash of lipstick across my lips. I am about to wipe it away when Olivia grabs my hand.

"I am fatally serious, Manderley. Please don't joke."

Olivia can be like a bullmastiff with a knotted-rope toy when she is *fatally* serious.

"Of course you are," I say, squeezing her hand. "We are in Cannes because your screenplay was nominated for a Palme d'Or. You don't need me to write a screenplay."

"I don't need you to write a screenplay. I want you to write a screenplay with me. Will you think about it?"

She is trying to pick me up, dangling a writing job like a carrot before my downtrodden, dragging nose, and I appreciate it.

"Yes."

"Think about it," she says, linking her arm through mine. "We could be like Joel and Ethan."

"Who are Joel and Ethan?"

"The Coen brothers!"

You can't live or work within a two-hundred-mile radius of Hollywood without knowing the names Joel and Ethan Coen, but it's fun to wind Olivia up a bit. I look at her and frown.

"The Coen brothers. Of course. The figure skaters who took gold at the last winter Olympics. I loved their costumes."

"Are you kidding me? Tell me you are kidding. They wrote *The Big Lebowski. O Brother, Where Art Thou? True Grit*—"

She stops reciting the Coen brothers' filmography when she feels my side shaking with repressed laughter.

"You are such a—"

There is a knock on my door. I press my hand to my stomach and look at Olivia through wide eyes. "Should I feel this much angst? Should my stomach feel as if someone used it to practice origami? Shouldn't things be easier, more relaxed? Maybe it's a physical sign I shouldn't be going on a date with a stranger in a foreign country. Maybe—"

She unhooks her arm from mine and turns to face me. "Maybe, schmaybe. Listen. You are young and beautiful and you have had a *helluva* bad year. This is the time in your life when you should be grabbing on to any good opportunity that comes your way, especially if that opportunity is tall, dark, and lethally handsome."

She reaches inside the bodice of her jumpsuit again and pulls out a small pack of breath strips.

"How many things are you carrying in there? Your La Perla bodysuit is like Mary Poppins's magical carpet bag."

"Never mind about my bodysuit. Here." She slides one of the blue strips out of the package and holds it to my mouth. "Put this on your tongue, pull on your big-girl thong, and let's do these Frenchmen."

"Olivia!"

She takes the opportunity to push the strip into my mouth, before walking over to the door and peeking through the peephole.

"It's Monsieur X," she whispers. "He has brought you flowers and his designer stubble is looking particularly spec this evening."

The contents of my stomach—one *citronnade*, an apple, and a breath strip—begin burbling up my throat. I duck around the partition separating my bedroom from the foyer and pray I won't be violently ill. I listen as Olivia opens the door and greets Xavier with a purring, "*Bonsoir*, Monsieur X."

"*Bonsoir*, Mademoiselle Tate."

"Don't be so formal," Olivia teases. "Why not call me Madame O?"

Time to pull on my big-girl thong, as Olivia said. I swallow the acidic bubble rising up my throat and step out from behind the partition.

Olivia was right. Xavier does look particularly spectacular tonight. He is wearing his tuxedo without the tie and he's left the top two buttons of his shirt undone. He looks like a male model in a diamond jewelry advert.

"Good evening, Xavier," I say, smiling.

He looks at me and his eyes widen. He nearly drops the bouquet of jasmine and pale pink peonies he is holding.

"Manderley?"

Behind him, Olivia nods her head, urging me to say something, do something. What would Lauren Bacall do if Humphrey Bogart showed up at her door with flowers? She wouldn't hide behind a partition like a timid schoolgirl. I walk over to Xavier with my head held high and kiss both his cheeks.

"Are those for me?" I ask, nodding at the flowers.

"Of course." He hands the flowers to me. "You look beautiful tonight, *ma bichette*. Truly, breathtaking."

"Thank you. You look rather breathtaking yourself."

He gazes deep into my eyes and his lips curve in a smile. For a moment everything else fades away—my nerves, Olivia, the room—and all I can do is stand motionless, transfixed.

"I will just pop into the bathroom and put these in some water," Olivia says, taking the flowers from me. "Be right back."

"Thank you for the flowers, Xavier. They are lovely."

"You're welcome."

He reaches out and lifts a lock of hair from my shoulder, gently twisting it around his long finger, and his expression changes, his smile fades, his eyes appear somehow dimmer, filled with melancholy.

"You are a different Manderley tonight."

"What do you mean? I am the same Manderley."

"Are you? I hope so."

He releases my lock of hair and smiles again.

Olivia returns. "Well, you kids better get going," she says. "And remember what Zelda Fitzgerald said, 'Be cautious in life and reckless in love.'"

"I don't think that is a Zelda Fitzgerald quote."

"Isn't it?"

"No."

"Oh well." Olivia shrugs. "Then learn from Hemingway. He said, 'My only regret in life is that I didn't have more sex.'"

My cheeks flush with heat.

"Wine," Xavier says. "I believe he said he regretted not drinking more wine."

Olivia laughs boisterously. "You are right, Monsieur X. So, be sure to drink a lot of wine and have a lot of sex tonight. Just in case you are to die a horrible, unexpected death tomorrow."

"Good night, Olivia."

"Good night, Manderley." She grabs my shoulders and gives me a quick hug. "Mmm, you smell good. What is that perfume you are wearing?"

"Essence of Jasmine."

"Yummy. Where did you buy it?"

I look at Xavier and smile. "It was a gift."

"Lucky you."

"Yes," I murmur. "I am lucky."

Chapter Fifteen

Text from Emma Lee Maxwell:
Would you please order me a pair of tall Hunter Wellington boots in black gloss as soon as you possibly can? (Like, now.) If you order them from Amazon they will be here in two days. I promise I will pay you back.

Text from Emma Lee Maxwell:
Oh yeah! Don't forget to order the shine kit.

Text from Tara Maxwell:
Did Emma Lee ask you to buy her rain boots? She tried to get me to buy them for her by saying "everyone wears Wellies in the Cotswolds." Are you sure we should be encouraging her matchmaking scheme?

I wonder what I would have been doing right now if Olivia hadn't been nominated for a Palme d'Or. I wouldn't be driving in a beautiful sports car with a beautiful man in the South of France. I would be spending this evening the same way I spend every Friday evening: soaking in a rose-scented bubble bath while listening to Nat King Cole or Bing Crosby croon one of their dreamy love songs. Later, Olivia would text me to say she wished I had gone out with her to the club of the month. She would tell me how great the DJ was and how she saw Leo or Gigi or Liam. And I would fall asleep watching *The Ghost and Mrs. Muir* starring Gene Tierney and (sigh) Rex Harrison.

With Xavier, I am able to step over the cultural line that has divided me from the beautiful, glamorous people, a line I never thought I wanted to cross. At least, I never wanted to cross before coming to Cannes. I have never thought myself a part of Hollywood culture—pool parties where the guests are too busy making deals to swim, VIP parties with red ropes separating the "important" from the "insignificant," hazy nightclubs where celebs do coke or smoke weed in the bathrooms. The drug scene is pervasive in Hollywood, because actors and actresses are often deeply flawed people riddled with anxieties. Johnny Depp doesn't talk about it a lot, but it is well-known in Hollywood that he suffers from panic attacks. Emma Stone has agoraphobia. Scarlett Johansson confessed in a magazine interview she suffers serious anxiety before each film. And Nicole Kidman said she has crippling stage fright. Some actors snort lines, smoke weed, or pop pills to fight the deep doubt and depression associated with all types of artists. The first party Olivia and I went to was in the Hills. The host was a famous studio exec who told me he often holds gutter-glitter parties for his teenagers and their friends, so they can "learn how to do cocaine responsibly."

I never stepped over the cultural line separating me from the beautiful, glamorous people because I never felt it was a line I wanted to cross. Xavier makes me think differently, but then he is a different sort of beautiful, glamorous person. Isn't he?

"You're awfully quiet tonight, *ma bichette*."

"Am I?"

"Is anything the matter?"

"Not at all."

I look at him. His dark profile against the window lit by street lamps reminds me of one of those Jane Austen–era silhouette portraits, the kind Marianne Dashwood sketched of John Willoughby in *Sense and Sensibility*. I feel the same way Marianne felt when she looked at Willoughby, the consuming belief that she had found her someone special, her soul mate.

Xavier takes his gaze off the road for a moment, just long enough to steal my breath.

"What you are you thinking?"

"I am thinking about Marianne Dashwood."

"Is she a friend?"

I smile. "She is a character in a Jane Austen novel. In the film version, she sketches her lover's profile with a charcoal pencil. When I saw your profile just now, it reminded me of Marianne sketching her Willoughby."

"You were sketching my profile in your mind?"

I look down at my hands, embarrassed.

"Does that mean I am your Willoughby?"

"I hope not."

"You don't want me to be your lover?"

My heart skips a beat. "Willoughby duped Marianne. He was not the hero she believed him to be."

"That sounds ominous."

"Despite his charm, Willoughby had a scandalous past."

"Don't we all."

Now what does that mean? How am I to interpret that statement, as a glib response or a confession?

"What happened to Marianne and Willoughby?"

"He abandoned her in favor of Miss Grey, a dazzling beauty with a better social pedigree and larger dowry. Poor Marianne."

"Poor Marianne? She was better off without Willoughby."

"That is true," I say, arranging the layers of my dress. "She was better off without Willoughby because his departure made room for Colonel Brandon, an older, kinder, truer gentleman. Willoughby was without standing or fortune. Colonel Brandon could take care of Marianne."

"So, Marianne was a social climber?"

Out of the corner of my eye, I notice he is clutching the gearshift so hard the blood appears to have drained from his knuckles. They are as white as his tuxedo shirt.

"What? No!"

"Standing and fortune. Are these what matter most to women?"

"Is that a rhetorical question?"

"Answer me, please. Are they what matter to *you*?"

The air leaves my lungs in a sudden rush. "I thought we were talking about Marianne and Willoughby."

"We were, but now I want to know what matters to you, Manderley. Do you value standing and fortune over everything else?"

"Of course not." Tears prick the corners of my eyes. How did a pleasant conversation about two Jane Austen characters suddenly turn into something strangely personal? "When I commit my life to someone—*if* I ever commit my life to someone—I want to know we share the same values. Trust, honesty, loyalty, family. These are the things that matter to me. Fortune and standing might matter greatly at the beginning of some love affairs, but their value often diminishes over time."

He relaxes his hold on the gear shift. "I am glad to hear it."

He says nothing more. He offers no explanation for his pointed, personal question, merely stares out the window, his brow knitted as he concentrates on a series of sharp turns. I look away, because I do not want to see that scowl on his face when I can still hear his accusatory tone in my head. I want to study the sheer fabric of my skirt and pretend we are back in my hotel room and Xavier is telling me how beautiful he thinks I look in my new dress.

My instincts tell me Xavier is not a dangerous or unbalanced man. There is something deeper at work here, some invisible emotional thorn lodged in the paw of this great beast. I just need to find out what is causing his sudden, unexpected mood changes.

He downshifts and pulls off the road onto a narrow gravel overlook. I glance out the window at the smooth black sea and the moon reflecting golden on the surface.

"Manderley. Please, look at me."

I turn to him.

"I am sorry, *ma bichette*. I did not mean to be so brusque with you. You see"—he sighs and runs a hand through his immaculately combed hair—"I have spent most of my life surrounded by men. Boarding schools. The naval academy. At sea. Boardrooms. I have become accustomed to speaking to men, bluntly and plainly."

"That isn't all of it, though, is it?"

He inhales sharply. "What do you mean?"

"You weren't just brusque. You were . . . suspicious."

"Suspicious of what?"

I notice he didn't deny feeling suspicion.

"Me."

"I have reasons to be suspicious of people and their motives for wanting to grow close to me. Millions of reasons."

"I am sorry to hear it."

"No, I am the one who is sorry." He puts his hand on my face, stroking my cheekbone with his thumb. "It was unfair of me to bring the ghosts of my past with us tonight. Will you forgive me? Can you forgive me or have I ruined the evening for you?"

I nuzzle against the warmth of his hand. "We all travel with the ghosts of our past, Xavier. From time to time, they try to spoil things, but only if we let them. I forgive you."

I want to share with him about my father's debt and the humiliation of discovering the IRS planned on seizing all of his property, the disappointment I felt in realizing my father hid things from me, from all of us. I know what it means to have ghosts that make it difficult to trust.

"*Merci*," he says, stroking my cheek again.

He shifts the car into gear and we take off again, racing along a narrow road hugging the coastline. He pushes a button on his steering wheel and soft classical music fills the compartment.

"Are you hungry?"

"Yes."

"*Bon.*"

"Where are you taking me for dinner?"

"It's a surprise." He winks at me. "Our reservation isn't until nine, though. I thought we might stop for drinks and dancing before dinner."

We arrive at a small coastal village and Xavier pulls to a stop in front of a one-story white stucco building. A valet appears from the shadows. Xavier leaves the engine running, but opens the door and climbs out.

"We will only be an hour," Xavier says, handing the valet his key fob.

He walks around the car and opens my door. I take his hand and step out of the cool car into the balmy night air. The sound of bluesy music and tinkling laughter spills out of the building.

"Where are we?"

"This is La Grotte du Pastis, but most people just call it La Grotte," Xavier says, placing his hand on the small of my back and leading me down a long, dimly lit stone corridor. "It has a remarkable collection of wines and cocktails, but it is famous for its aperitifs."

As it turns out, La Grotte is French for *the cave*. The bar is located in an actual cave, with three stone walls, a vaulted limestone ceiling, and one side open to the sea. Tables set into alcoves offer private places to sip wine, but the big draw appears to be the glass dance floor jutting out of the mouth of the cave and offering a view of the surf crashing on the rocks below.

Xavier leads me to a table close to the dance floor. He pulls my chair out and I perch on the edge, watching the dancers sway in the lantern light to the bluesy music.

"This is breathtaking."

"I am glad you like it, *ma bichette*. I thought you might."

A waiter arrives to take our order.

"Would you like some champagne?" Xavier asks.

"I have never liked champagne. The bubbles give me a terrible headache. What would you recommend?"

"La dame prendra un cocktail de citronnade avec de la vodka, un zeste de citron, et des glaçons," he says to the waiter. *"Je voudrais signle-cask de whisky écossais avec une goutte d'eau, merci."*

The waiter nods and hurries back to the bar.

"I think you are the first woman I have met who doesn't like champagne."

"You must think me childish and gauche."

"Not at all," he says, smiling. "I think you are unpretentious. You are unlike anyone I have ever known and I like you, very much."

"Thank you, Xavier. I like you, too."

Our gazes meet in the darkness and the world fades away again. Xavier and I are alone, two lovers swaying to a tune as old as time. Is it lust or love? I am not sure, but I don't want the tune to ever end.

The waiter returns with our drinks. I look away, afraid I might be caught with my emotions on naked display. He puts my glass on a napkin on the table in front of me.

"Take a sip and tell me if you like what I ordered you," Xavier says when the waiter disappears into the shadows again.

I lift the glass to my lips and inhale before taking a sip. It has almost no scent except for the hint of lemon from the twist floating between the ice cubes and tastes like a grown-up *citronnade*.

"What is it?"

"*Citronnade* cocktail. Lemon juice, honey, and vodka served over ice. Do you like it?"

"It's delicious. I think I will make it my signature cocktail. Each time I drink it, I will remember sitting in this magical cave with you."

"That is sweet of you to say."

"Is it? I am only being honest."

"Which makes it all the more sweet."

We are dancing again. Dancing without touching, that's what I like to call our flirting. I hear the notes of a distant song, something primal and urgent, deep inside of me, something that makes me want to move closer to him, to close the distance between us.

He hears it, too, I think. He stands and holds out his hand.

"Will you dance with me, *ma bichette*?"

I answer him simply by standing and taking his hand. He leads me to the throng of dancers already swaying together and we dance to a slow, mournful blues tune. The wispy layers of my skirt flirt with our legs with each movement, brushing against my bare thighs, wrapping seductively around Xavier's tuxedo pants.

It's hypnotic, the sound of the sea crashing against the rocks, the breeze blowing softly through my hair, the keening of the saxophone, and Xavier humming near my ear. The song ends, but Xavier keeps his arm around me until another one begins.

I look up into his handsome face and my heart aches with happiness, with longing, with the poignancy one feels when they are experiencing a joy they know can't last forever.

He kisses my forehead.

"What is wrong, *ma bichette*? You are frowning so much you have worry lines stretching across your forehead."

"I was just thinking about something my aunt said to me once. She said, *Every happy moment is a breath away from dying and becoming but a memory*. It makes me sad to think this happy moment will soon die. I want it to go on forever."

He slides his hand up to the middle of my back and holds me tighter. "So do I, *ma bichette*. So do I."

The world around us fades away again and we are alone, dancing over the sea beneath a velvety black canopy adorned with a trillion stars. He lowers his head and presses his lips to mine. We kiss as if we truly are the only people left in the cave.

"Do you remember how you said you would think of this evening every time you taste a *citronnade* cocktail?" he murmurs, brushing his lips over mine.

I nod.

"Well, I will think of you every time I taste honey. I will think of your warmth, your sweetness, your purity, and how much your lips taste like drops of honey." He kisses me again, softly. "I have never been a sentimental man. I never would have thought to wish for a way to bottle up memories like perfume."

I shift my gaze to my feet. He tips my chin up, forcing me to look at him. "Not all memories are worth saving, but this one, *ma bichette*, is definitely bottle worthy."

"Excuse me." We look over our shoulders and discover a man with a camera standing beside us. "Would you mind if I snapped your picture?"

Xavier nods, but he does not release his tight hold on me. I smile. There is a bright flash. The photographer thanks us and hurries away.

"I think his flash blinded me." I laugh, blinking. "Either that, or I have fallen and am staring up at the starry sky."

Xavier laughs. "Come on," he says, relaxing his hold on me. "Let's finish our drink before we have to leave for dinner."

We return to our table and are sipping our drinks when a boisterous, fashionably dressed crowd enters the bar. The women are tall and leggy, their beautiful bodies poured into tight Versace gowns. The men are handsome, tanned and athletic, with breeding oozing from their immaculate pores. They do not wait for the hostess to show them to a table, but instead claim several small tables and pull them together to create one large surface. They order several bottles of Veuve Clicquot.

I am so engrossed in studying the beautiful ones, it takes me several seconds before I realize Xavier has not said a word. I find him tipping his glass of scotch back and forth, staring moodily at the amber liquid sloshing around inside. The mood feels heavier somehow, as if someone has dumped a pile of bricks into our cozy hot-air balloon basket.

"I wish I had the confidence to wear a backless Versace gown and sparkly heels and guzzle expensive champagne like it was water."

I had been aiming for self-depreciating humor, but my comment lands far from the mark.

"You wouldn't be here with me if you were in a Versace gown guzzling champagne," Xavier says, standing. "Shall we go?"

We are walking by the boisterous newcomers when a beautiful one, a brunette with model-sharp cheekbones and sleek black hair, looks at Xavier and gasps.

"Xavier!"

Xavier keeps his hand on the small of my back, urging me to keep walking.

"Xavier de Maloret!" The brunette stands, blocking our path with her size two Versace-clad body. *"Je pensais que c'était toi, chéri!"*

She flicks her cool gaze in my direction and her upper lip curls as if I am a bug she wishes to squash beneath her Christian Louboutin stiletto heel. I suddenly recognize her as the woman in the sparkly dress, the one who confronted Xavier in the hotel parking lot. She continues to stare at me as she speaks to Xavier in clipped French.

Xavier responds in equally clipped French. I listen to the exchange without understanding a word.

"Où est Marine?" she shouts. *"Où est Marine?"*

Xavier removes his hand from the small of my back and grabs her arm, hissing in her ear. They stare at each other, locked in a silent battle of wills, until she finally pulls her arm free of his grasp and walks back to her seat, sinking into her chair like a scolded child.

Xavier puts his hand on the small of my back and we leave the bar. The valet brings the car around and we climb in, but Xavier does not pull away. We sit in the dark, listening to the purr of the car's expensive engine. I keep hearing the woman's final question in my head, a question I was able to translate: Where is Marine?

"Manderley?"

"Yes?"

"I know how that must have looked to you."

"It's okay. You don't need to explain."

He turns to look at me.

"I want to explain."

I want to press my hands to my ears hard enough to block out the words he is about to speak. *La, la, la. I can't hear you. I can't hear you telling me you are a playboy with lovers scattered from one end of the French Riviera to the other.*

"I already know what you are going to say."

"You do?"

"Yes," I say, swallowing a lump of emotion. "That woman is your girlfriend, isn't she?"

"What?" He laughs harshly. "No. That woman is not my girlfriend. I told you she has never been my lover. I did not lie."

"Who is she?"

"Her name is Jacqueline. I was *involved* with her best friend, Marine. I have not seen Marine in over a year, but Jacqueline has misconceptions about how things ended between us. She believes by publicly challenging me she will get me to"—he sighs and runs his hand through his hair again—"I am only sorry her misguided, juvenile behavior has embarrassed you and spoiled our evening."

People do not use the word *undone* much anymore, but it is the word I would use to describe Xavier's current demeanor. He appears positively undone by this latest encounter with Jacqueline, alternately running his hand through his hair or gripping the leather steering wheel until the blood drains from his knuckles. I am Southern born and bred. Jacqueline's scathing looks and loud scene should have humiliated me. Yet, my only concern is for Xavier.

"Our evening will only be spoiled if we allow Jacqueline to spoil it," I say, putting my hand on his elbow. "I won't give her the power to ruin our happy memory, will you?"

He relaxes his punishing grasp on the steering wheel and the color slowly returns to his fingers.

"You are right," he says, turning to look at me. "This is our evening and I don't intend to let anyone spoil it. Thank you, Manderley. You are unlike anyone I have ever known."

He shifts the car out of neutral and we are off again, speeding around serpentine curves.

I meant what I said. I don't want to allow Jacqueline to ruin this special evening, but I can't deny her outburst has left me feeling a little undone. The ghost of Xavier's girlfriend past now has a name to go with her amorphous shape . . . Marine.

Chapter Sixteen

"Close your eyes."

"You're serious?"

"Absolument."

Xavier has pulled to the side of the road again and is dangling a black silk eye-mask, the same type of eye-mask found in the gift shop of the Hôtel Le Majestic.

"You want me to wear an eye-mask?"

"Oui. I have planned something special for you and I do not want the surprise ruined before we even get there."

I take the mask, hold it to my eyes, and fasten the Velcro straps behind my head. Xavier makes sure I can't see anything, before driving on. We aren't driving for long when the car stops and Xavier kills the engine.

"We are here," he says.

"Can I take my mask off?"

"Soon."

The driver's-side door opens and closes. My stomach flutters with nervous excitement. What could Xavier have planned? Slow dancing and sipping cocktails in a cave by the sea was the most romantic experience I have ever had and I can't imagine what could top it.

My door opens. Sultry, sea-scented air invades the compartment, moving over my skin as seductively as the layers of my gossamer gown. Xavier helps me out of the car. I am wobbly after the vodka cocktail and disoriented without my sight. Xavier wraps his arm protectively around my waist. We begin walking over what feels like a garden path of brick pavers bordered by grass. Every second step, my heel sinks into soft ground.

"Relax," he says, squeezing my waist. "I have you."

I listen for clues that might reveal our location, but hear only the soft *thwack-thwack* of palm fronds blowing in the breeze and waves hitting the shore somewhere in the distance.

Finally, Xavier stops walking, puts his hands on my shoulders, and turns me around. *"Voilà,"* he whispers in my ear, his warm breath teasing my hair. "We are here. You can take the mask off and open your eyes now."

I reach behind my head and unfasten the eye-mask. When I open my eyes, I discover I am standing on a wide gravel path facing a beautiful Napoleon III–style château with whitewashed façade, blue painted shutters, wrought-iron balconies, and a mansard roof. The gardens surrounding the château are filled with towering Aleppo pines, waxy-leaved magnolias, citrus trees heavy with fruit, and oleander bushes. I have never been here, but I recognize it as easily as I would recognize my family home in Charleston. We are standing on La Grande Allée leading from the sea to . . .

"Hôtel du Cap-Eden-Roc!"

"Oui," he laughs. "We are at the Hôtel du Cap. Are you happy? Is it a good surprise, then?"

"Are you kidding me? Do you know how many post-cards my aunt sent me from this hotel? I still have them tied up with the ribbon from the box of chocolates she sent me from the hotel's chocolatier." I impulsively throw my arms around Xavier and hug him like he's the Macy's Santa. "This is the best surprise you could have given me."

He laughs again and kisses my forehead.

"Thank you, Xavier."

"You are welcome."

I turn back around and stare at the hotel, its windows glowing golden against the night, and recall the many snippets my aunt wrote to me about her visits. *The mojito baba, so refreshing after a day in the sun . . . Their* pavé de loup à la plancha *is divine . . . Played tennis with Robert Redford yesterday . . . The concierge confessed he believes the ghost of F. Scott Fitzgerald haunts the hotel . . . You do realize Fitzgerald based the hotel in his novel* Tender is the Night *on Cap-Eden-Roc . . .*

A pang of sadness echoes in my heart as I realize how much larger and impersonal the world now seems in the wake of my aunt's death. Tears fill my eyes, blurring the postcard-perfect picture of Hôtel du Cap-Eden-Roc at night. I blink them away before my contact floats off my eyeball and down my face.

Xavier wraps his arm around my shoulders.

"You are thinking of your aunt, aren't you?"

"Yes," I whisper.

"You loved her much."

I nod my head.

"What made her so special? What did you admire most about her?"

I smile. "Some people color with their favorite crayons. Aunt Patricia colored with all of the crayons in the box.

Bold, rarely used colors extending far beyond the lines. Her vibrancy and audacity inspired many. I like to think it inspired me—or, at least, it is inspiring me now."

"My family is from Brittany, a land of legends and many superstitions. My grandfather believed the dead continue to enjoy the hospitality of friends and loved ones long after they have stopped walking this earth. He said their spirits return to us whenever we speak kindly of them, that they flit unseen amongst us, happy to have been resurrected through love." His rubs my collarbone with his thumb, a gentle, comforting gesture. "If that is true, your words and love resurrected your aunt just now, here, in one of her favorite places."

"That is such a nice thought. Thank you."

"You're welcome."

We turn around and begin walking down the Grande Allée toward the hotel's world-famous pool and the sea, breathing in the sharp scent of pine needles commingled with the heady, incense-like scent of magnolia blossoms. We follow the path until it veers to the right, and come to the hotel's poolside restaurant, with floor-to-ceiling windows that offer sweeping views of the sea.

"I have wanted to visit this hotel ever since my aunt told me it was built by a newspaper mogul for writers seeking inspiration. This is a dream come true."

"I tried to get reservations at their restaurant, the one your aunt wrote you about, but they are hosting a special event." I am about to thank him for even trying when he raises my hand to his lips and kisses my palm. "So, I booked their sky-top champagne bar instead. For the next two hours, we will be dining by ourselves. How does salty pan-fried *panisse*, grilled lobster, and chilled rosé sound?"

"It sounds perfect."

* * *

Later, after I have savored the buttery lobster and chilled rosé, after we have talked about everything and nothing, we are walking up the Grande Allée on our way to the parking lot, when Xavier grabs my hand and pulls me into a secluded corner of the garden. Hidden between walls of oleander bushes, we kiss until I am clutching the front of his tuxedo shirt and we are both gasping for breath.

I rest my head on his chest and we stand locked in each other's arms in the moonlight, the heady scent of spring in the South of France filling our senses.

He reaches over my shoulder, plucks one of the pink flowers from the oleander bush, and hands it to me. I hold the flower to my nose and inhale the scent. Mmm. Roses and sweet pink bubblegum.

"My aunt always said the scent of oleanders carried on a sea breeze was what heaven would smell like."

He plucks another flower and brushes the powdery petals along the line of my bodice, over the swell of one breast, and then the other. Teasing. Tickling. Promising something more.

"What do you say, *ma bichette*?" he asks, holding my gaze. "Is this heaven?"

My breasts react to his slight touch, tightening. My nipples harden, straining against the wispy fabric of my bra. When he notices my hardened nipples, he lowers his mouth to the place between my breasts. A quick kiss that sears my skin with the intensity of a red-hot brand. I can't breathe.

"Is this heaven, Manderley?"

"Yes," I whisper.

He presses the flower to the place he kissed, slowly dragging the petals up my chest and throat, over my chin, around my lips. "And oleanders? How do you feel about oleanders?"

"I . . . love them."

"Do you?"

I can't move. I am paralyzed by the power of his gaze, knocked senseless by the intensity of my body's reaction to his touch. I am entranced by him, and if he asked, I would strip naked right here in the garden and offer myself to him just as he offered the oleander blossom to me. In my mind, I see him as a god. He is like the Greek god Pothos, the personification of yearning and desire, reducing mere mortals to quivering creatures consumed by hunger.

Unfulfilled yearning can drive a person mad, can't it?

The thirty-one-minute drive back to the hotel is excruciating as I try to imagine what will happen when Xavier walks me back to my room. Will he ask if he can spend the night? Will he try to make good on his promise to make "violent love" to me? What will I do if he does ask to spend the night making violent love to me?

Anxiety and lobster do not pair nearly as well as rosé and lobster. By the time we reach my door my stomach is threatening to demonstrate its rejection of the buttery meat and bitter nerves.

"I had a wonderful time tonight, Manderley," he says, brushing a lock of hair from my face. *"Merci."*

"Thank you, Xavier," I say, leaning against the door. "I will never forget this night."

"That was the plan." I think he is going to ask me to invite him into my room, but he leans down and kisses my forehead. *"Bonne nuit, ma bichette."*

"Good night, Xavier."

He turns to leave. "That's right," he says, snapping his fingers. "Could I use your mobile?"

I frown. "My cell phone?"

"S'il vous plaît."

I fumble in my evening bag, pull out my iPhone, enter my password, and hand it to him.

"Merci," he says, taking the phone.

His thumbs move over the screen and then he is typing something, perhaps a text or email. A few seconds later, my phone emits the swooshing sound it makes when a text is sent. He pushes the home button with his thumb and taps the screen again. Finally, he pushes the power button and hands the phone back to me.

"Merci."

I take my phone, but I don't slip it back into my bag. He winks and walks away. I wait until I hear the elevator ding before taking my key out of my bag and slipping it into the lock.

I step into my room and close the door behind me, leaning against it. I push the home button on my iPhone and enter my password. The Contacts app is still open.

Xavier de Maloret.

My heart skips a silly, girlish beat, like it did when I was in high school and would write my first name on my notebooks and then add my boyfriend's last name.

I feel like Liesel when Rolf kissed her in the gazebo in *The Sound of Music.* I want to spread my arms wide and let out a glass-shattering *Wheeeee*! I am not sixteen going on seventeen, but I definitely want someone older and wiser, a Frenchman who makes my heart burst with joy simply by adding his name and phone number into my contacts.

I have brushed my teeth and washed my face. My gorgeous gossamer Dior is hanging in its garment bag in the wardrobe. I am drifting to sleep when my phone vibrates. It's a text from Xavier, quoting *Bonjour Tristesse*. It's then I realize he sent himself a text from my phone so he could have my number.

Text from Xavier de Maloret:

I was rereading *Bonjour Tristesse* and came to the part where Cécile says she kissed Cyril hard enough to bruise him so that he would not forget her. I couldn't forget you if I wanted to, *ma bichette. Bonne nuit et de beaux rêves*, X.

Chapter Seventeen

The first thing I do when I wake up the next morning is reach for my phone to check for a message from Xavier. I hold my breath as I enter my password and then feel an exhilarating rush of adrenaline when I see a new text from him.

Bonjour. I have a business obligation this morning. Would you like to meet for lunch? La Palme d'Or, Hôtel Martinez, at 1:30?

Something comes over me, a feverishness, an unusual recklessness, and I answer yes before checking with Olivia to see if she has any plans. I am staring at Xavier's name on my screen, humming *I am sixteen going on seventeen*, when Olivia knocks softly on the connecting door.

"Come in."

The door opens and Olivia pokes her head through, focusing her gaze on the unoccupied side of my bed.

"You're alone?"

I sit up. "Of course, I am alone."

"I don't believe it. Not after the look he gave you when he saw you in that dress last night." She chuckles low in her throat and climbs into bed beside me. "Someone should alert the CIA. You have unparalleled powers of resistance. There is no way I could have sent that man back to his room alone after he looked at me with that smoldering gaze. He was sex in a tuxedo."

I find it best to quickly change the subject whenever Olivia gets a little too . . . Olivia-ish. "Did you have a nice time last night?"

She wrinkles her nose.

"That bad?"

"Turns out, I don't like jazz that much. No wonder they called it the Lost Generation. One hour of listening to all of those wailing horns and pounding pianos and I wanted to get lost. I was crazier than Zelda. True story."

I laugh. "What about the jazz singer? Do you like Gaspard?"

"The cat's meow." She holds her hand like a cat's claw and pretends to scratch me. "Me-ow!"

"I am glad. Maybe he will end up a character in your next screenplay. The handsome tennis pro who spends his days on the courts with society's elite and his evenings in a smoky club playing seductive and forbidden jazz to a lost generation of poets and artists."

"Ooo, that's good. good." She rolls over, snatches a pen and pad of paper from my nightstand and begins scribbling. "I am writing that down in case Gaspard takes me to the absinthe bar again and the green fairy steals my memories."

"So you tried absinthe? How was it?"

"Strong and bitter, like Jägermeister." She tosses the pad of paper and pen back onto the nightstand and rolls onto her side, propping her head up with her elbow. "So, I take it you had a nice time with Monsieur X?"

I grin and pull the covers up to my chin.

"That good, huh?"

"Oh, Olivia!" I cry. "It was better than good. It was the best."

"Even better than your date with Caden Foster?"

"Caden Foster? Who is that?"

"Wow!" Olivia whistles. "That must have been some date if it has made you forget all about Caden 'Away with your fictions of flimsy romance' Foster."

Away with your fictions of flimsy romance is one of the lines in a poem by Lord Byron. Caden Foster was my on-again, off-again college boyfriend. He asked me out the first time by reciting a Lord Byron poem. He had an artist's soul, beautiful and extremely volatile, which is why we were on-again, off-again throughout college.

I tell Olivia about La Grotte du Pastis, how Xavier held me close as we danced over the sea, and about the romantic dinner for two at Hôtel du Cap-Eden-Roc.

"Hold on! He reserved the entire champagne bar at one of the world's most luxurious hotels in France? Who is this Monsieur X?" She hops out of bed, runs to her room, and returns a few seconds later with her MacBook. "I think it's time we employed a little Mr. Robot action."

"No! We definitely do not need to employ Mr. Robot action." I reach for her MacBook, but she swats my hands away. "Didn't you learn anything from your botched attempt to play the vigilante hacker? Besides, anything I need to know about Xavier I will learn from . . ."

I let my words trail off because Olivia probably can't hear me over the wild *tap-tap-tapping* noise her fingernails are making on the keyboard and because I am a little curious to see what she uncovers. To be more precise, I am curious to see if she uncovers a photograph of Xavier with *Marine*. In my mind, Xavier's phantom ex is everything I am not: a tall, willowy slave to fashion, a Glamazon who commands attention with the power of her personality and the awesomeness of her beauty.

"Found it!" Olivia's eyes widen and her mouth hangs open. "Oh my God, Manderley!"

"What? What is it?" I sit up quickly. "What did you find?"

She lifts the MacBook and I press my hands to my face, covering my eyes. "No, don't show me. I don't want to see. It's a picture of Xavier with some gorgeous woman, isn't it?"

"Yep."

I feel sick to my stomach. That little worm of curiosity that was nibbling on my resistance suddenly turns ravenous, devouring what is left of my insouciance. I pull my hands away from my face and look at Olivia's computer screen. Displayed is a French website called Beaux Rêves. The bold azure masthead and neat columns of French text leave no doubt that it is the website of some type of news outlet.

"Hold on. Let me switch the language." Olivia positions the pointer over a small British flag icon at the top of the screen and clicks the button. The page reloads. "'Beaux Rêves, a weekly lifestyle magazine capturing the luxury and glamour of the Riviera.'"

She scrolls down, past articles about luxury yachts, designer timepieces, and boutique hotels, until she comes to a gallery with photographs of beautiful people at glamorous parties. A svelte blonde sipping a glass of champagne, a distinguished elderly gentleman laughing at the camera, a couple with their arms . . .

"Wait! Is that me?"

"Yes!" Olivia clicks on the picture and it grows to fill the screen. "You asked me if I found a photo of Xavier with a beautiful woman, and here it is. Look at you two! You belong on the pages of a swanky lifestyle magazine."

I grab my eyeglasses off my nightstand and put them on. I look at the picture and my heart skips a beat. The photographer at La Grotte didn't just snap a picture of two people dancing, he captured a fleeting, intimate moment between a man and a woman. He captured one of the most intimate moments of my life. Xavier has his arms around my waist. He is looking down at me instead of into the camera, a confident smile coaxing the corners of his mouth, a dimple barely visible beneath his stubble. The dark background lends to the impression that we are alone even though we are surrounded by other dancers.

"Look at you, gazing into the camera through your eyelashes like a little sex kitten, chin down, lips pouting."

It's not the Lauren Bacall "look," but it is as close to sultry as I have ever been. It is sultry-ish.

"It was dark and I had my contacts in," I say. "I was squinting to see the photographer."

"You don't look like you were squinting. You look like you were flirting with your tall, dark, demonstrably devoted lover."

"It is a beautiful picture."

"It's a keeper," she says. "I would make it my screen saver."

She right clicks to save the photograph and then opens iMessage. She clicks on my name, attaches the photograph, and hits return.

"Can you read the caption under the picture?"

"I will read it only if you promise you will send the

photograph to Reed Harrington and her squad with the message: Bonjour Bitches!"

"I am not sending that message."

"Will you at least make the photo your Twitter profile picture?"

"Olivia!"

"Fine," she says, turning the screen back and clicking on the caption. "'Xavier de Maloret, CEO of Théophilus, the oldest luxury ship builder in the world, was photographed at La Grotte du Pastis last night, dancing with an unidentified companion who wore a diaphanous Dior gown.'" Olivia stops reading and slaps my shoulder. "Unidentified companion! You're the unidentified companion, Manderley! Oooh! That's so mysterious. So film noir. I love it."

"What else does it say?"

Olivia continues reading aloud. "'It is rumored Monsieur de Maloret is in Cannes finalizing a lucrative deal to build a fleet of superyachts for perfume billionaire and hotelier, Thierry Lambert. The first, a 170-meter megayacht with submarine and helipad, is expected to be ready for delivery in three years.'" Olivia stops reading and whistles. "One hundred and seventy meters! How many feet is that?"

"Over five hundred."

"Five hundred feet? Your boyfriend is building superyachts nearly as long as the *Titanic*."

"It is pretty amazing."

"I'll say. A rich boat builder who gives you a Dior bag before your first date and looks way, way hotter than Mister Andrews."

I look at her blankly.

"Mister Andrews. The man who designed the *Titanic* in the James Cameron movie. Remember, he told Rose

DeWitt Bukater the ship was going to sink and there weren't enough lifeboats?"

"Yes, I remember. But, Xavier is not my boyfriend."

"What is he then?"

"I don't know."

"Well, you better lock that shit down, Manderley!"

"Why? Because he is rich?" I look at her the same way my nanny would look at me when she caught me reading books under my covers at night instead of sleeping.

"Please." She rolls her eyes. "Don't even give me that face. Money might not buy happiness, but wouldn't you rather be miserable on a superyacht than a row boat?"

It's terribly crass and gauche of Olivia to suggest I pressure Xavier to make a commitment just because we have discovered he is incredibly wealthy. I would point out the tastelessness of her comment, but I love my best friend and understand her obsession with wealth; and the security it provides stems from a childhood spent in poverty. She told me once they were often without utilities. One desperate winter, her mother cooked Christmas dinner on a camping stove and they wore Wonder Bread bags over their shoes because they couldn't afford boots.

Instead, I tell her to keep reading.

"'Since taking over as chief executive of Théophilus after his father's death, Monsieur de Maloret has been full steam ahead, helping to revive his family's foundering business. First came the triumphant purchase and integration of Italian boat builders Titan-Donati. He expanded Théophilus's reach by acquiring the Dubai-based luxury yacht manufacturer Samilyah Marine. By shrewdly anticipating trends—such as larger platforms, infinity pools, panic rooms, anti-paparazzi shields, and the integration of jet engines—he has transformed sea travel to a decadent pastime for the world's most discerning clientele. As annual profits climbed from $532.4 million in 2008 to an astounding $2.3 billion last year . . .'" She drops the MacBook to her lap. "Holy Cal Hockley!" Olivia sputters. "Two-point-three billion dollars? This article says your Monsieur X made two-point-three billion dollars last year? And I called him Xavier the Malaria!"

Xavier's question about whether I value standing and fortune above all else suddenly makes sense. He is probably accustomed to people currying his favor simply because of his fortune. My daddy used to call people like that ticks. *Beware of the ticks, Mandy darling, they survive by feeding off the largesse of others.* We had a few ticks in Charleston, hangers-on hoping to make the right connection that would allow them to move up the beast that is society.

It also explains Xavier's unwillingness to open up about his life, and his anger when he thought his privacy had been invaded.

I feel a connection with Xavier. I might not have grown up with billions of dollars, but I was a member of a wealthy and prominent family. I understand the pressure that comes with trying to maintain your privacy when you live in an intrusive society. There's a saying in Charleston: What happens in your backyard today will be discussed on your neighbors' front porches tomorrow.

Charleston has many porches.

"Do you know how lucky you are?" Olivia says, closing her MacBook. "Of all the cliffs, in all the countries, you somehow visit the one that has a billionaire sporting designer stubble and an incredible six-pack. Oooh, let's go to Monte tomorrow. Maybe your luck will hold out."

"It's supposed to be beautiful tomorrow. Wouldn't you rather go to the beach?"

"I can go to the beach in California! I want to go to Monte Carlo, that magical place where fortunes are made and sizzling-hot love affairs kindled."

She closes her MacBook and reaches her hand out, rubbing my head.

"What are you doing?"

"I am rubbing your head."

"I know you are rubbing my head," I say, slapping her hand away. "Why?"

"For good luck. I am going to stop at the cliff on my way to Monte tomorrow and I want the universe to bring me a handsome billionaire with designer stubble," she explains, reaching her hand toward my head again. "Share the luck, Manderley!"

If I have learned anything in my twenty-seven years on this planet, it is that luck is like a bad boyfriend, full of charm and promises in the beginning, but eventually he will disappoint you with his inconstancy.

Chapter Eighteen

Luck might be a bad, faithless boyfriend, but over the next few weeks Xavier proves that he is good, true, and unstintingly generous.

We fall into an easy, comfortable pattern. While Xavier attends business meetings, Olivia and I have brainstorming sessions on the beach or go on inspirational adventures.

We visit the whitewashed Villa Santo-Sospir in Saint-Jean-Cap-Ferrat, where the famous French writer, director, and filmmaker Jean Cocteau entertained Orson Welles, Charlie Chaplin, Marlene Dietrich, Yul Brynner, Pablo Picasso, and Coco Chanel.

One afternoon, Xavier arranges a special outing to the Castle of la Croix des Gardes, a beautiful estate near the port, where Grace Kelly, Cary Grant, and Alfred Hitchcock filmed the ballroom scene in *To Catch a Thief*.

A little internet digging and I unearthed several other filming locations used by Alfred Hitchcock, including a villa in Saint-Jeannet that served as the home of the character played by Cary Grant. The elderly owner wouldn't let us tour the inside of the villa, but she was kind enough to allow Olivia to stand on the back terrace and snap selfies with craggy Baou de Saint-Jeannet looming in the background.

"I am standing where Cary Grant stood," she said. "Go ahead, push me off the terrace. Let me fall to my death on the rocks below. There's no reason for me to go on. Nothing will ever beat this moment."

We reenact the famous chase scene in *To Catch a Thief*, racing our rented Peugeot through the village of Le Bar-sur-Loup just as Cary and Grace did.

When I tell Olivia that Cary stayed at the Carlton Inter-Continental hotel in Cannes during the filming—that Hitch shot the beach scenes on the hotel's private beach—she insists we go there so she can collect some sand to take back to California with her. I try to tell her it isn't the same sand because Cannes spends 650,000 euros each year hauling in "fresh beach," but she won't listen. "I am getting that sand, Mandy. Even if there is only one grain that was there in 1955, that is still a grain of sand touched by the great Alfred Hitchcock while filming my favorite movie with my favorite actor!"

We spend days exploring the Vaucluse, a department of Provence where the classic French film *Jean de Florette* was filmed. We admire rolling hills covered in bright red poppies and stone farmhouses set amidst vineyards. We visit a charming village, walk down its cobbled streets, peek into courtyards, and toss coins into a fountain.

When he isn't busy with his work, Xavier takes me to secluded, off-the-tourist-track places in Provence and along the Côte d'Azur. We have a picnic of crusty *fougasse* bread filled with olives, Italian sausage, and creamy French cheese, and drink rosé on a beach near Villefranche-sur-Mer and watch the fishermen tossing their nets into the sea.

He patiently carries my basket through village markets as I buy soap flecked with lavender buds for Emma Lee, bottles of Herbes de Provence for Tara, and a sheer pink pashmina for Olivia.

We drive in his convertible through mountainous passes and along the coast from Cannes to Saint Tropez. We sun ourselves upon the ramparts of Château de La Napoule, an old military fort built on the edge of the sea in 1387 by the counts of Villeneuve. In a quayside café in La Napoule I try absinthe. While the bartender performs the absinthe ritual—attaching a flat, perforated spoon to the rim of a glass, placing a sugar cube on the spoon, and slowly pouring the green liquid over the cube—Xavier translates the words printed on a small plaque on the café wall: *In 1898, following his release from the Reading Gaol, where he had served two years hard labor for homosexual activities, the poet Oscar Wilde came to this café to drink absinthe and befriend the local fishermen.*

In the evenings, as the day is fading into night, we wind our way through the city's labyrinth of narrow streets in search of a new restaurant, one that will become our place. We eat goat cheese soufflé, fish soup with spicy sauce, grilled sea bass brushed with Provençal olive oil and sea salt, summer berries and fresh cream.

Then, we stroll barefoot along the beach, kissing in the lantern light. Or, we lie together on a deckchair, listening to waves whispering against the shore. These are my favorite times, the moments I treasure and press to the pages of my mind like snapshots. I treasure the quiet, end-of-day moments the most because they are when Xavier is at his most candid, relaxed and open, holding me in his arms while he tells me about his childhood in Brittany, his love of the sea, or the pressure he feels to preserve a family business that has been operating for over two hundred years.

I gather all of these little bits of information like scraps of paper blowing in the breeze, snatching at them, flattening them out, and pasting them to the scrapbook in my mind labeled *Xavier*.

The sunny days of summer do not last forever. Soon, the clouds will roll in, the temperature will drop, and I will find myself in a land far from Cannes. Perhaps it will be a Friday night in October. Olivia will be at some club and I will be at home, soaking in my rose-scented bubble bath, listening to Bing Crosby or Nat King Cole, remembering the way the Mediterranean looked like a mosaic of blues and greens. When the bubbles go flat and the bathwater turns cold, I will climb out of my tub, wrap myself in a robe, and pad into the living room. I will click on my gas fireplace and sit on my sofa. Then, I will reach into my mind, pull the Xavier scrapbook off the shelf, and flip through the pages. I will remember the snapshots of us together, strolling down the Croisette, Xavier's hand on the small of my back. I will remember the scraps of paper and all of those little bits of information. *Xavier played Rugby in college. Xavier prefers single-cask scotch with a splash of water. When Xavier was eight, he stole his father's sailboat and tried to sail to Madagascar because he read about a band of pirates who made their home in a cave on the island. Xavier tastes like warm cinnamon when he kisses me.*

Chapter Nineteen

Text from Emma Lee Maxwell:
Hypothetically speaking, if an American citizen were to move to another country, say, England, for example, would they need to obtain a work visa before traveling there or could they apply for one after they were settled in? Would they even need a work visa if they were planning on starting their own business?

Text from Tara Maxwell:
Has Emma Lee told you she is definitely moving to England, or is she avoiding it because she knows you will try to talk some sense into her?

I return to our rooms after breakfast one morning to find Olivia frantically tearing things out of her dresser drawers and tossing them into her open Louis Vuitton suitcase. High heels, tubes of lipstick, lacy La Perla panties, and pilfered bottles of Fragonard toiletries litter the floor. (Olivia has been asking the maid to leave extra each time she refreshes our room, and now she has an impressive stock of travel-size hotel toiletries.)

"Thank God you are here!" She says, shoving bottles of Fragonard into her sneakers. "We have reservations on the four-fifteen to Paris and I don't know how we are going to make it. I still have to finish packing, and shower, and put on my face, and . . ."

She sinks to her knees beside her open suitcase and tries to fit the sneakers into an overfilled compartment. I kneel beside her and take the sneakers from her shaking hands. Then I remove a pile of wadded-up T-shirts from her suitcase, shaking them out and folding each one into a neat little square. I put the T-shirts back into the suitcase, turn the sneakers so the soles face away from the garments, and efficiently fit everything back into the suitcase with enough room for several more bottles of pilfered toiletries.

"Our flight isn't until next week, Olivia."

"Didn't you hear what I said? We have reservations on the four-fifteen. We are leaving today!"

"What? Why?"

"Didn't you read my text?'

"What text?"

Olivia reaches into the pocket of her robe and whips out her iPhone. She pushes the home button and holds the screen in front of my face, too close for me to read. I take the phone, hold it farther away, and read the text.

Text to Manderley Maxwell:
  Spec news.

"That's it? It just says spectacular news."

Olivia grabs the iPhone from my hand and slips it back into her robe pocket before hurrying into my room. She returns a few seconds later, breathless, holding more hotel toiletries.

"It is spectacular news. The most spectacular news." She tosses the shampoo and lotion bottles onto the folded pile of T-shirts and sits down beside me, wrapping her arm around my shoulder. "Go ahead, guess what it is."

"You're in love with Gaspard and you are going to stay in France permanently."

"That would be divine, wouldn't it? But this is even better news."

"What could be better than love?"

"Success."

"You already have that."

"Well, *we* are about to have some more."

"We?"

"I sort of pitched our screenplay idea to my agent, and he sort of pitched it to a few execs, and now Warner Brothers is talking about offering us a contract!"

"That's fantastic!"

She claps her hands excitedly. "You haven't even heard the best part yet."

"I haven't?"

She shakes her head and squeals. "They are talking about getting Leo to play the part of the tennis-pro jazz musician." She doesn't wait for my reaction. She hops up and begins pacing the length of the room. "We need to go back to LA immediately. We need to meet with my agent and . . ."

Her voice fades to a distant hum. All I can think about is saying goodbye to Xavier. I knew this time would come—it was like a dark cloud hovering far, far away on the horizon, moving closer, closer, each day—but I thought we still had a few more days together. What am I going to do? The dark cloud that has been threatening my happiness for weeks has finally arrived and all I want to do is run to Xavier, wrap my arms his neck, and cry, *Please, please don't make me go. I don't want to go back to Los Angeles. I want to stay with you!*

My iPhone chimes. I pull it out of my pocket.

Text from Xavier de Maloret:
I have a business meeting this morning. Would you like to go for a swim this afternoon? I know a secluded beach not too far from here.

Tears cloud my vision. I blink them away and send a text to Xavier telling him I have something important to say. I hit return and hold my breath until my phone chimes again.

Text from Xavier de Maloret:
I just stepped out of the shower, but you are welcome to come up now.

I leave my room without telling Olivia where I am going, panic spurring me on, prodding me to run, run down the hall and up the flights of stairs, run to Xavier's door and into his arms.

Hurry. Hurry. If you don't hurry, you might get there and discover he has already left the hotel. You might lose the chance to look him in the eyes, those beautiful Mediterranean-blue eyes that sparkle one moment and hint at darker, enigmatic depths the next. *Hurry!*

I am out of breath and flushed all over by the time I reach his door. A frantic, frizzy-haired mess of a woman terrified at the thought of missing her opportunity to say goodbye to the man she . . .

. . . loves.

And there it is. The awful, agonizing truth of the matter. I am in love with Xavier de Maloret.

I knock on the door and Xavier answers, his hair damp, a towel around his neck, a smudge of shaving cream on his cheek near his ear. He is wearing pajama bottoms without a top, his muscular chest tanned to a rich brown from all of our days swimming in the sea.

"Bonjour, ma bichette," he says, pressing a quick kiss to my cheek. "This is a nice surprise."

My eyes fill with tears as soon as I hear him call me his little deer. The literal translation of *ma bichette* is "my little doe," but I recently discovered it is also a term of endearment, meaning *darling* or *sweetheart*. I realize the name might rankle some feminists, but it makes me feel warm inside, like when I used to drink hot cocoa after trudging through the snow from my classes to my dorm room. He notices my tears.

"What's the matter?" He opens the door and gestures for me to come in. "Have you had bad news?"

I step inside and close the door. "The worst."

"Come," he says, taking my hand and leading me to a chic sitting room decorated in tones of gray, black, and white. He gestures for me to sit on a velvet sofa while he sits on the coffee table across from me. "What is it?"

"I have come to say g . . . goodbye." My voice catches and I have to look away from him before I burst into tears. "We are leaving this afternoon."

"Leaving? So soon? I thought you were going to be here until the end of the month."

"We were supposed to be, but Olivia needs to go back to Los Angeles to meet with her agent. She pitched an idea we had for a new screenplay and Warner Brothers is interested. It's a tremendous opportunity."

"But that is marvelous, isn't it? It's your chance to

write the stories you want to tell, instead of editing some-one else's."

"I know, but . . ."

"But what?"

"I don't want to leave."

He sighs and runs his hand through his damp hair. "Then don't."

"I have to."

"Because you are her life preserver?"

"Well, yes," I say, shoving my glasses up my nose.

"Stop doing that," he says, grabbing my hand. "Wouldn't you rather do something else?"

"Like what?"

He stands up, walks over to the window, crosses his arms over his chest, and stares out for so long I worry he has forgotten I am here. Finally, he turns back around and walks over to me.

"Marry me."

"Marry you? Are you crazy?"

"Perhaps."

"I can't marry you."

He crosses his arms over his chest again and looks down at me. "Why not?"

"Because I don't even know you."

"What would you like to know?"

"Well, to start, I don't know your full name."

"Girard Fortune Xavier de Maloret."

The panic I felt when I saw the Balmain blondes flirt with Xavier returns, viciously clawing at my frail confi-dence. My chest itches and it takes all of my control not to scratch. Xavier is a rich, handsome man from an aris-tocratic family who probably lives in a grand mansion and runs with a grand set. Why would he want to marry me? Plain, socially awkward Manderley Maxwell. Sure, I came from wealthy parents, but I have never been part of a set.

"Unless you do not want to marry me," he says.

I look up and fresh tears fill my eyes.

"Perhaps you do not find me attractive."

"Are you serious? You're gorgeous."

"Okay then." He laughs. "Maybe you don't like me."

"Like you? I love you."

My cheeks flush with heat. I look down at my Tiffany-painted toenails peeking out from the tops of my sandals and wish I could call *Cut!* and redo this scene.

"Did you mean that?"

I look into his eyes and realize this is the time to put it all on the line. I might not have another chance to tell Xavier what meeting him has meant, how it has brought into sharp focus a yearning previously ignored.

"A little less than a month ago, I stood on a cliff on the Côte d'Azur feeling alone in the world, wondering how I would ever find the strength to take my next breath, and then the unimaginable, the unbelievable happened: You stepped up and took my hand and I learned to breathe again."

"Then marry me." He wraps his arms around my waist and kisses my forehead. "Take a chance on me, Manderley Maxwell. You won't be sorry, I promise."

"It is difficult to think clearly when you are holding and kissing me."

"*Bon!* I don't want you to think clearly, *ma bichette.*" He brushes his lips over mine and I inhale the clean, soapy scent of his shaving cream. "I want you to be mad with passion, reckless in your desire. I want you to follow your heart where it is telling you to go."

"You want to marry me?"

He chuckles. "*Oui.* Is that so hard to believe?"

"Well, yes."

"Why?"

"Because you hardly know me."

"I have seen glimpses of your soul and those glimpses were beautiful. You are kind, honest, and selfless. Everything else is distraction. Everything else I will learn over time."

"But . . ."

"What?"

"Aren't there things you want to know before you ask me to marry you?"

"I have already asked you to marry me, *ma bichette*." He grins. "However, I will ask you a few questions if it will make you feel better."

"It will."

"Besides fidgeting with your eyeglasses, do you have any bad habits I should know about?"

"Each morning, I make a comprehensive to-do list and I cannot go to bed unless I have checked off every item."

He frowns. "You're organized and driven. That's hardly an annoying habit. Try again."

"If I am reading a book or watching a movie I don't find enjoyable, I won't stop reading it or leave the theater. I have to finish it. Also, I steal socks."

He laughs. "You steal socks?"

"My feet turn icy at night if I don't wear socks to bed. But, I have this thing about wearing the same pair of socks two nights in a row. So, if I run out of fresh socks, I will take a pair from my family, friends, or boyfriends. There is always a pile of discarded socks beside my bed."

Xavier whistles. "That is serious."

"See?"

He laughs. "I don't think you will have to worry about cold feet when you are in bed with me, my love. Nevertheless, you have my permission to borrow my socks whenever you want. Better yet, we will sail to Ireland and I will buy you enough woolen socks to last a lifetime."

I cast my gaze across the sitting room to the bedroom beyond, the king-size bed with the rumpled sheets, and my pulse quickens.

"Thank you," I say, heat flushing my cheeks at the thought of sharing a bed with Xavier. "What other questions do you have?"

"Do you want children?"

"Yes."

"Bon." He hugs me tighter. "I wouldn't want you to sacrifice one passion for another, so will you promise to continue to write the screenplay with Olivia? I am sure it can be accomplished via the internet."

"I promise."

"Bon. I don't have any other questions right now. Do you have any for me?"

"Only a million."

He chuckles, lifting my hand to his lips. "Start with one. We have a lifetime for the rest."

"Why didn't your relationship with Marine work?"

"You don't really want to hear about my relationship with another woman, do you? Wouldn't you rather talk about what we want out of our marriage?"

"My father remained alone after my mother died. I asked him once why he didn't date. He said when he married my mother it was forever, that death hadn't altered his affections. I want that kind of love. How do I know you will be as committed to me as I will be to you?" I drop my head to his chest and listen to the thud of his heartbeat against my ear, seeking courage in the strength of the sound. "Divorce is not a path I ever want to tread."

His body tenses. He puts me back on the couch. I worry I have pushed him too far.

"Do we ever know another person, really? I would like to promise you that we are a perfect match and we will make each other so deliriously happy, so content, we won't ever think of divorce. I can't promise that, Manderley." He leans his elbows on his knees, reaches for my hands, and looks deep into my eyes. "I can promise I won't ever betray you. Remember when we were at La Grotte and you said you wished you could be more audacious? Wearing a scandalous designer gown and guzzling champagne is not audacious, *ma bichette*. Following your heart when your head is telling you to take a different direction is audacious. Be audacious."

Be audacious. If I were writing the script for this scene, I would have typed those words for Xavier to say. Does he know how lonely I have been living in the shadows, watching everyone around me reap the spoils of their daring? I want to be daring. I want to be reckless. I want to step on the tightrope even if I fall. *Do it! Take a risk. Otherwise, you are going to die in the shadows, yearning, unfulfilled, and alone.*

"Okay. I will do it! I will marry you."

I do want to marry Xavier, even if there is a little maggot of doubt wriggling inside the tender, developing fruit of our love, a maggot that could so easily be squashed if only Xavier would tell me about my predecessor—*Marine*.

Chapter Twenty

"What do you mean, you are eloping with Xavier?" Olivia isn't taking the news of my impending nuptials well. I am in my room, packing my suitcase while she paces in front of my open closet doors. I reach past her for a sundress still hanging in my closet. She snatches the hanger from my hand. "Stop! Would you please stop packing for just a minute and tell me what is happening?"

She hangs my sundress back up in the closet before taking my hand and leading me to her suite. Olivia sits on the sofa, curling her legs underneath her.

"Xavier asked me to marry him," I say, sitting on the chair across from the sofa, "and I said yes."

"This is insane. *Shutter Island* insane! You hardly know him."

"Do we ever know another person, really?" I say, repeating Xavier's logic. "I love him, Olivia. I love him so much it physically hurts when I think about leaving him here to fly back to Los Angeles."

"Are you saying you are marrying him because you

don't want to go back to Los Angeles? You hate it that much?"

"It's not about hating Los Angeles, Olivia. Well, not entirely."

"What?" she cries. "What is it about, then? Help me understand how you, the most levelheaded woman I know, could even consider running off with a man you have known for less than a month. It's so . . . so . . ."

"So what?"

"Irresponsible."

"What's wrong with being irresponsible once in a while? Tara has been irresponsible most of her life. Emma Lee is still irresponsible. I want to be irresponsible. Just once."

"Fine!" She uncurls her legs and hops to her feet. "Then stay in bed all day and eat greasy takeout. Go to bed before you have crossed off everything on your to-do list. I know! We will go to a club and get stinking drunk. You can pick up the first hottie you see and have dirty, dirty sex with him. That's irresponsible . . . for you."

"I don't want to have dirty sex with a stranger. I want to marry Xavier and let him make sweet love to me."

"Assuming it is sweet."

"What does that mean?"

"What does it mean?" She snorts and throws her hands up. "What if he is a freak? What if you get to Italy and he whips out a Christian Grey contract and manipulates you into agreeing to be his submissive sex slave? He could beat you!"

"He's not going to beat me."

I cross my arms in front of my chest and stare at Olivia over the tops of my eyeglasses so she can see her words are not going to alter my course. I am resolute.

"I am going to marry Xavier, Olivia." I anxiously look at the clock on Olivia's nightstand. Xavier is due in a little over an hour and I still have a lot to do before then. "I know you love me, O, and you are worried I am making a big mistake. Maybe I am. I just know if I don't do this, I will spend the rest of my life wondering what might have happened if I'd had the courage to take a chance, to follow my heart."

"You love him?"

"I do," I say, excitement fluttering in my belly. "I love him and we are eloping to Lake Como."

"Well, it doesn't look like you are going to have any problem saying those words when you get to the altar," she says, sinking back down onto the sofa. "If this is what you want, to elope with Monsieur X, I will do everything I can to help you get to the altar. Let me make a quick phone call to my agent. I will tell him I need to postpone the meeting with Warner Brothers because I am going to Lake Como to serve as my best friend's maid of honor!"

"No!"

"No?"

"You can't postpone your meeting with the studio. They might change their minds about optioning the screenplay."

Once Warner Brothers discovers Olivia's writing partner is an unknown with no screenwriting experience, they will most certainly pass on the project, but Olivia is energized and I don't want to drain that energy with my doubts and negativity.

"You're my best friend, Mandy. I can't let you get married to a virtual stranger in a foreign country without at least holding your hand as you walk down the aisle, especially now that your dad is . . ."

Dead. My dad is dead. This is the first time I have thought about him since Xavier asked me to marry him. I try to imagine what my father might have said if I had phoned him all breathless from the first flush of love and told him I planned to elope. My father was a sensible man, but he was also a marshmallow-soft romantic. I want to believe he would have said, *Follow your heart, darlin', as long as it eventually brings you, and that young man of yours, back home.*

Home. My heart shrinks for what it misses even as it expands at the hope of what might be.

"Thank you, Olivia," I say, sniffling. "It means the world to me that you want to stand by my side when I marry Xavier, but I wouldn't be happy knowing you sacrificed an opportunity to achieve your dream just to help me achieve mine."

"But isn't that what you have been doing these past four years?"

She has me there.

"Ha! I have you there, don't I?"

I brush a stray tear from my cheek and laugh. "Yes."

"So you will let me come with you to Italy?"

I don't want to hurt my best friend's feelings, but I don't want her at my wedding. I don't want anyone at my wedding. There is something romantic about two lovers running off to get married in secret. No wedding planners. No family drama. No rubbery dinner in a banquet hall. No drunk second cousins doing the Chicken Dance or the Electric Slide on the dance floor.

I get up and walk to the sofa.

"I have a better idea," I say, sitting beside Olivia. "Why don't we both go after our dreams? Then, when you have secured your Warner Brothers contract and I am a newly-wed, we can celebrate together. You can come to Brittany and we will—"

"Brittany?"

"Xavier's home is in Brittany."

"Oh." Her shoulders slump. "I guess I didn't realize marrying Xavier means you will be moving to France. We have seen each other nearly every day for the last eight years. I am going to miss you."

"I am going to miss you, too."

I drop my head onto her shoulder. She gives me a quick side hug before hopping to her feet. She grabs my hand and pulls me up.

"Let's go. You have to finish packing before your Prince Charming arrives to whisk you off in his Jaguar." She walks back into my room and I follow her. "Speaking of Cinderella. What were you planning on wearing on your elopement day?"

I reach into my suitcase and pull out the white eyelet-lace sundress I wore the day I met Xavier. Olivia looks at the dress and wrinkles her nose.

"You're joking?"

"No."

"Manderley! You can't wear that tired dress."

"Why not?"

She tilts her head and her bangs fall over her eye. "Do you think Carole Lombard wore a Madewell sundress when she eloped with Clark Gable? Do you think Marilyn Monroe wore eyelet when she eloped with Joe DiMaggio?"

"I am not Carole Lombard or Marilyn Monroe."

"Pish," she says, waving her manicured hand. "You're as beautiful as a classic Hollywood actress—or you would be if you would put a little more *jhusj* into your appearance."

Jhusj is Olivia's made-up word for glitz and glamour.

"Wait here."

She hurries back into her room, returning a few minutes later with her garment bag slung over her arm. She unzips the bag and removes the Chanel dress she planned on wearing to after-parties if she had won the Palme d'Or, an ivory silk sheath dress with flutter sleeves, tiny, prim buttons marching up the sides, and a plunging back. She found it in a vintage store on Melrose in West Hollywood. The store owner told her Angelina Jolie's designer used it as inspiration for a dress he designed for Angie to wear to the Academy Awards—though he removed the sleeves and added a plunging neckline to go with the back.

"I want you to have this," Olivia says, handing me the gown. "Wear it on your wedding day."

"Oh, Olivia. Are you sure?"

She nods. "It will be your something old and borrowed. Now you just need something new and blue."

Forty minutes later, I have my something new. While Olivia finished packing my toiletries, I popped down to the Dior store and purchased a lacy bra and matching panties to wear under my wedding dress.

Now, I am sitting in my room waiting for Xavier to arrive, shredding a fresh Kleenex, a pile of shredded Kleenex on the table beside me. My suitcase and garment bag stand at the ready beside the door.

Olivia departed for the airport a few minutes ago, sniffling and repeatedly reminding me that she is only a call, text, or Leo's private jet ride away. Olivia might have concerns, but secretly she is happy her conservative best friend is about to do something *scandaleux*.

I look anxiously at the clock on the nightstand. Xavier is fifteen minutes late. What if he doesn't come for me?

I am imagining myself rushing to the airport to join

Olivia on the flight back to Los Angeles, the scalding humiliation I will feel when I have to confess that I was jilted before even making it to the altar, when there is a knock at the door.

Dropping the Kleenex I am clutching onto the pile, I stand, smooth my hair, take a deep breath, and walk on shaky legs to the door.

Please, dear Lord, let it be Xavier.

I clutch the door knob, my palm damp with perspiration, and peer through the peephole. My heart skips a beat as I recognize Xavier standing on the other side of the door. I open it.

"Thank God you are still here," he says, a note of worry clearly recognizable in his voice. "I was afraid you had lost faith in me."

"No," I whisper, my mouth suddenly dry.

He pulls me into his arms and kisses me hard on the lips, a leg-lifting, dizziness-inducing kiss. I wrap my arms around his neck. I expect it to be a quick, chaste peck since we are still standing in the hallway, but Xavier has something else in mind. He puts his hands on my waist, urging me back into the room, and kicking the door closed behind him.

Then, I am pinned to the wall, the proof of Xavier's desire evident beneath his linen trousers, a big, solid promise of what to expect on our wedding night.

He raises his head, grinning down at me.

"What was that for?"

"All couples have rituals." He lets his hands drop from my waist and my skin feels colder at the loss of his touch. "I think kissing you good and hard is what I am going to do every time I come home late."

I laugh, drunk with his kiss and talk of rituals. "Do you plan on coming home late often?"

"*Oui*, if it means I get to kiss you like that." He glances over at my suitcases. "All ready, then?"

"Yes."

We are walking to the elevator when my iPhone chimes. I reach into my Lady Dior bag to see if it is a text from Olivia or my sisters, but Xavier stops walking, drops my suitcase, and takes my phone out of my hands, slipping it back into my purse.

"This our time, *ma bichette*."

"What if it's important?"

"More important than marrying me?"

The air leaves my lungs in a rush. "When you put it that way . . ."

He tucks an errant lock behind my ear, smiling. "I don't want to control you, Manderley, but when we met you said you were exhausted from being everyone's life preserver. Don't you think now might be a good time to make a change?"

"What do you mean?"

"When you slip my ring on your finger, I will become *your* life preserver. It will be my duty to cherish and protect you. I don't ever want to see you as overwrought as I did that first day on the cliff, and I will do anything I can to prevent that from happening, even if that means urging you to let your sisters and friends float on their own for a while."

A lump of emotion forms in my throat. Xavier's pledge is the most thoughtful, romantic thing any man has ever said to me.

"What if they sink?"

He strokes my cheek with his thumb. "What if they learn to swim?"

"You're right," I say.

"I usually am," he says, winking.

He picks up my suitcase and we continue walking to the elevator. I push the down arrow.

"Xavier?"

"Oui?"

"Thank you."

"For what?"

"Saying you will be my life preserver."

"You're welcome."

Chapter Twenty-one

It is just after dawn when the rattle of a room service trolley in the hallway outside our suite pulls me from my slumber. I open my eyes and stare at the sixteenth-century fresco painted on the ceiling over my bed, an angel surrounded by a band of plump cherubs in a sky awash with golden sunlight, and wonder if I am still dreaming.

I pinch my arm beneath the covers just to be sure I am truly awake and breathe a sigh of relief when it hurts. I have had wonderful dreams before, the sort of dreams that linger after you wake up and make you grieve for the loss of them as they fade from your memory, but waking up in Italy knowing I am getting married in a few hours is a dream come true.

We arrived at the Palazzo della Ferrante several hours after sunset. The luxurious boutique hotel situated on the shores of Lake Como was originally built as a palace for an Italian Renaissance prince. Our two-bedroom suite has wrought-iron Juliet balconies with panoramic views of the lake and snow-capped mountains.

When Xavier said we could elope to Italy, where it is easy for foreigners to be legally wed in civil ceremonies conducted by a public official, I pictured a nondescript government building in an ancient village. I never dreamt we would be married in a Renaissance palace.

I certainly never dreamt we would spend our wedding night with cherubs gazing down upon us, but soon Xavier will climb into this bed and we will make love for the first time beneath the watchful gazes of angelic children. I try to imagine what it will be like to have Xavier's naked body atop mine, his hands cupping my bottom, lifting me against him. His tongue tracing my lips, the faint taste of scotch in my mouth.

There is a knock at my bedroom door and my body flushes with heat, as if my thoughts have been projected on the ceiling for anyone to see.

"Come in."

The door opens and Xavier strides in, dressed in black trousers and a summer-weight light cashmere sweater, the sleeves stretching around his large biceps.

"Bonjour, ma bichette," he says, leaning over the bed and kissing my forehead. "Did you sleep well?"

I am not a virgin, and yet, I pull the sheet up to my chin, suddenly feeling modest, self-conscious beneath the covers. Is my hair a frizzy bird's nest? Did I remove all of my mascara last night? Do I have morning breath? Lawd, please not morning breath.

"I slept well, thank you. Did you just get up?"

The sheet isn't covering the left side of my body. My bare leg is exposed; one sock-covered foot is sticking out.

"I have been awake for hours," he says, smiling at my thick, fuzzy sock. "I have already been to the gym and spoken with my assistant to confirm everything is set for the ceremony this evening."

I sit up quickly and one strap of my baby-doll nightgown slips down over my shoulder. I pull the blanket up.

"This evening? We are getting married this evening?"

He chuckles. "That is why we are here, *ma bichette*."

"I know," I say, exhaling. "I just didn't think it would happen so fast."

"The mayor agreed to officiate the ceremony. He was scheduled to leave on a trip this afternoon, but he offered to delay his departure so he could marry us."

Who am I marrying that he has the connections to rent out an entire champagne bar at an exclusive resort and arrange a last-minute wedding in Italy?

"That was kind of him."

"He is a family friend."

"Ah."

"Are you getting cold feet?" he asks, quirking a brow. "If so, you can borrow my socks."

He makes me smile. Lawd, he makes me smile. "I am not getting cold feet."

"You are sure?"

"Promise."

"Bon." He smiles, handing me the robe that I tossed over a chair before going to bed last night. "I ordered breakfast. Scrambled eggs and orange juice. It should be here soon. Get dressed and meet me in the sitting room."

He closes the door and I fall back on the bed. My head is spinning around. I am not thinking straight. Am I seeing things as they are or tinting them with the brush of infatuation? Am I in love or lust? Whatever the answer, no other man has ever made me feel so dizzy and disoriented, so reckless and ready to abandon responsibility.

That bold voice inside my head, the one that has kept me from making impulsive, emotional decisions, has stopped guiding me and is humming one tune over and over again: *I think I wanna marry you. I do. I do. I do. I do.*

I shower, scrape my hair into a sleek ponytail, and slip on a black sundress, the nicest in my suitcase. In the sitting room, Xavier is reading the newspaper at a table set for two. He smiles when he notices me.

"There you are," he says, folding his newspaper and tossing it on the table. "Another minute and I was going to make sure you hadn't fallen back asleep."

"I am sorry," I say. "I hope I haven't kept you waiting too long."

He stands and pulls my chair out. "It was worth the wait. You look beautiful."

Lauren Bacall would have received such a compliment with insouciance. I nearly knock the water glass over when I sit and reach for my napkin. I know there will come a time when I am at ease in Xavier's presence, when his unexpected touches or compliments are as familiar as my reflection, but for now they make me clumsy and self-conscious. All I can do is mumble my thanks.

Xavier pours orange juice into my empty glass and removes the silver dome over my breakfast plate. The scent of scrambled eggs and potatoes roasted with tomatoes, peppers, and onions fills my nose.

We talk about Xavier's home in Brittany while we eat breakfast. He tells me about the many responsibilities that go with taking care of a large estate. I want to tell him I will help him, but it feels somehow presumptuous.

"I am sorry we won't be able to have a proper honeymoon," he says, stirring his coffee. "I have a business trip to Dubai later this month and I have to meet with an official with the department that monitors the restoration of historic properties in France before I go."

"I don't mind, really."

"Hmmm"—he lifts his coffee to his lips, inhales, and takes a sip, placing it back on the saucer and looking at me through narrowed eyes—"I wonder. Don't all women want an elaborate wedding with all the frills, followed by an extended honeymoon to some exotic place?"

I look out the open French doors to the snow-capped mountains in the distance, the ancient village on the distant shore, the intricate wrought-iron fretwork of the Juliet balcony, and sigh.

"Have you looked out the window?" I say, smiling at him. "This *is* an exotic location."

"You're happy then? You don't wish we were getting married in a church, you in a white gown, your friends weeping into their hankies?"

"In case you haven't noticed, I am not comfortable being the center of attention."

He chuckles. "I've noticed."

"Besides, I have always thought exchanging vows is a deeply personal event, an intimate union between two people who are promising to spend their lives forsaking all others. I have been to elaborately produced weddings and I always left feeling a little . . . sad. I feel the same way when I watch those reality television shows about wealthy housewives. Do we need to live our lives out loud?" I shake my head. "I don't think so."

"I am glad to hear it, *ma bichette*."

"What about you?" I ask, reaching for my orange juice. "Are you sorry we aren't having an elaborate wedding?"

"I had an elaborate wedding the first time I got married. *C'était une expérience misérable*."

My hand trembles and orange juice spills onto the table, splashes on the napkin covering my lap. *First marriage? Did Xavier just say he has been married before?* A sour taste fills my mouth and it's not from the orange juice.

Chapter Twenty-two

"First time?"

Xavier reaches across the table, dabbing the spilled orange juice with his napkin.

"Oui."

"You were married before?"

"Oui."

He tosses the stained napkin onto his plate and sits back, staring at me with the sort of bored expression one wears when they discuss the weather with a grocery store cashier. I realize I am fairly naïve, having only dated a few men, and from a conservative part of the more puritanical United States, but Xavier's confession is as stunning as his matter-of-fact delivery. Is this how things are done in Europe?

"You have nothing to fear, *ma bichette*. Marine is not a part of my life." He plucks a tangerine out of the bowl of fruit on the table between us and slices it in half with his butter knife, a slightly ominous act that seems to hold a deeper, metaphorical meaning. "She will never be a part of my life again."

A sudden gust of wind causes the French door to rattle against the doorstop. The sheer white curtains billow, fluttering, floating above our table like a specter. I shiver and cross my arms. *Marine*. It could be my imagination—for it can be overactive in times of stress—but it feels as if Marine is looming over us, as if she has been looming between us all this time.

Marine.

The first Madame de Maloret.

I suddenly remember the conversation we had about my visiting Cap-Eden-Roc and his strange, far-off expression, and how I felt he was thinking of someone else as he spoke to me.

You are afraid retracing your aunt's footsteps will only remind you that she is further from you than ever before. You worry that you will visit the places she loved only to discover they aren't as magical as they were in your memory, and then you might wonder why you ever thought them magical in the first place. Is that it?

Now, I wonder if he had been thinking about Marine, about the places they visited together.

"Are you in love with her still?"

He drops the tangerine wedge onto his plate and wipes his fingers on his dirty napkin before standing and coming around to my side of the table.

"Mon Dieu, non!" he says, squatting beside me, holding my hands. "I do not love Marine. I do not hate her, either. I feel nothing for her. Nothing at all."

The hairs on the back of my arms stand up straight. "That frightens me."

"Do you want me to have feelings for her?"

"No, but it scares me you once loved her enough to marry her and now your feelings have moved from great passion to a place beyond hatred, a place that is cold, barren. How do I know you won't say the same about me one day?"

He stands, pulling me up with him, wrapping his arms around my waist, brushing his lips against my ear. "Because you aren't Marine. You are nothing like her."

A wave of love and longing washes over me and I am ripped out to sea on a current of emotions. I love him. I do. I know it sounds ridiculous to say I love someone I have known only a month, but when he holds me in his arms, I lose myself in the depths of my desire, rationality becomes a distant place on the horizon. When I am with Xavier, I feel a spark of courage to be the person I have always longed to be, the confident, spontaneous, cultured woman hidden beneath the layers of uncertainty.

And so, I make the choice to believe him when he says our marriage won't end in divorce, that he won't one day say he feels nothing for me, *nothing at all*.

Chapter Twenty-three

After breakfast, Xavier suggests we tour the Palazzo della Ferrante's gardens until it is time for us to get ready for our civil ceremony. It is a beautiful sunny morning, with a slight mist lingering over the dew-speckled grass. The air is heavy with the scent of oranges and cypress. The perfect day for a wedding.

We follow a gravel path bordered by tortuously clipped box hedges until we arrive at a fountain. A statue of Cupid embracing Psyche stands on a pedestal in the center of the fountain. Psyche is reclining on her side, her arms reaching up for Cupid, hovering above her, his wings outstretched as if he is about to pluck his lover off her plinth.

We pause to admire the statue.

"I wish I read Italian," I say. "I would like to know what the words carved into the pedestal mean."

"*'Ho saziato la mia sete alla fontana dei tuoi baci,'*" Xavier says in flawless Italian. "'I quenched my thirst at your fountain of kisses.' This is the La fontana degli amanti. The Lovers' Fountain. I had a motive for bringing you here."

"You did?"

He reaches into his pocket and removes a small midnight-blue velvet box. He opens the box. An engagement ring with a large grayish-blue, pear-shaped stone surrounded by diamonds is resting inside.

"Will you marry me?"

For the second time today, I pinch myself to make sure I am not dreaming and say a little prayer of thanks when I realize I am not. My eyes fill with tears.

"Yes. I will marry you."

Through the haze of my tears, I watch Xavier take the ring out of the box and slip it on my finger. He cups my face and stares into my eyes deeply.

"Are you happy?"

"Incredibly happy. I wish it could stay like this forever."

"Me, too."

A smudge of sadness darkens his sparkling gaze and he presses his lips together as if trapping unspoken thoughts in his mouth. I look up at him, waiting for him to share what he is feeling, but he bends down and presses his lips to mine instead. It's a poignant kiss, filled with a mélange of unspoken emotions—yearning, wonder, hope, and the fear that always shadows new love, the fear we will fall too fast and not survive the fall.

He stops kissing me. When I open my eyes, he is watching me, smiling.

"What?"

"I like the way you look after I have kissed you, sleepy-eyed, as if you are just waking up from a wonderful dream. I hope you always look like this when I finish kissing you." He lifts my hand and kisses the knuckle above my engagement ring. "Do you like your ring?"

"I love it. Is that a sapphire?"

"Blue diamond."

"I didn't know there were such things."

"Oui." He puts his hand on the small of my back and we begin walking back to the palazzo. "They're extremely rare. Fortunately, a jeweler in Monaco happens to deal in rare gems. I told him I wanted a stone that looked like the sky before a winter storm, to match your eyes. He sent three rings to our hotel yesterday afternoon by courier and I chose this one. The courier was delayed in traffic, which is why I was late picking you up."

"You went to all that trouble just so you could get me an engagement ring?"

"It was no trouble," he says.

"It is more trouble than anyone has ever gone to on my behalf, and I will treasure this ring even more because of it." I stop walking and turn to face him, standing on my tiptoes and pressing a kiss to his cheek. "Thank you, Xavier."

It is only later, as I am soaking in a tub of hot, bergamot-scented bubbles, that I realize Xavier has given me my something blue.

> *Something old.*
> *Something new.*
> *Something borrowed.*
> *Something blue.*
> *And a lucky silver sixpence in her shoe.*

I also realize, with a pang of anxiety, Xavier didn't say he loved me when I told him how much I loved him.

Chapter Twenty-four

It took twenty-seven years to find the man I wanted to marry and only twenty minutes to unite my life with his. The brevity of the ceremony stunned me almost as much as the enormity of what it meant: Manderley Maxwell was gone forever, and in her place, a new, unfamiliar creature. Manderley de Maloret. Would she emerge from her uncertain cocoon a bolder, more confident butterfly, secure in her unique beauty because of the love of her new, still unfamiliar husband? Would she fly to her new land, content, or would she long for what she had left behind?

The look Xavier gave me when I walked onto the terrace wearing Olivia's gown, the slow, satisfied smile that spread across his handsome face, the way his eyes narrowed with obvious approval, and his chest rose with a sharp inhalation of breath, is a look that could embolden the most timid butterfly. It certainly gave confidence to my faltering feet. It gave me the confidence to walk past the hotel staff and guests who had assembled to watch the ceremony.

It was a warm evening, with long amber rays from the setting sun stretching over the lake and a light breeze sending orphaned geranium blossoms skittering across the terrace. If there were other details worth remembering, I did not notice them in the few seconds it took me to reach the place where Xavier stood with the mayor and the interpreter. I kept my gaze firmly focused on the tall, dark, handsome Frenchman who would become my husband before the sun slipped behind the distant Monte San Primo. His dark wavy hair combed back. His startling blue eyes sparkling as brilliantly as the diamond ring on my finger. The dark stubble on his angular jaw. The crisp white collar of his dress shirt. His charcoal suit coat stretched over his broad shoulders. His hand, tan and steady, reaching out for mine. The warmth and strength of his fingers laced together with my fingers.

The next few minutes passed in a blur. A stronger breeze, swirling geranium petals, my fluttery sleeves fluttering against my skin, gooseflesh on my arms, Xavier squeezing my hand in reassurance. Blinding flashes of light and *the click-whir, click-whir* of the hotel photographer's camera. The mayor prattling on in Italian about civil codes and marital duties, the interpreter murmuring the translation in English. And then, finally, the moment was upon me. The interpreter smiled and translated the mayor's words.

"Does Miss Maxwell declare she wants to take as her husband Mister de Maloret here present?"

"Yes."

Xavier slipped a diamond band on my finger, looked into my eyes, and said, "I, Girard Fortune Xavier de Maloret, take you, Manderley Grace Maxwell, as my wife and promise to be faithful to you always, in joy and in pain, in health and in sickness, and to love you and every day honor you, for the rest of my life."

I made my vow. We kissed. The onlookers clapped. The hotel photographer snapped a few more pictures.

And that was it. Twenty minutes from the time I stepped onto the terrace and let Xavier take my hand until we walked arm in arm, Monsieur et Madame de Maloret, into the hotel manager's office to sign the various documents required to make everything legal.

Twenty minutes is all it took to step out of one life and into another.

Chapter Twenty-five

"You're trembling. Are you cold?"

"A little."

Xavier shrugs out of his jacket and wraps it around my shoulders before I can answer. We had dinner with the mayor, his wife, and their family—a lovely, convivial gathering under a wisteria-covered pergola in the garden—and now we are walking back to our suite.

I am not cold. I am terrified. My anxieties about our wedding night started during the marriage toast, when the mayor dropped a small piece of toast into a double-handled glass filled with champagne, an ancient French custom symbolizing health and fertility, and wished us a home filled with laughter and the happy patter of many little feet.

The unnaturally fast pace and out-of-sequence order of our courtship means we haven't had the usual progression. We haven't had time to ease into each other; we are jumping in, feetfirst, without testing the waters.

By the time Xavier slips the key to our suite into the

lock, I am a bundle of nerves in an expensive, borrowed vintage gown and high heels.

"After you, *ma bichette*," he says, pushing the door open and standing back.

The scent of melted wax and fresh flowers greets me the moment I step over the threshold into the sitting room. The room is aglow with the light of dozens of candles. A bottle of champagne and a massive bouquet of flowers have been positioned on a table near the balcony. A fire is crackling and hissing in the log fireplace. Through the open bedroom doors I spy a trail of oleander petals strewn over the floor and bed.

Xavier follows me into the room, closing the door behind him with a decisive click. I jump at the sound. Xavier comes up behind me. His hands on my hips. His lips against my ear.

"Finally," he murmurs, his voice low and thick with desire. "I have wanted to be back in this room, just the two of us, since the moment I saw you walk onto the terrace, looking so beautiful in your gown I thought I would die if I didn't take you in my arms and make you mine."

I let my head fall back, resting it against his solid shoulder. I wish I could match his ease, but I am a novice when it comes to seduction, a trembling, terrified novice. He pulls his jacket off my shoulders and it falls in a pool of expensive fabric at my feet. My legs shake and I have to grab Xavier's wrists so I don't fall.

"Don't be afraid, *ma bichette*," he whispers, turning me in his arms, looking deep into my eyes. "I would sooner die than hurt you."

He kisses me and then takes my hand, leading me to the sofa facing the fire. I sit, stiff as a Carolina reed, while Xavier walks over to the table and pulls the wine bottle out of the silver bucket. He opens the bottle with a nerve-rattling pop and fills two glasses with light pink liquid. He carries the glasses over to me.

"Rosé"—he hands me a glass—"because champagne gives *mon amour* a headache."

"Thank you," I say, taking the glass.

He sits beside me and we sip our wine in the orange light of the fire. We don't talk. We don't touch. We just sip our wine and savor the heady effects of our desire for each other. I am certain he can feel it, taste it, my desire for him.

I drain the contents of my wineglass and set the empty vessel on the table in front of us. I am not a drinker, so the glass of rosé—my third of the evening—has transported me to a warm, safe place. I am not intoxicated, but I am skating on the edge of coherency. Aware of my surroundings, but happily disconnected. I kick my heels off and rest my head on the back of the couch, closing my eyes and stretching my legs. It doesn't take long before I am floating on a warm sea, soft, sensual waves washing over my body. I am floating, floating, floating away from all cares, all fears.

I am vaguely aware of Xavier lifting me in his arms, carrying me. I open my eyes and see his handsome face, his angled jaw that makes me want to run my finger over it, feel the stubbly beard on my skin, those unreadable blue eyes that make me want to dive into them, again and again, until I solve the mystery hidden in their depths.

"I love you, Xavier," I say, speaking from my heart, my throat clogging with emotion. "I know it is too soon for me to say it, but I do. I love you so much my heart hurts when I look at you because I don't think you love me half as much as I love you."

"Merci." He bends his head and presses his lips to mine. "That is the nicest thing anyone has ever said to me."

We are on the bed, sinking into the mattress, surrounded by oleander blossoms. Xavier is on top of me, kissing me, touching me, grinding the proof of his arousal against my thigh.

"Make love to me, Xavier. Please, make love to me. I want to be yours."

"You are mine," he says, kissing my lips, nibbling my neck, biting my shoulder. "Till death us do part."

The hiss of a zipper. Silky fabric moving lightly against my skin like a whisper. The taste of strawberries and currants dipped in honey on his lips, tongue, on my mouth, tongue. The scent of citrusy cologne and heated skin. The sound of his heavy breathing against my breast, neck.

"Mon Dieu," he growls against my lips. "I have never wanted someone as much as I want you right now."

"Prove it," I gasp, emboldened by my desire and the wine. "Make love to me. Now."

A pained moan. Mine or his?

Lacy fabric scratching my thighs, calves. Cool air blowing over my breasts, teasing my hardened nipples, coaxing goosebumps on my legs. Buttons being unbuttoned, zipper unzipped. Fabric tearing. The warmth of Xavier's naked body pressing me into the mattress.

"Look at me, *ma bichette*."

I open my eyes and a swell of emotion has me biting my lip, blinking back tears. Xavier pushes into me, his long, thick member parting my gentle folds, pushing deep, deeper inside me, claiming my soul as his rightful possession.

I am Manderley Grace de Maloret.

Madame de Maloret.

Truly loved and claimed by Girard Fortune Xavier de Maloret. I float along on the current of drugged desire until the motion becomes overwhelming, the feelings aroused too powerful, and then the compulsion to move, to touch, to taste, is too strong to ignore. I arch my back, move my hips around and around, thrusting, inviting him deeper, deeper into me.

I blink until the fog of desire clears enough for me to make out shapes: the carved wooden poles of the four-poster bed, the angels frolicking on the ceiling over our heads, the small indentation of Xavier's throat, the splinters of silver radiating from his pupils.

He notices me watching him and groans, thrusting his hips harder, pushing deeper into me. I wrap my legs around his lean waist and squeeze. He slides his hand under my bottom, cupping my cheek, lifting me against him.

The clumsiness, the awkwardness I felt when we stepped into the suite is a distant memory, barely recognizable traits of the woman I was before I became Manderley de Maloret. Madame de Maloret.

Xavier looks into my eyes and my heart aches with emotions I can't articulate. He tenses. A fine sheen of perspiration covers his skin. He grows thicker, harder inside me. I cry out. He groans, convulses inside me, thrusts one last time, and then collapses on top me, heaving, drawing jagged breaths against my ear, murmuring incomprehensible words in French.

Finally, when I feel my lungs incapable of inflating enough to draw life-sustaining breath, Xavier rolls off of me and we lie side by side, staring up at the Pietro Liberi fresco.

Xavier pulls me closer and I rest my head on his shoulder. We lie together, our breath syncopated, our limbs entwined so that I cannot tell where my body begins and Xavier's ends.

"Thank you for the oleander blossoms," I say, holding one of the bruised petals to my nose, inhaling the sweet scent.

"You said they were the scent of heaven." He kisses my forehead. "I want you to feel as if you are in heaven when you are with me."

"Xavier?" I say, curling against his side. "Why do you call me *bichette*?"

He pulls the blanket over us and kisses my forehead.

"Do you remember the first time we met? You looked so frightened, so hunted, it stirred in me a fierce desire to protect you." He holds me tighter. "Then, when I learned you had an equally protective nature, I thought you reminded me of a doe, a wide-eyed, graceful doe."

I close my eyes and press my hand to the place on his chest where his heart is thudding, thudding, thudding. The strong, empowered woman in me should rebel against the notion of a man wanting to protect me, but the soft, slightly wounded girl who just lost her father yearns to be held close and shielded from life's sharper edges.

I look at the small crescent-shaped scar barely visible beneath the stubble on his jaw and my heart swells. I trace the white mark with my fingertip.

"How did you get this scar?"

He chuckles. "You don't really want to hear about that, do you?"

"Yes, I do."

Xavier's voice rumbling in his chest reminds me of summer nights I spent sleeping on our porch, listening to distant thunder rolling over the dunes. I close my eyes and listen as he tells me about being ten years old and standing on the deck of his father's sailboat, the salty spray on his cheeks, and the sun on his head.

"My father and uncles went sailing every other Saturday from May until September. This was the first time they let me join them and I wanted to show them all, but especially my father, that I could be a capable deckhand." He presses his hand against the small of my back, making slow, lazy circles with his thumb, lost in his memories. "My father called out, but I wasn't paying proper attention. The boom swung around, cracked against my skull, and I woke up in the car on the way to the hospital. I was so ashamed, I bit my lip when the doctor was stitching my face. Didn't shed a single tear."

"Your father must have been proud of your courage."

"If he was, he never said. My father didn't share his feelings freely. He believed emotions were best kept secured in a cask, somewhere deep inside. He would say *Boys feel, men act*. Crying about a crack to the skull was pointless. It was more important I should learn not to repeat the same mistake that caused the crack in the first place. "

Boys feel, men act. I remember Xavier's response when I told him I was leaving Cannes early. He didn't take me in his arms and tell me how sad he was that our love affair was ending sooner than we had hoped, nor did he smother my face with kisses while declaring his consuming love for me. He took action by asking me to marry him.

How much we reveal about ourselves, our inner workings and motivations, just in sharing a single memory.

It suddenly occurs to me this man lying next to me, this wonderful, complex, naked man holding me in his arms, was once another woman's husband.

Marine.

Did he tell her he loved her when he asked her to marry him? Did he get down on one knee and proclaim his passion for her, vow that he would die if she didn't agree to become his wife? Or did he keep his feelings for her as tightly secured as he has kept his feelings for me?

Crying is pointless. It is more important that you should learn not to make the same mistake.

Did he grow up with Marine? Did they play together as children, share their first kiss at a school dance? Was she the love of his life?

Could that be why he asked me to elope with him after dating such a short time? He had a great love with Marine and it ended. Is he making sure he doesn't repeat his mistake by marrying someone he hardly knows, someone he does not love?

A chill trickles down my spine. I want to move closer to my husband, to benefit from the warmth of his solid body, but that awkwardness has returned. I feel myself stiffening, pulling away mentally and physically.

Xavier's hand has fallen off the small of my back. His breathing is slow and shallow.

"Xavier?"

"Mmm?" His voice is thick with sleep. "What is it, *ma bichette*?"

"Why did you marry me?"

He chuckles softly.

"I am serious."

He lifts his head, his eyes flutter open, and a drowsy smile curls the corners of his mouth. "I married you because I am a sailor and a sailor could always use another life preserver."

His eyelids flutter shut and his head falls back on the

pillow. He is asleep within seconds, his muscular chest and flat abdomen slowly rising and falling with each breath.

My throat clogs with emotion. Xavier didn't marry me because I stoked a raging inferno of passion within him. He didn't marry me because he found himself so attracted to my magnetic personality he couldn't imagine pulling away. He didn't marry me because he thinks I am exciting, sexy, and charming. He married me because he thinks I am responsible, sensible, and dependable.

What a fool I am! Imagining myself to be as glamorous as Rita Hayworth or Ava Gardner, capturing the heart of a handsome man while on holiday in the South of France, making him fall so deeply in love with me that he begs me to run off with him. I am not a Rita or an Ava. I am a plain, dependable June Allyson. I am an average, reliable Joan Fontaine.

There's a reason June Allyson starred in movies like *Little Women* and *The Glenn Miller Story* instead of *Carmen* or *Gentlemen Prefer Blondes*.

Rita Hayworth, Ava Gardner, Betty Grable, they were World War II pinup girls, every GI's fantasy girl. June Allyson and Joan Fontaine, they were women the GIs went home to marry.

Just once, I wanted to be the fantasy girl.

Chapter Twenty-six

"*Bonjour,* Madame de Maloret." I am tiptoeing by the bed, my sandals in hand, when Xavier reaches out and grabs my wrist, pulling me on top of him. "Where do you think you are going?"

My heart skips a silly girlish beat when I hear him call me by my married name, and the awkwardness I felt waking up naked beside him evaporates like the morning mist hanging over the lake. I drop my sandals and they clatter to the floor beside the bed.

"I was going to check my email to see if the photographer sent the pictures from our wedding yet. I promised Olivia I would send a photo."

"Olivia can wait," he says, unbuttoning my blouse. "I have thought of another tradition I think we should begin this morning. Right now, in fact."

"You have?"

He drops my blouse onto the floor beside my sandals and reaches around, deftly unclasping my bra with a flick of his thumb.

"Yes, I have."

He slides the bra straps down my arms and my breasts spill onto his chest. He takes one of my nipples into his mouth, sucking, flicking it with his rough tongue.

"Tradition?" I moan, clutching his shoulders.

He removes his mouth from my breast and looks up at me, frowning.

"What?"

"You said something about a new tradition."

"Oh, yes." He snakes a hand between us and pulls my skirt and panties off in one fell swoop. "I suggest we start each day of our married life by making mad, violent love to one another. I am happy to start the tradition today and allow you to continue it tomorrow. *D'accord?*"

Instead of waiting for me to agree, he rolls me over, braces himself with his forearms, and slides down my body, taking my sex in his mouth, licking, flicking my clitoris the same way he licked and flicked my nipple moments before. His mouth tells me what I am aching to hear; that he thinks I am sexy as a pinup model, that the world beyond our bedroom has ceased to exist, we are alone, wrapped in sheets of lust. Time has ceased to exist. There is no past, no future, only this moment. I clutch his hair, silky black strands slipping between my fingers, and moan low in my throat as waves of pleasure roll over my body, warm waves rocking me, carrying me to a distant place.

"Xavier. Xavier."

"What, *mon amour?*" he asks, looking up at me through the thick fringe of his lashes, a teasing smile on his wet lips. "Do you like this?"

I answer him by closing my eyes, arching my spine, and inviting his tongue back into my body. Later, I might remember this uncharacteristically bold response with embarrassment, but right now later is an abstract concept.

I am moving, my hips, hands, legs, instinctually, responding to his touch in some ageless way, as if we have been lovers since the beginning of time. Xavier pushes his tongue inside me, thrusting, withdrawing, thrusting, withdrawing, until I am trembling violently, my legs shaking with the sweet trauma of his touches.

Chapter Twenty-seven

What a strange place was this home on the strand. This forlorn pile of stones clinging desperately to the falaise. How much longer will it hold against the unrelenting waves threatening to sweep it into the sea? How long before a seeker of truth ventures into the dank cellars, lifts his torch, and exposes the secrets crouching like shadows in every forbidding corner? Will the secrets, once brought to light, skitter across the flagstone floor, horrid and naked, trying in vain to return to the darkness? And then—

"Dashing."

I stop writing and look over at Xavier, reclining on the lounger beside me, a slender volume of poems open in his hand.

"I beg your pardon?"

"The word you are trying to think of is *dashing*." He grins. "You're writing about me in your journal, aren't you?"

I laugh. "I am not writing about you."

"Is that so?" He closes his book and crosses his arms, looking at me from behind his dark sunglasses. "We've only been married a day and you're already writing about another man? Cruel woman."

"I am not writing about a man."

"Is it a journal entry?"

I wish I hadn't brought my notebook and pen to the pool. "It's nothing."

He frowns. "It's something."

"I thought . . ." I look at the last sentence scrawled across the page. "I am going to try to write a novel."

"Non."

"No?"

He removes his sunglasses and stares deep into my eyes, so deep I think he can see all of the secrets written on the pages of my heart.

"You're not going to *try* to write a novel. Trying is passive, it is yielding to the possibility of failure before you have even begun. You *will* write a novel."

Now I know how Xavier was able to dramatically increase his company's earnings in less than ten years. His fortitude is as powerful as his physique.

"I *will* write a novel."

"Bon. That's better." He smiles, slipping his glasses back on. "Can I read it?"

"It's not worth reading. It's nothing."

He holds his hand out. I consider lying. *Oh, these scribbles? They're my to-do list."* I consider tossing the notebook into the lake, letting it sink to the bottom to feed the fish. Instead, I hand him the notebook and study his profile as he reads the entry. He looks over at me and back at the notebook, reading the entry a second time.

"It's good, Manderley."

"Really?"

"I wouldn't have said it if I didn't mean it," he says, handing me the notebook. "It's an intriguing beginning. I want to know more about the house on the strand and the secrets hidden in her cellars."

"Thank you." My heart swells with his praise.

"De rien." He looks over his shoulder, smiling. "Tell me, are the secrets of a romantic nature? Is this to be a tale of forbidden love, full of heaving bosoms and ripped bodices?"

I frown. "Why would you assume it's going to be a romance novel?"

"I am French, *mon amour*. Romance is our lifeblood, running through our veins, at the heart of every great story we have ever told, the motivation of our greatest feats."

"I would like to hear a few of your stories," I say, closing my journal and staring at my toenails, the pool sparkling beyond my feet. "Tell me about your romances."

He laughs and the sound disturbs a swan waddling on the lawn nearby. The bird hisses.

"Those are stories better left unwritten, *ma bichette*." He chuckles, but the sound is less natural. "Besides, you are clearly the writer of the family and your story sounds far more interesting. Are you sure it isn't going to be a romance?"

"Positive."

"What's the secret then?"

"Murder."

"Murder?" He sits up and takes his glasses off again, fixing me with a curious stare. "Who was murdered?"

"The wife of the man who owns the house on the strand."

The words come out of my mouth without thought, as if something deeper and darker is compelling me to speak. Xavier pushes his sunglasses back on his face and stares out at the lake. I feel colder, bereft, as if the sun has moved behind the clouds. I hug the notebook to my chest.

"Why?"

"Why?" I repeat.

"Why did he murder his wife? What was his motivation?"

"Is there ever a good motive for murder?"

"Oui. Occasionally."

I glance at his profile, notice the muscle working frantically along his jaw, and an uneasiness comes over me, a feverish, queasy, sick feeling. I assume Xavier was talking about motives for a fictional murder. Wasn't he? *Change the subject, Manderley. Ask him about sailing, about his home in Brittany, about that little book of poetry . . .*

"Betrayal," he says in a cold, flat tone. "There's a powerful motive for murder. Betrayal can drive a man mad with rage, make him do things he would not normally consider. The deeper he loves the person who treated his trust so capriciously, the more insane their betrayal makes him."

Something tells me Xavier is not speaking theoretically when he speaks about the rage of betrayal. Did Marine betray him and did his love for her drive him to the point of madness? I want to ask him. I should be able to ask him—after all, we are husband and wife, bound together for all eternity—but I am afraid to hear his answer. My confidence in Xavier's love for me is still so fragile, as paper-thin as the tissue that was in my Dior gift bag, that I am afraid to test it.

I lift the hem of my cover-up and stick my finger through a hole in the eyelet lace. How much easier would my life be if I had the courage to say what I was thinking and to ask the questions fear keeps me from asking? Instead, I am tortured by the unknown, haunted by the what-ifs.

"Stop fidgeting," he says, reaching over and pulling my finger free from the hole. "Do I make you that nervous? I am sorry. I am afraid I can be sullen, sometimes."

Whatever clouds skittered across his mental sky must have skittered away again because he doesn't appear sullen or distracted. My smiling, attentive husband has returned.

"You don't make me nervous," I lie.

He looks skeptical, but doesn't argue. "Are you going to finish your novel?"

"I don't know."

"Finish it, Manderley. Always finish what you begin, even if the journey is not a pleasant one and you end up somewhere you never expected to be." He squeezes my hand. "Believe in yourself to see it all the way through. I know you can do it."

"Thank you."

"De rien." He grabs the sunscreen lotion off the table and stands, towering over me, his broad shoulders blocking the sun. "You're starting to burn. Roll over. I will rub lotion on your back."

I shrug out of my cover-up and roll onto my stomach. Xavier sits on the edge of my lounger. His thigh presses against my side and a frisson of desire passes through my body. Will it always be this way, I wonder? Will my body always react to his slightest touch?

He moves my hair to the side, exposing my back and part of my neck, squirts lotion onto his hand, and rubs it into my skin with his fingertips. Slow, firm circles moving down my spine, working the tension from my muscles. I close my eyes and feel myself drifting to the warm, happy place between awake and sleep.

"Tomorrow is our last day here," he says, leaning down to kiss my shoulder. "I have something special planned."

"Mmm."

"Do you want to know what it is?"

"Mmm-hmm."

"I rented a boat. We are going sailing."

"Sailing?"

I scoot up, wide-awake now.

"*Oui*. Is there a problem?"

Xavier grew up near the sea. He was in the French navy. He is the president of a major boat-building corporation. I don't want to disappoint him, so I swallow the bile rising up my throat, and blink back the tears.

"No, no problem at all." But it is a problem. A big problem.

Chapter Twenty-eight

We are preparing for bed when Xavier drops a slender volume onto his nightstand—the same slender volume he brought to the pool. The cover is worn blue leather and the title, *Poems for Seafarers*, is embossed upon it in swirling silver letters. The swirly letters reflect the lamplight like a lighthouse beacon, beckoning me closer or warning me of impending disaster, I don't know which.

When Xavier steps back into the bathroom, I lift the book of poetry in my hands, holding it as if it might suddenly turn to dust and blow away. I open to the middle and find a poem by Lord Tennyson; the yellowing page is dog-eared and the type smeared from someone—presumably Xavier—running his finger over the words.

> *Break, break, break,*
> *On thy cold gray stones, O Sea!*
> *And I would that my tongue could utter*
> *The thoughts that arise in me.*

Oh Tennyson! What kindred souls are we? Would that my tongue could utter the thoughts bothering me. Would that I could tell Xavier the truth: that I don't ever want to step foot on a boat of any kind—sailboat, speedboat, ocean liner, or kayak.

At the bottom of the page, someone has put a small mark, this in pencil, beside the poem's final stanza.

> *Break, break, break*
> *At the foot of thy crags, O Sea!*
> *But the tender grace of a day that is dead*
> *Will never come back to me.*

Such a melancholic poem, so full of nostalgia for what was loved and lost. I read the lines again and it becomes clear Tennyson was writing about the loss of a lover or dear friend. Sixteen lines of carefully chosen words to convey a deep sense of mourning.

I touch my finger to the yellowing page, trace the faint pencil mark beside the last stanza, and wonder what Xavier had been thinking when he highlighted "Break, Break, Break." Who had he been mourning?

Marine.

I hear the name whispered in my head and quickly turn the page. I close the book and open to the frontispiece, an engraving of a ship being swallowed by a dark, stormy sea. Moonlight illuminates the ship and the wave it rides upon—the last ray of light before eternal darkness. My attention is held not by the haunting scene, but by the inscription, written in elegant, loopy penmanship on the title page.

> *To Xavier,*
> *My most beloved seafarer.*
> *Love Always,*
> *Your darling,*
> *Marine*

A maggot of doubt begins wriggling into my heart, spoiling the sweet, unsullied trust I've had for Xavier. He does not love me. I am but a placeholder for the one he lost. He still loves Marine. Why else would he carry a maudlin book of poems given to him by his *darling* Marine?

I close the book again and put it back on the night-stand, but I can still see the words *my most beloved* and the large, looping M of Marine's signature seared on the back of my eyes.

I press my hands to my face, pushing my fingertips against my eyelids as if the act will blot Xavier's first wife from my mind, from his heart. I don't want to think about her, to wonder why she gave Xavier a book of poems written in English. Did they have English terms of endearment for each other? Did they dream of one day moving to England or America, retiring to a quaint fishing village in Cornwall or Massachusetts? Did she read to him from *Poems for Seafarers*? Did they lie in bed, Marine stroking his head, running her slender, manicured fingers through his hair as she murmured the words of Whitman or Dunbar?

Xavier emerges from the bathroom in a cloud of soap and citrus-scented steam, his hair damp from the shower he takes before bed, his chest bare, a towel wrapped around his waist.

He stops to press a kiss to my forehead before circling around to his side of the bed. I grab my iPhone and pad into the bathroom. As soon as I have closed and locked the door, I slide to the tile floor and push my phone's home button, as if possessed by the spirit of another woman, a jealous, insecure woman.

Marine de Maloret.

I type the name into the search bar and hold my breath

as I wait for the returns. The first hit is an article from a French language newspaper out of Quimper. I click on it and a bold, black headline appears—**La bataille la plus âpre de l'Europe se poursuit**—followed by a photograph of an unsmiling, tuxedo-clad Xavier standing beside a striking brunette in a sleek black cocktail gown, her hand resting casually, but proprietarily, on Xavier's forearm. They are standing on a neatly clipped lawn, a towering gray stone château in the background. The caption beneath the photo is in French, but the names *Monsieur et Madame Xavier de Maloret* need no translation.

I enlarge the photo and stare at the woman standing beside my husband, the creature who has been a ghostly presence these last few weeks, sensed, not seen, and immediately regret using the power of the internet to exorcise her. Striking might not be a potent enough word to describe Marine. She is everything I am not—confident, stylish, gorgeous, at ease with her beautiful, lithe body. If I were in Monte Carlo, I would wager a small fortune Marine moves with the singular grace that seems the divinely bespoke trait of tall, slender women. All of the evidence is here—in this single photograph—the tilt of her chin, the posture subtly emphasizing her long, lean legs, the serene smile. How can I ever hope to compete with the memory of Marine?

The lights are off and the drapes closed when I finally return to the bedroom. Xavier lifts the blankets and I climb into bed beside him.

"I thought you would never be finished in there," he says, pulling me against his hard, naked body. "It feels like an eternity since I did this"—he kisses my lips—"and this." He takes my bottom lip into his mouth, nibbling and sucking on the plump flesh, while his knee spreads my thighs.

"Xavier?" I gasp.

"Oui, mon amour?"

"What are you doing?"

He chuckles low in his throat, the sound seductive in the night-darkened room, with his chest pressed against my breasts. "I am going to make love to you."

And he does. Slow and hot, groaning as he holds me tight around the waist and eases his body into mine. He is maddeningly restrained in his lovemaking, patiently stoking the flames of my desire until I clutch his waist and push him deep inside me, deep into my womb, silently urging him to increase his tempo.

"Mon Dieu. Tu me rends fou."

Beads of perspiration drop on the pillow beside my head, echoing in my ears like spring rain pattering on a tin roof. Still, Xavier keeps his rhythm slow and achingly gentle.

"Tu es à moi, Manderley."

Mon-de-lee.

Hearing him pronounce my name the way only he does, with his heavy French accent, so that it sounds like a sensual moan uttered by a lover in the throes of desire, touches a raw place in my heart and I begin to cry. Hot, silent tears slipping out of my eyes and down onto the pillow to mingle with his beads of perspiration. I weep for what I have and what I fear is not mine to hold.

Chapter Twenty-nine

I am walking down a gravel driveway lined with tall plane trees, their trunks mottled with gray, green, white, and yellow bark. Golden rays of sunlight penetrate the thick canopy of waxy leaves, creating lacy shadows on the ground.

I pause in a beam of light so I can feel the warmth of the sun on my face. I feel nothing. Not the warmth on my cheeks nor the breeze ruffling my hair.

In the distance, I hear the surf crashing against the rocky shore. I lick my lips, hoping to taste the salty tang of sea air. I taste nothing.

I continue walking, suddenly anxious to reach the end of the drive. A strong gust of wind blows through the branches and rattles the leaves so that it sounds as if they are whispering to me—a welcome or a warning, I cannot tell.

Suddenly, the wind plucks the trees from the ground in a great shedding and swirling of waxy leaves. The trees spin around in the sky, roots dangling, bare branches grasping the air like skeletal hands. Through the mael-

strom of leaves and branches, I recognize Xavier's home at the end of the drive just ahead.

"Xavier!" I cry, running toward the château. "Xavier."

The silhouette of a person suddenly appears in one of the windows—its features too indistinguishable to determine if it is a man or a woman—and my pulse quickens in terror.

I run across the courtyard and up the stairs, into a grand foyer aglow with the light of a thousand slender candles in a tinkling crystal chandelier.

For a second, I wonder if my simple cotton sundress is too plain for such magnificent surroundings, too plain for a man as magnificent as Xavier, but the anxiety passes quickly, as soon as I notice the trail of oleander blossoms leading from the front door and up the stone staircase.

"Xavier?"

He appears at the top of the stairs, looks down, and notices me standing in the foyer. He hurries down the stairs, happy, no, relieved, to see me.

I turn to check my appearance in the cloudy baroque mirror hanging near the door, but it is not my image I see reflected in the glass. It is Marine, dressed in a billowy black gown, her glossy black hair floating around her shoulders—my shoulders—as if weightless.

"Marine, darling," he says, reaching for me. "I thought you would never arrive. I've missed you."

I try to pull away, but I can't move my feet. I look down and see the gnarled, earth-encrusted roots of a plane tree wrapped around my ankles.

"Marine, what is it, darling?"

I am not Marine!

I try to speak the words, but my mouth appears to be frozen in a grotesque smile. I look in the mirror again, at my pale, almost lifeless skin, my lips tinged blue like the corpse of a drowning victim, and Xavier standing behind me, his eyes as deep and dark as the sea crashing on the rocks nearby.

He leans forward, as if to kiss me, and I am falling, falling into his eyes, splashing into a black, stormy sea, icy waves washing over my head, pushing me down, down, down . . .

"Xavier!" I cry, reaching my hand out for him. "Xavier, please. Save me."

"Wake up, *ma bichette*." Xavier's strong arms are around me, his warm breath on my shoulder, scented with cinnamon. "Wake up."

"I am drowning," I gasp, my chest tight.

"Shhh," he soothes, folding me into him. "You aren't drowning, *ma bichette*. You are safe. It was only a nightmare."

My limbs are trembling and my skin feels cold, so very cold. The memory of the dream is still powerfully present, lingering in such a way as to make me question whether I am truly awake or lost in another, sweeter nocturnal fantasy. I wrap my arms around Xavier's neck, bury my head against his shoulder, and cling to him so the icy waves can't drag me to the depths of the ocean.

He holds me against his chest, murmuring words in French I don't understand, until my tears stop falling and my trembling limbs relax.

"You are safe, *ma bichette*. I promise," he whispers in my ear, his lips brushing my lobe. "Now, won't you tell me what that was all about? What did you dream about that made you cry out for me in your sleep?"

I tell him about my dream, about the angry wind, the swirling trees, the icy sea, but I leave out the part about my inhabiting Marine's body, taking over her life.

"Have you had this nightmare before?"

"Not this particular nightmare, no, but I have had other frightening dreams about the sea."

"When did they begin?"

"I don't remember," I lie.

"Recently?"

"Yes."

"I see." He smooths the damp hair off the back of my neck and leaves his hand there, rubbing the bumpy ridge under my ear with his thumb. "*Mon amour*, have you been sailing since your father and aunt had their accident?"

"No."

"Were you happy when I told you I was going to take you sailing tomorrow?"

"No."

"Why didn't you tell me?"

Hot stinging tears nettle my lids and I close my eyes tight because I know if one tear falls, many will fall.

"Manderley? Why didn't you just tell me?"

"I have always loved the sea, felt connected and calm when near it, but ever since my father's death, I have developed a powerful fear of the ocean. I didn't want to disappoint you."

He presses his lips to my forehead and his stubble scratches the place between my eyes.

"That you felt a need to hide the truth from me disappoints me far more than a canceled sailing trip. A marriage is like a castle tower. If it is built strong and true, it can stand many assaults. Lies, even small deceptions, weaken the walls." His touch is gentle, but his tone has a harsher edge to it than it did a moment ago and my heart aches, knowing I caused it. "I don't want you to be the

Manderley you think I want you to be; I want you, the real Manderley de Maloret, fears, faults, and all."

"Yes, Xavier."

"You must be honest with me. Otherwise . . ." He tightens his hold on my neck and takes a deep breath. "I don't want to think about what would happen if I discovered you haven't been truthful with me. Just promise—"

"I promise," I say, pressing a teary kiss to his chest. "I promise to be honest with you, Xavier. Always."

Chapter Thirty

Text from Tara Maxwell:
This is a joke, right? Seriously. Who is that man? Why were you wearing an old wedding dress in that picture? Why aren't you answering your phone?

Text to Tara Maxwell:
Not joking. The man is my husband, Xavier. I got married in that beautiful old dress. I will call to explain soon.

Text from Tara Maxwell:
Have you lost your damned mind? You're supposed to be the responsible one. What am I going to say to Emma Lee?

Text to Tara Maxell:
Tell her being the responsible one is overrated.

Text from Emma Lee Maxwell:
Please, pretty please with a mess of sugar on it, tell me you aren't joking. Tell me you really eloped with some

smokin' hot, hot, hottie. Tara has been pinging so hard since we got your email with the pic, she hasn't said a word about my move to England.

Text to Emma Lee Maxwell:

Not joking. I am now Madame de Maloret, wife of the smokin' hot, hot, hottie. Go after your dreams, darlin' Emma Lee. Move to England and become a matchmaker, if that's what you truly want. Tara will be just fine. Daddy would want you to follow your dreams.

Since the drive from Lake Como to Xavier's home on the western coast of France takes fourteen hours, we divided the journey into two days, stopping for lunch the first day at a quaint fondue restaurant on the shores of Lake Geneva. We dip crusty bread into bubbling cheese, sip chilled white wine, and walk along the shores of the lake, skipping rocks, and learning more about each other. We make love on a blanket beneath a pine tree beside the lake. Xavier holds me in his arms after, whispering promises in my ear. We will travel to La Trinité-sur-Mer each April, where I will watch him sail a single-hull in the Spi Ouest-France regatta. We will visit Switzerland in the winter and wander through Christmas markets, drink hot spiced wine, eat Chräbeli cookies flavored with anise seeds, and go skiing down alpine covered mountains. He is surprised when he learns I can ski.

"South Carolina isn't exactly known for its white winters, *ma bichette*," he says, chuckling. "Forgive me if I doubted your proficiency on a slope."

"You forget I went to boarding school in Vermont and college in New York. Besides"—I boldly slide my hand under his shirt and teasingly run my fingers over his rippled abs—"you will soon learn I am proficient at many, many things."

He laughs and heat flushes my cheeks.

"Who is this brazen woman I suddenly find myself married to?"

I start to pull my hand out from underneath his waistband, suddenly shy again, but he grabs my wrist and pushes it back until I feel his manhood against my fingers.

"Finish it, Madame de Maloret," he says, reaching his free hand under my blouse and cupping my breast. "Finish what you started. I promise, you will enjoy the journey."

"We just . . ." My breath catches in my throat as I feel him stirring under my hand, growing hard with rekindled arousal. "Aren't you tired?"

"I am a Frenchman, *mon amour*. I am never too tired for lovemaking, especially when I am married to a beautiful, proficient woman."

We are driving through the heart of France the next day, only hours from his home near Saint-Maturinus-sur-Mer, when I notice the shift in his mood. Animated and charming, the perfect travel companion becomes quiet, broody, his long, lean fingers wrapped around the steering wheel, gaze fixed intently on some distant point on the horizon.

The abundant sunshine we enjoyed in the South of France and Lake Como has been replaced by flannel-gray skies thick with clouds. When fat raindrops begin pattering the windshield, I untie the cardigan knotted at my neck and wrap it around my shoulders. I am trying not to view the change in weather as a bad omen. I don't want to believe the gloomy clouds portend darker, less cheerful times, but the dreary weather combined with Xavier's bleak mood make it difficult.

I remember the slinky woman at La Grotte and wonder if Xavier is used to women whose conversation sparkles as bright as their diamonds. He seems content to drive in silence—his eyes hidden behind a pair of expensive sunglasses, but I worry . . .

I am anxious. I can feel the nervous energy building inside, the quivery, twitching muscles, and I know it won't be long before hot, itchy hives erupt on my chest and spread up my neck. Some of what I am feeling is natural. I have married a man I met on holiday and he is taking me home to meet his family, friends, and neighbors for the first time. They will be curious, perhaps even angry at having been excluded from sharing our wedding day. What if they take one look at me, the drab little American with the drab dishwater-blond hair, in the drab little sundress, and wonder what Xavier was thinking when he married me? If the roles were reversed and I was taking Xavier back to Charleston to meet my loved ones, he would feel the same amount of tension I am feeling now, wouldn't he?

I look at the man I promised to love, honor, and obey, and swallow a hysterical burble of laughter. Girard Fortune Xavier de Maloret wouldn't know a panic attack if it crept up and choked the confidence out of him.

He looks over his shoulder and catches me staring at him. "Do you regret marrying me?"

"What?" The question takes me as much by surprise as his sudden mood change. "Why would you ask such a thing?"

He stretches his arms, locks his elbows, and grips the steering wheel tighter. "Answer me."

"No, I don't regret marrying you."

He stares at me, his face pale, drawn, his lips pressed together in a grimace, the half smile, half frown skeptics wear upon hearing something they believe outrageous. The rain is coming down harder now, the drops graduating from patters to pounds. I want to urge Xavier to return his attention to the road, but I am afraid he will perceive it as subterfuge or evasion.

"You're certain?"

"Absolutely."

He stares a second longer before returning his attention to the road. My mind begins whirling as it searches for a reason for his question. Did I say something to make him think I don't want to be his wife? Have I not been affectionate enough? Is it because I haven't told him I love him since our wedding night? But then, he hasn't ever told me he loves me . . .

It's not you, Manderley. It's him.

When we first met, I likened Xavier to a sleek jungle cat because of his dark looks and intense gazes. Now, I wonder if he might be a jungle cat with a thorn stuck in his paw, something too sharp and too painful to discuss. I inhale, but his next question knocks the breath from my lungs and the reason from my hypothesis.

"Why did you cry the other night?"

"What? When?"

"The night you had the bad dream—before you had the bad dream. You cried when I made love to you."

"I was overcome with emotions."

"Regret?"

"Fear."

"Fear?" He pierces me with a look far sharper than a thorn. "You are afraid of me? Why?"

I shrug, feeling suddenly foolish.

"Have you heard something to make you believe I would harm you?"

"No," I whisper. "Fear I will lose you. That I will wake up one day and this will all have been a wonderful dream. I will be back in Los Angeles wishing someone noticed me, wishing I had someone like you in my life."

His face softens, his grip relaxes. "I hope you always feel that way."

"I will always love you."

He makes a noise in his throat that people make when they don't believe what you are saying but have decided to humor you. "One day you might wake up and realize your life with me is not the dream you imagined . . . that it is something else, something mundane and . . . lacking."

"Lacking?" *What an odd word.*

"If you ever start to feel that way"—he reaches for my hand without taking his gaze from the road, lifts it to his lips, and kisses my knuckles—"bored, disillusioned, restless, I hope you will tell me. If, after some time together, you decide I am not the man you want to spend the rest of your life with, tell me, just as I will tell you if I begin to question our compatibility."

We drive for several miles before he speaks again, and when he does, the clouds that hung like a pall over our previous conversation seem to have evaporated. The animated, charming travel companion has returned.

I, on the other hand, feel as if the life has drained out of my body. My aunt Patricia went big-game hunting in Zimbabwe once, a fifty-thousand-dollar, ten-day safari that promised the opportunity to "bag a trophy lion."

When the moment to pull the trigger finally arrived, my aunt found she didn't have the fortitude. She said she would have fallen to the ground if not for the marrow keeping her upright. She said she looked into the beast's eyes and realized it was a special type of insanity that made anyone believe they could encounter such a wild, magnificent creature and walk away unscathed.

That's how I feel now, sitting beside Xavier. Only my marrow is keeping me from collapsing on his leather seat and sliding down into the wheel well. *I will tell you if I begin to question our compatibility.* Why? Why did he give words to a vague feeling, a fear that should have remained unspoken? For I do not believe every thought, every emotion, should be shared, not even with one's spouse. Some feelings should be kept private, kept secreted in the basement of your heart, until they fade away.

He tells me about the village near his home, the whitewashed shops lining the wharf, the chapel with the Celtic cross in the yard, the small fishing museum with a Gauguin drawing of women in traditional Breton dress. The closer we get, the more sites he points out.

I only half listen because in my head I hear a continuous loop of him saying *I will tell you if I begin to question our compatibility.*

"Manderley?"

"I am sorry. What did you say?"

"I reminded you I will be leaving for Dubai next week, but you won't be alone. Madame Deniau will be there if you need anything."

"Madame Deniau?"

He frowns. "My housekeeper. She doesn't speak English and she can come off as a little strange, but she has been at the château since the first stone was pushed in place and is terribly proud of her connection to the de

Malorets. She will see to your needs." He shifts into a higher gear. "I will introduce you to my family when I return from Dubai. My sister will be annoyed I didn't drive you to her home before leaving on my trip, but she is usually annoyed with me about something or other."

We have turned off the autoroute and are traveling on a rural two-lane road, zipping by a dizzying succession of white, red, and black signs announcing villages with strange names like Bénodet, Combrit, Plomeur. The air inside the Jaguar is colder, heavier with moisture, and I realize we must be close to the sea.

"Your family doesn't live near the château?"

"*Non*. Amice has an apartment over the old kitchens, but her work makes it difficult for her to visit the château as much as she might like. She lives in Paris. She is an *avocat d'entreprise* with a large multinational firm." He notices my confusion and explains that an *avocat d'enterprise* is a corporate lawyer. "My uncles are scattered around Brittany, close enough to visit when they wish, but not so close that you will see them while I am gone.

"It would be easier if you spoke French, but, never mind. There is a language institute in Quimper. I will ask my assistant to enroll you in the next class."

I consider reminding him that I graduated from Columbia University and worked as an assistant to a successful Hollywood screenwriter, that I am quite capable of making my arrangements for an immersion class, but we are minutes from arriving at his home and I don't want to spoil the moment with my petulant indignations.

"Yes, Xavier."

I close my eyes and rest my head against the headrest. My stomach is twisted in an intricate macramé of knots. I wish I could turn the clock back a day, to that moment when we were lying in each other's arms on the banks of

Lake Geneva, the scent of pine needles heavy in the air, and the taste of Chardonnay on our breath and each other's lips.

"We're here," Xavier says, grabbing my hand. "*Bienvenue à Château de Maloret, ma bichette.*"

Chapter Thirty-one

My first view of Château de Maloret will forever be etched upon my mind, like the coat of arms etched into the stone posts on either side of the wrought-iron gates preventing curious tourists from trespassing. My first view of my new home was, in fact, through those magnificent gates, ornate panels with curling vines, blooming roses, and sparrows caught in flight. While Xavier opened the gates to allow us to pass, I gazed through the rain-splattered windshield at a castle out of a storybook tale, with a drawbridge over a moat, towers, chapel, and partially ruined dovecote. Several of the windows are glowing, warm and golden, against the gloomy day.

Unlike the driveway in my dream, the real drive to Château de Maloret does not feature serpentine twists and turns. It is a straight line from gates to front door, with clipped yew bushes creating an impenetrable hedge running alongside. Xavier follows the drive until it branches off in two directions. He turns left and we continue driving until we arrive at a low stone building with a steeply pitched mansard roof and a series of arched wooden doors.

"Here we are," he says, rolling to a stop. "These were once the stables, but my great-grandfather modified the building when he replaced his horse and carriage with a 1938 Daimler Roadster. Today, the bottom story is used as a workshop and garage. The top story has been transformed into guest apartments."

"This is where Amice has her apartment?"

"That's right. It's also where your sisters will stay when they come for visits."

He begs my pardon and leans over to open the glovebox, his arm resting on my leg. He removes a garage door remote from the compartment and pushes the button. Two wooden doors swing open. Xavier pulls into the garage and kills the engine. He climbs out of the driver's seat, stretching his arms over his head and groaning, before walking around the front of the car to open my door. The scent of wood shavings and car wax is heavy in the still air.

"You said this was a garage and a workshop. What kind of workshop?"

He answers me by taking my hand and leading me deeper into the darkened garage. He flips a switch and dozens of overhead lights flicker on to reveal a massive space filled with gleaming automobiles. He leads me to the first, a futuristic-looking silver sports car with a contoured nose, low, narrow doors, and a panoramic glass roof. He opens the driver's-side door—which swings up instead of out, like a butterfly's wing—and gestures for me to get in. I slide into the narrow seat and run my hand over the red leather dashboard, admiring the cockpit's many gauges and dials.

"The McLaren 570GT," he says, squatting beside me.

"It's framed in carbon fiber, so it is strong, but light-weight. The top speed is only 328 kilometers per hour, but it's so low-slung you feel like you are flying over the ground."

"Two hundred and four miles per hour? You're a race-car driver?"

"*Non.*" He laughs, helping me out of the car and closing the door. "I have a friend who works for McLaren. He invited me to their technology and production center in Surrey and let me take one of the first 570GTs for a test on their track at Dunsfold. I put my name on the waiting list that day."

He shows me the other cars in his collection until we arrive at the last one in the row, an antique convertible roadster with a deep burgundy paint job and running boards.

"Is this your great-grandfather's roadster?"

He grins. *"Oui."*

"It looks like the car Laurence Olivier drove in *Rebecca*," I say, resisting the urge to run my hand over the fawn leather seat. "It's beautiful."

"It is rather special."

"So, you're a collector of fine cars?"

"Non," he says, shaking his head. "I am an enthusiast."

"Is there a difference?"

"Oui." He crosses his arms and leans against one of the old rough wooden posts supporting the ceiling. "An automobile collector is interested in acquiring and displaying. An enthusiast appreciates the function as well as the beauty of the vehicle. An enthusiast wants to drive, to feel the freedom that comes when it is just you and the car. It's the same freedom and sense of escape I get when I am sailing."

"You drive all of these cars?"

"Oui."

"Is there a car you don't own that you wish you did?"

"That is a good question." He smiles. "The Petersen Automotive Museum in Los Angeles has Steve McQueen's 1956 Jaguar XKSS in their collection. I would love to own that car."

"Why? Because you like Steve McQueen's films?"

"I do like his films, but that's not why. McQueen was a skilled race-car driver and a tremendous enthusiast. The XKSS was his favorite. There are stories about him racing it through the canyons and hills around Hollywood, the whine of the engine waking residents, and police chasing him down Sunset Strip, once with Natalie Wood in the passenger seat."

"What a wonderful story."

"Have you ever raced through the Hollywood Hills in a vintage convertible?"

"I can't say I have."

"Add it to the list."

"What list?"

"The list of things we will do together. Put it right after sipping spiced wine at a Christmas market in Lake Geneva, but before having children."

My heart skips a beat. "Children?"

He pushes himself off the post and sweeps me up in his arms, carrying me to the roadster. "Many, many children," he says, dragging his lips over mine.

He climbs onto the running board and steps over the passenger door into the car. He sits on the leather bench and we kiss until we are tripping over ourselves, frantically fumbling with buttons, snaps, zippers, tearing at our clothes, aching, shaking with a feverish need to taste and touch each other.

"Xavier," I gasp. "Stop. We can't."

"Who says we can't?" he asks, raising one brow. "I am master of Château de Maloret and if I want to make violent love to my wife in the stables, nobody is going to stop me. Now, take off those damnable lacy panties."

Before leaving the stables I learn why the scent of shaved wood permeates the air in the garage. When Xavier said he descended from a long line of boat builders, he meant actual boat building, planing wood, gluing joints, brushing turpentine.

"Boat building is a skill that has been passed down in my family, from father to son, for hundreds of years. My father taught me how to build a boat with my own hands and I will teach my son."

Chapter Thirty-two

As soon as we leave the stables, a pair of shaggy black beasts come bounding up to us, tongues lolling, tails wagging. Xavier whistles once sharply and the pair sit, tongues still lolling, tails still wagging.

Xavier drops our suitcases and ruffles their furry heads, first one, and then the other. He glances up at me.

"Do you like dogs, *ma bichette*?"

"I am frightened of dogs."

"You have nothing to fear with Jacques and Jules. They are the sweetest souls you will ever meet—despite their mangy appearance." He takes my hand and pulls me down beside him. "Jacques is named after Jacques Cartier, the famous Breton sailor who discovered Canada, because he likes to wander, and Jules is named after Jules Verne, because he likes to—"

"—write novels?"

He laughs. "Jules likes to curl up beside the fire in the library. The lazy bag of bones would stay there all day, if he didn't have Jacques chasing him around." He takes my hand, turns it over, and urges me to hold it out toward the dogs. "They are Breton water dogs."

Jules briefly presses his nose to the back of my hand, like a gentleman kissing a lady's hand in greeting. His long, droopy whiskers tickle my skin and I laugh. Jacques follows Jules's lead and presses his leathery nose to my hand.

"Most people teach their dogs to use their paws to shake visitors' hands, but you taught yours to kiss hands?"

"They only kiss ladies' hands."

"Charmer."

"We try, don't we, *garçons*." Xavier laughs.

Jacques, clearly the more energetic of the pair, leaps up at the sound of his master's laughter, barking and spinning in circles.

"Alors, vas-y," Xavier says, standing. *Okay, let's go.*

Jacques races off. Jules remains at my feet, soulful chocolate eyes fixed on my face, tail sweeping back and forth across the gravel. He is awfully charming.

"Would you like to pet him?"

"Would it be alright?"

"Of course, *ma bichette*," he says, helping me stand. "Jacques and Jules belong to you, too, now. They will expect you to let them accompany you when you walk on the beach, and Jules will probably want to sleep with you when I am out of town. He's a naughty boy that way."

I carefully reach out and touch the wavy black fur on Jules's head and he moves closer, nuzzling my leg.

"That's it," Xavier murmurs encouragingly, resting his hand on the small of my back. "He has a tickle spot just below his ear."

I bond with Jules until Xavier retrieves our suitcases and urges me to follow him. We walk across a cobbled courtyard to a set of tall, narrow, gilded wooden doors. Xavier tucks my suitcase under his arm and is reaching for the brass knob when the door opens, the hinges screaming like a banshee.

A tall, painfully thin elderly woman appears in the doorway, her face so gaunt her cheekbones appear as sharp as knives, her grizzled hair worn in a thick braid at the base of her neck. She is clutching her weathered hands at her waist. Her cloudy black eyes fix on me immediately and don't leave my face, even as she greets Xavier in thick French.

I smile nervously and press my hand to my throat as the skin begins to tighten and itch while Xavier speaks to his housekeeper.

"Manderley, *mon amour*," he says, placing his hand on the small of my back again. "This is Madame Deniau."

"*Bonsoir*, Madame Deniau," I say. "*C'est un plaisir de rencontrer vous.*"

Her thick gray eyebrows knit together and she finally shifts her gaze off of my face. She looks at Xavier and says something in French. Xavier replies.

Madame Deniau looks at me and huffs, "*Vous!*"

She lifts one of the suitcases and disappears down a hallway, her footsteps strangely silent despite the polished stone floor. Xavier waits until he is sure she is out of hearing before laughing.

"I told you she could be rather . . . odd."

"*Vous?*"

"You inverted your pronoun when you told her you were happy to meet her. You said, *C'est un plaisir de rencontrer vous*. You should have said, *C'est un plaisir de vous rencontrer*."

I scratch my neck. "She was correcting my French?"

"*Oui,*" he says, grabbing my hand so I don't scratch

myself raw. "She is a stickler about grammar. You will find she is a stickler about a good many things. Bérenger is much easier to deal with and he speaks a bit of English."

"Bérenger?"

"He is our caretaker. He manages the estate and the army of workers we employ part-time to keep it from turning to rubble and tumbling into the sea. He is off on his annual holiday this week and next, but you will meet him when I am in Dubai." He takes my hand, lacing his fingers through mine. "Now, shall I give you a tour of your new home?"

"Yes, please."

"This is really just a service corridor. Originally, it was part of the dungeon. Two hundred years ago, this was where riders would have returned after a day spent hunting." He gestures to a room with dark wood paneling where rows of leather riding boots with boot-stays sticking out are lined up along the wall. "This was where they would have removed their boots and left them to be polished by underbutlers. Today, you will find rain boots and slickers. Be sure to wear them when you take Jacques and Jules for a run along the beach or you will return covered in sand and seawater after they dash into the sea and then return to shake off their wet coats all over you."

Xavier shows me the old kitchen, with an iron stove and gleaming copper pots hanging from the ceiling, but tells me there is a smaller, more manageable kitchen on the first floor in our apartments. We continue down the corridor and climb up a circular staircase, the same kind of narrow, dank staircase my aunt Patricia has in her home in Ireland. Xavier pushes a scarred wooden door open and we are in a cavernous room with a wooden ceiling, tapestries covering the walls, and a massive fireplace.

"We are now in the oldest part of the château," Xavier

says. "This was the great hall, where banquets would have been held. Today, we rent the space out for weddings."

Xavier leads me back to the circular stairway and we climb up the stairs to the gallery, a long room with parquet floors and a coffered ceiling. Mullion glass windows on one side offer a view of the inner courtyard and the sea beyond. We visit the chapel before heading back to the private apartments.

"You wouldn't have a map of the château, would you?"

He chuckles. "I will ask Bérenger to make you a copy. In the meantime, just remember the château originally formed a box with four towers, one in each corner. The west wing is no longer standing, so the château is now a U. The east wing is the great hall. The south wing is the chapel. The north wing is the private apartments. All of the towers have ground level doors that open to the courtyard. Does that help?"

"Yes."

Xavier stops in front of a mirror framed in gilt. He pushes on the glass and the mirror swings in, revealing a hidden door. We step through the door into a hallway and Xavier closes the door behind us. This part of the château has been tastefully renovated and updated. The wood paneling has been painted white, the ceiling beams and wood floor stained dark gray. On one side of the hallway, tall windows look out on the courtyard.

Xavier opens a door and steps back so I can enter. It's a masculine living room, with dark gray walls, a black leather sofa that looks like it came from the cover of a Restoration Hardware catalog, tall leather wingback chairs beside a fireplace, and a scarred, salvaged wood coffee table with stacks of sailing and car magazines. One wall is covered with framed antique nautical charts.

"What a lovely room."

"I just had several of the rooms on this wing redecorated, but I understand if you want to add your touch."

"No," I say. "It's beautiful just the way it is."

A miniature poodle asleep on a tweed blanket on the sofa suddenly wakes up, barks, and then leaps down and runs over to me, hopping up on its back legs.

"Hello," I say, holding my hand flat the way Xavier taught me. "What's your name?"

"That's Coco."

"As in Coconut?"

"No, as in Coco Chanel."

I laugh. "You named your dog after a designer?"

"I did not name Coco," he says, his face tight. "She was . . . abandoned by her previous owner."

"How sad. She's so tiny."

My fear of dogs disappears as I look down at the tiny poodle with the heart-shaped nose. I squat down and Coco jumps onto my lap.

"Who would abandon such a sweet little dog?"

"Someone who is selfish and heartless," he says, his tone cold.

I stand, cradling Coco in my arms. "It was good of you to give her a home."

He doesn't respond. Instead, he walks over to an armoire and opens the doors to reveal a well-stocked liquor cabinet. He splashes a generous portion of scotch into a heavy cut-crystal glass, raises it to his lips, and drains it in one swallow.

He deposits the empty glass in the armoire and turns back to me, his expression more relaxed.

"It's getting late. Are you hungry?"

"A little. Are you?"

"Oui." He takes Coco from my arms and deposits her

on her blanket on the couch. "I'll ask Madame Deniau to prepare something."

"No!" My protest bursts out of me. "It is getting late and I wouldn't want to impose. Madame Deniau is probably getting ready for bed. I can make something for us if you show me how to get to the kitchen."

"You're sure?"

"Absolutely."

"The kitchen is the last door at the end of the hall," he says, rubbing his neck. "I am sore from the drive. Would you mind if I took a shower first?"

"Go on," I say, standing on my tiptoes and pressing a kiss to his lips. "I'll manage fine."

When he leaves, I stand in the living room, glancing around at the strange belongings that will one day be as familiar to me as my own, and feeling like a tourist who slipped away from the group and is trespassing in the lord's private apartments. It's surreal. The eighteenth-century paneling on the walls. The incense-like scent lingering from hundreds of years of fireplace smoke permeating the floors, ceilings, walls. On the table in the corner, the framed photographs of a family I don't know. The little white dog on the couch staring at me with her shiny black-button eyes.

I feel as if I am a character in an old Bette Davis movie, a woman with amnesia who finds herself in a strange home, an interloper pretending to be someone she is not. I wonder if Marine felt this way on her first night at Château de Maloret.

A bolt of lightning splits the sky outside the window, bright white light flashes like a strobe in the room. Coco leaps up, stares at the window as if she suddenly sees a ghost, and barks, a shrill yap that raises the hair on the back of my neck.

Chapter Thirty-three

Text from Tara Maxwell:
Winter called to remind me that the terms of Aunt Pattycake's last will require that I spend three months living in Tásúildun. I don't remember hearing that at the reading, do you? What am I going to do? I can't leave Charleston.

Text to Tara Maxwell:
Why not?

Text from Olivia Tate:
Monsieur X leaves for Dubai today, doesn't he? I know you will miss him, but spend the time working on your novel. The portion you sent me is spec. Absolutely spec, Mandy. If you get too lonely, call me.

"In French, we don't say *I miss you*." Xavier leans down to kiss my forehead and the spicy scent of his expensive cologne wraps around me like an embrace. "We say *tu me manques*, which means *you are missing from me*. That is how I will feel while I am away from you, as if part of my heart is missing."

I turn my head, nuzzling against his shoulder. "I wish you didn't have to go."

"Je suis désolé, mon amour," he murmurs against my ear. "I would send someone else, but I have been working on this deal for over a year and it is too important to—"

"I know how important it is," I say, turning my head and pressing my lips to his. *"Tu me manques."*

He smiles. "Your French is improving already."

"Merci." I yawn and stretch my arms. "Xavier?"

"Oui?"

"What made you decide to end things with Marine?"

"Merde," he mutters under his breath. "You know I have to leave in a few minutes, Manderley. Honestly, now is not a good time for a discussion about Marine."

There never seems to be a good time. Why is he so reluctant to open up to me about his first marriage? It's almost as if he is hiding something.

"But—"

"Go back to sleep now." He tucks the blanket under my chin and stands. "I will fly back as soon as I close the deal, I promise."

He kisses me one last time and then he is gone, his confident footsteps echoing down the hallway.

"I love you," I whisper to the darkness, wishing he would hear it and hurry back to tell me he loves me, too.

A few minutes later, the Jaguar's purring engine can be heard revving in the stables. I climb out of bed and move to the window facing the stables, pull back the curtains, and watch the Jaguar back out of the garage and disappear around the corner.

Watching Xavier drive away reminds me of the day my father dropped me off at my boarding school in Vermont, the gripping loneliness and irrational fears of abandonment I felt, the hot, salty tears that clogged my throat.

I climb back under the covers and hug Xavier's pillow to my chest. The last thought I have before falling asleep is how extreme it is to be in love, raised to the heights of pleasure one moment, and plunged to the depths of despair the next.

Somebody has made a pot of coffee.

It takes me a while to register, and when I do, I sit up in bed, brushing my hair out of my eyes, half expecting Xavier to walk into the room carrying two steaming mugs. The apartment is silent, though.

Ridiculously disappointed, I shower and dress before making my way to the kitchen attached to our apartments in search of the coffee that drew me from my slumber. Coco suddenly appears at my heels, her little nails *click-click-clicking* on the parquet floor. I scoop her up and carry her into the kitchen, only to find the coffeepot clean and dry. In fact, a thorough search of the pantry reveals two orphaned beans in the bottom of a foil coffee bag. I consider going in search of Madame Deniau, but the sun is shining so brightly I decide I would rather go to town for coffee.

"Want to go for a walk, Coco?"

She cocks her head and her ears pull back.

"Marche?"

She yaps excitedly, her tail thumping against my side.

I find a tiny white harness and a crystal-encrusted Chanel dog leash in the back of a drawer in the chest in the hallway, and set off with my new friend.

An hour and a half later, I walk into the village, Coco fast asleep in my arms, as would be expected of a Chanel-wearing dog. She perks up when we pass a boulangerie, the buttery scent of crusty baguettes and flaky croissants teasing her little nose.

"Behold! Her Majesty Coco has arisen," I say, setting her back on her feet. "Let the royal *levée* begin."

She shakes, stretches, and raises her nose in the air as if to say *we are not amused*.

In truth, had I known the château was located so far from the village I wouldn't have brought her. Before leaving, Xavier showed me the cabinet in the stables containing the keys to the cars, each labeled in his strong, sure script, and told me to use whichever I preferred.

"Can you drive a manual?"

"Yes."

"Bon," he said, smiling. "The Aston Martin is easy to maneuver on these narrow roads, and a sexy ride, but the Range Rover is more comfortable for longer drives. I would advise against taking the McLaren."

I am sure the Aston Martin would have been a sexy ride and cut my journey to a fraction of the time, but the less time I spend at the château means less effort to avoid Madame Deniau, or, as Olivia has taken to calling her, Madame Vous.

The village is postcard perfect, just as Xavier described it. The whitewashed shops lining the wharf and forming the main thoroughfare. The chapel with the Celtic cross in the yard, covered in lichen.

Two elderly women huddled together outside the charcuterie are eyeing me suspiciously. I smile as I pass. Their gazes shift from me to Coco and back to me again.

"Scandaleux," one of them hisses.

Thanks to Olivia, *scandaleux* is one of the few French words I know, so I assume they are mistaking me for someone else and keep walking.

"Excusez-moi," I say, stopping the next person I pass, a man in a striped shirt and beret. *"Où puis-je acheter le café, s'il vous plaît?"*

He stares at me blankly, making me wonder if I have inverted another pronoun and butchered my simple request for coffee, until Coco yaps and hops on his leg.

"Oh, la!" he says, bending over and scratching Coco's head. *"Bonjour, Mademoiselle Coco."*

He stands and jerks his thumb at a glass-fronted shop with an old metal sign hanging above the door.

"Merci," I say.

He nods brusquely and walks away.

The shop appears to cater to tourists, selling handmade baskets filled with picnic items, tins of sardines, jars of olives, wheels of cheese, and bottles of the locally produced *chouchen*, an alcoholic beverage made from fermented honey and served as an aperitif.

I take two bags of coffee off a shelf and walk to the cash register, queuing up behind two women who look to be about my age. They don't notice me until they have finished paying and turn to leave. One looks down at Coco and frowns.

"Êtes-vous Madame de Maloret?" she asks sharply.

"Oui."

The women exchange glances.

"Tu te moques de moi," the other one says, staring at my chest. *"Elle est plate comme une limande."*

She is flat as a dab.

"Chloé!" the cashier gasps.

The one named Chloé rolls her eyes at the cashier and they both start talking at once, a rapid fire exchange of words I can't comprehend. The women give me dirty looks and leave the store.

"Don't mind them," the cashier says in a British accent. "Chloé and Vivienne are a pair of daft cows."

"You speak English?"

"Whenever I can."

"Thank God," I say, dropping the bags of coffee on the counter. "I am Manderley Maxwell. I mean, Manderley de Maloret."

"I know who you are."

"You do?"

She laughs. "I don't know where you are from, but this is Saint-Maturinus, luv. This fishing village might have Wi-Fi and a Carrefour Express, but the residents are stuck in the Middle Ages. When their liege lord returns from the South of France with a new wife, it creates a stir at the well."

Heat flushes my cheeks. It never occurred to me what people might think about the hastiness of our wedding. I don't like knowing people are viewing the most important event in my life through jaded lenses.

"My name is Caroline Gaveau, but my friends call me Caro," she says, running the bags of coffee over a bar scanner. "I own this shop along with my husband, Yves."

"It's nice to meet you, Caro. What brought you to Saint-Maturinus-sur-Mer, if you don't mind me asking? It seems far from the beaten path."

"A man," she says, laughing. "What else would motivate a woman to leave her home in favor of life in a medieval fishing village?"

"A medieval fishing village with Wi-Fi," I say, ironically.

"And a Carrefour Express!"

We laugh.

I pay for the coffee and Caro gives me back a handful

of coins. She reaches under the counter and pulls out a reusable sack, sticks the bags of coffee inside, and hands it to me.

"I didn't pay for the sack."

"It's a gift. They're made locally using seagrass and recycled paper. You might want to remember to bring it when you come to the village because none of the shops give those plastic bags you Americans are so fond of."

"Thank you."

"You're welcome, luv. Stop in if you get lonely."

"I will."

The bells on the door tinkle and a man with a camera strung around his neck walks into the store. I turn to leave and then stop.

"Caro, what did Chloé say about me?"

She inhales and the air whistles between her teeth. "You don't want to know, luv."

"I do."

"She said *elle est plate comme une limande*. It's a French saying, which, roughly translated, means *she's as flat as a flounder*."

A tingling heat sweeps up the back of my neck and over my cheeks. I thank Caro for telling me and hurry out the door, scooping Coco into my arms, and not stopping until I have a stitch in my side.

Back in our apartments, I unhook Coco from her leash and lean against the door until the pain in my side goes away.

I am putting Coco's leash back when I notice a photograph on the floor near the chest, which wasn't there when I took the leash out of the drawer. I pick it up and gasp when I see it is a photograph of Marine. She is sitting cross-legged on a bed, a sheet covering her private areas, her black hair hanging over her bare shoulders, a seductive expression on her face as she stares into the camera.

An ache begins to build deep in my chest.

That's when I see the little white dog curled up on the pillow on the bed behind Marine. Coco! I look down at the sweet dog spinning circles at my feet and the pain shoots to my heart with the speed and devastation of a bullet.

I hear Xavier's voice in my head. *I did not name Coco. She was . . . abandoned by her previous owner.*

It barely registered at the time, but now I think about the way Xavier hesitated before saying Coco was abandoned, as if he weren't being truthful.

I look at the photograph again and my vision blurs with unshed tears. It never occurred to me Marine might be Coco's owner. Xavier had described Coco's previous owner as heartless, and, indeed, it would take cold person to abandon a helpless little dog, but . . .

. . . but something doesn't feel right. There are hundreds of puzzle pieces to this picture and I feel as if I am missing most of them. I have been trying to fit the wrong pieces together, hoping for a clear picture.

The woman in the photograph doesn't look cold. Her eyes are sparkling. Her cheeks are flushed. Her swollen lips are parted in a smile. Her seductive gaze suggests a deep desire for the person taking the picture.

I feel sick.

I take the photograph into the living room and toss it into the fireplace. With trembling fingers, I light a long match and toss it onto the picture. The corner curls black and I feel a stab of guilt. I pull it out of the fireplace and blow on the corner, crying out at the futility of the situation. If Xavier is still in love with Marine, burning a picture will not change his feelings. It just marks me as a jealous, insecure girl.

Marine has been the ghost between us, and I don't think she will be exorcised anytime soon.

I toss the picture into the liquor cabinet, beside the bottle of scotch, and close the doors as if I am locking the ghost in the closet.

I go into the bedroom to get my iPhone.

Olivia answers on the second ring. "You can't be missing Xavier already," she says, laughing. "Girl, you got it bad."

I don't say anything.

"Manderley? What's wrong?"

"I am having a bad day."

"Tell me about it. Life is tough when your château is too big and your prince is a handsome millionaire. Don't let the tiara weigh you down, darling, it's just one of the burdens of the blessed."

The tears I have been holding back spill down my cheeks and I draw a jagged breath. The words spill out of my mouth as fast as the tears spilling down my cheeks. I tell Olivia about the women in the village—all of them. I tell her about Coco and the photograph. I confess my doubts.

"What do you think?"

"It is rather strange," she concedes. "Usually couples fight over custody of their pets. I've never known a woman to walk out on her man *and* her dog. Maybe . . ."

Olivia let's her words trail off, but I know the direction they were headed.

Maybe Marine didn't walk out on her man and her dog. Maybe she didn't walk out at all.

Chapter Thirty-four

Text from Xavier de Maloret:
My heart stopped beating the moment I left you sleeping in our bed and won't start beating again until I have you in my arms. *Tu me manques.* X

My nights are a quick succession of fractured dreams. I wake disoriented, and sometimes I think I can feel Xavier sleeping beside me, smell his breath on my neck, scented with scotch. Then, the light of dawn fights its way through the gap between the curtains and chases away the lingering magic.

My days are longer. I try to stay busy, working on my novel and taking the dogs for long walks, but I find the idle life frustrating and lonely. I miss working.

It is during these lonely times I call Olivia and we laugh about Hollywood gossip or plot our screenplay about the jazz musician living in '20s Cannes or I walk to the village and chat with Caro.

One rainy afternoon a week after Xavier's departure, I decide to explore the château further. I am wandering through a series of unfinished rooms near our private apartments, rooms with peeling plaster and floors in need of repair, when I find more pieces to the puzzle in the shape of boxes. Limp cardboard boxes filled with Marine's belongings—things a woman wouldn't dream of leaving behind. One box contains love letters tied with a Cartier ribbon and leather-bound journals, the pages filled with Marine's elegant, loopy script. School papers, a rag doll, and the trinkets of childhood fill another box. Five wardrobe boxes are stuffed with clothes—one filled entirely with Versace gowns. The last box contains a leather photo album resting on a crumpled-up Marchesa wedding gown. The album is like a portal to the past, giving me a glimpse of Xavier's life with the first Madame de Maloret—or at least a glimpse of the day he began his life with the first Madame de Maloret.

It looked like a romantic beginning. Xavier gazes lovingly at Marine in nearly every photo, his body positioned toward her, his eyes sparkling with a light generated by love—deep, devoted, forsake-all-others love. In a sad, masochistic act, I flip through each page until I reach the last.

I place the album on its taffeta bed and return to the apartments to find a stack of monogrammed stationery waiting on the hall chest. Heavy ivory paper and cards with gold interlocking M's embossed upon them. I trace the M's with my finger.

Manderley de Maloret. Marine de Maloret.

A cold sensation trickles down my spine—the sort of sensation my aunt used to say was caused by the touch of an unseen spirit. I hear my aunt's voice in my head. *A ghost has passed you by, my girl.*

I pull out my phone and compose a text to Xavier, asking him if he ordered me stationery.

His answer comes as I am climbing into bed.

Text from Xavier de Maloret:
No. It was probably Madame Deniau.

My eyes are fluttering shut when I realize this is the first night Xavier hasn't called me to say goodnight.

Chapter Thirty-five

"It was probably Madame Deniau," Olivia snorts. "Of course it was Madame Vous. Creepy old wraith."

My iPhone rang before my eyes were even open.

I look at the clock.

"It's only ten in Los Angeles. Shouldn't you be at some fabulous party flirting with tomorrow's next A-lister?"

"I am not in Los Angeles."

"You're not?"

She hesitates. "I meant to say I am in Malibu. Nathan let me use his beach house for the weekend."

"That was nice of him."

Olivia makes a rude noise with her mouth. "His commission for the sale of *A Quaint Milieu* probably paid half of his mortgage. Letting me use it for a weekend is the least he could do." A loud noise, like the roar of a jet engine, can be head in the background. "Ooh, the tide is coming in. Gotta go. Love."

The line goes dead.

She calls back as I am about to eat a late lunch, her name and picture popping up on my screen.

"*Bonjour*, Olivia," I say, holding the phone to my ear. "What's the matter? Can't sleep?"

"I will sleep just fine once you open your golden gates, Rapunzel, and let me sleep in one of your tower rooms."

"What?"

"I am at your front gates. You have sounded so depressed this last week I wanted to surprise you with a visit. So, surprise!"

I laugh.

I tell her how to open the gates and where to park, then hurry to meet her near the stables. She pulls up in a rented Peugeot, hops out, and we are hugging as if we haven't seen each other in years.

"Are you happy to see me?"

"Yes." I say, hugging her again. "You can't begin to know how happy I am to see you."

"Just a minute," she says, hurrying back to the car. "I come bearing gifts."

She opens the passenger door and returns with a bottle of champagne and a pair of socks.

"Here," she says, handing the gifts to me. "The champagne is for me and the socks are for Monsieur X. I figure you have probably pilfered most of his by now."

"Funny."

"I thought so."

She pulls her suitcase out of the trunk and we enter the château via an entrance to the private apartments, a narrow wooden stairway.

"Where are all of your burly footmen to lug my traveling trunks?"

"As luck would have it, Xavier's staff are gone for their annual summer holidays. It's just Madame Deniau, a gardener, and a part-time housekeeper who comes in from the village."

We spend the rest of the evening watching *Beaches* and drinking one of the bottles of wine we find in the liquor cabinet. When we have drained the last drop from the bottle and the credits are rolling up the screen, I show Olivia the boxes in the unfinished room. Marine's boxes.

"What do you think?" I say, pulling the Marchesa wedding gown out of its box and holding it up for her to see.

"What do I think?" she cries. "What do I think? I'll tell you what I think. Your Monsieur X murdered the first Madame de Maloret and buried her bones somewhere in this château."

"Be serious."

"I am serious," she says, snatching the dress from my hands and flinging it back in the box as if it is cursed. "It all adds up: his reluctance to talk about Marine, the abandoned pooch, the boxes, the angry villagers."

"You have spent too much time in La-La Land. People don't get away with murder in the real world."

"They do if they have a creepy, soul-sucking housekeeper to help them hide the body."

"So now you think Madame Vous . . . Madame Deniau is a murderer, too?"

"Madame?"

Olivia screams and I startle at the sound of Madame Deniau's papery voice behind us. My cheeks flush with heat as I turn to face her.

"Oui."

She gestures to the hallway and says something in French, but I can't understand her.

"She said you received a package and that she left it on the chest in the foyer of your apartment."

In my embarrassment I forgot Olivia speaks fluent French.

"*Merci*, Madame Deniau."

The woman nods her gray head and disappears as silently as she appeared. I look at Olivia.

"I didn't even hear her."

"Of course you didn't hear her. Stealth is a prerequisite to be a truly efficient murderer."

We return to the apartment.

The package, it turns out, is a jasmine bush in what looks to be an antique Sèvres pot, a wedding gift from Thierry Lambert. The message written on the attached card reads, *When you toured my fields you wisely said, "Scents can transport you to another time and place and evoke emotions hidden somewhere deep down." I hope this plant—grafted from a jasmine bush once used to make scents for Marie Antoinette—transports you to that day, when you were in the first blush of love for Xavier.*

I read the card to Xavier when he calls that night, but he sounds drawn and distracted. I try not to read too much into his tepid response, though it is beginning to feel as if we are separated by more than miles.

Chapter Thirty-six

"It has to be the McLaren," Olivia says, crossing her arms over her chest.

During breakfast this morning, Olivia asked if we could drive to the village so she could pick up some gifts from Caro's shop. Naturally, I agreed. I assumed we would take her rental, but she insisted I drive. The moment she saw the McLaren parked in the stall beside the Range Rover, she insisted we drive it into town.

"Olivia, I can't," I say, moving back toward the Ranger Rover. "Xavier advised against driving this car."

"Psh." She waves her hand dismissively. "He said you could drive any car you wanted, didn't he?"

"Well, yes."

"The McLaren it is!"

She opens the passenger door and it swings up.

"I don't know," I say, looking at the metallic silver paint glittering in the overhead lights.

"We are making a statement," she declares. "You need to claim your spot, show those snooty bitches *you* are

Madame de Maloret and you will not be intimidated by their baseless insults. This car makes that statement."

I look down at my chest and grimace. "Well, maybe not entirely baseless."

"Baseless, I say." Olivia climbs into the passenger seat. "There's nothing wrong with your sisters, Manderley. They are pert and proportionate—and best of all, they are silicone-free. Now, let's go! Let's drive this sexy beast."

She pulls the door closed with a soft thud, leaving me to stare at the black side vents set behind the door. I have never driven a car with side vents.

Isn't that the point? I eloped with Xavier because I was tired of living in the narrow confines of my perfectly boring, perfectly predictable life. I wanted to break out of the safe little box I constructed for myself and experience the world beyond the same four walls.

Olivia wants me to drive the McLaren to make a statement to the villagers; I want to drive it to make a statement to myself, a reaffirmation that I am not going to let fear force me into a monotonous existence. I might not be as audacious as Olivia, as determined as Tara, or as beautiful as Emma Lee, but does that mean I can't work to emulate them a little from time to time?

Walking back to the cabinet housing the keys of all the cars in the stables, I hang the Range Rover key back on its hook and remove the pebble-shaped key marked *McLaren*.

We encounter our first problem before we have even pulled out of the stables—and it isn't that the McLaren's steering wheel is located on the right instead of the left side. I push the round start button located on a console between the driver and passenger seats, where the stick shift is usually located, but can't figure out how to shift into reverse to back out of the garage.

"Where is the gear shift?"

Olivia googles it and finds a page that describes the "exhilarating experience of driving a supercar."

"Supercar?"

"A high-performance sports car," Olivia says, reading from the site. "Supercars are focused on performance with little regard for accommodation or cost. If it weren't for their advanced safety features, these vehicles would only be operated by professional drivers on a track."

"Professional drivers? This is crazy!" Panic squeezes my chest and I force myself to take slow, deep breaths. "Let's just take the Rover."

"Relax," Olivia says, patting my arm. "It says the McLaren is designed for touring. We are touring."

I frown at her.

"We are touring the village."

"That's hardly the same thing."

"Okay, here it is," she says, reading from the website again. " 'The drive, neutral, and reverse engage buttons are located on the center console of the cockpit. The MacLaren has a seven-speed seamless-shift gearbox that can be engaged by using the steering-wheel-mounted rocker-shift paddles.' "

I lean sideways and discover plastic levers affixed to the underside of the steering wheel.

"Of course!" Olivia cries. "Why didn't I think to look on the steering wheel? I test-drove a Mercedes that had gear-shifting paddle thingies."

Olivia continues reading from the website about the McLaren's unique features while I quietly worry about shifting smoothly and avoiding potholes in a car with such a low clearance.

"Oh, it says here you can adjust this dial"—she turns a small black and silver nob on the center console—"and it will stay in automatic mode so you never have to shift. Isn't that spec?"

"Absolutely," I say, unable to keep a note of sarcasm from creeping into my tone. "When we crash Xavier's high-performance sports car, at least we will know it wasn't because I shifted improperly."

"Drive on, Madame Andretti," Olivia says.

My legs are shaking before we have even driven past the château gates. Whereas the Jaguar's engine purred like a contented cat, the McLaren's engine growls like a ravenous predator. Just turning out of the drive onto the main road happens with a squealing of tires and a spray of gravel. I drive slow, keeping one eye on the speedometer.

"Hit it, Vin Diesel. Let's get fast and furious!" Olivia says.

"I am not getting fast and furious," I snap, palms damp on the wheel.

"Come on! A Mini Cooper passed us."

I give the McLaren a little gas, the engine growls, and we shoot forward, gaining on the Mini Cooper in a matter of seconds.

"Whoo-whoo!" Olivia hollers, punching the air. "That's what I am talking about. Get it, girl. Get your speed on."

"Stop it," I say, easing off the gas. "I am not getting my speed on. When did you turn into such an adrenaline junkie?"

I take my gaze off the road just long enough to shoot her a *grow up, please* look, but she just grins a toothy grin, and I intuitively know what she is going to say next.

"What can I say? I feel the need."

I groan and roll my eyes. "Don't say it."

"The need for speed!"

I have become accustomed to Olivia's frequent movie references in the eight years we have been best friends— I even occasionally enjoy them—but I don't appreciate the reference to *Top Gun*, a movie about fighter pilots, especially since, as I recall, one of them dies in a crash.

By the time the sign appears announcing our arrival in Saint-Maturinus-sur-Mer, I am a trembling, nauseous, sweaty mess. I drive to Caro's store, but there aren't any parking places wide enough for my comfort.

"There's a spot," Olivia offers.

"Too narrow."

I put the directional indicator on, slow down, and turn onto a less congested road.

"There's a spot."

"There's a puddle."

"So?"

"So, I don't want muddy water to splash onto the paint."

Olivia groans. "Just let me out and circle the block."

"Are you sure?"

"Positive."

I pull closer to the curb and push the hazard lights. Olivia hops out.

"I won't be long," she says, opening the passenger door. "Circle the block a few times, but roll the windows down and turn the radio on to a noticeable level. Make it EDM or something you would dance to at a club."

"Go!"

She closes the door and I drive off.

Forty minutes and dozens of laps around the block later, Olivia emerges from Caro's store, grinning, a reusable bag flung over her shoulder. Maneuvering Saint-Maturinus's narrow roads might not have given me the confidence of a race-car driver, but my nerves have definitely relaxed.

She hops in, clutching her purchases to her chest.

"Find a place to park," she says, reaching behind her and stowing the bag in the shallow boot behind our heads. "We need to talk."

"I will drive back to the château."

"No! Not there. I don't want to risk Madame Vous overhearing what I am about to tell you."

I follow the main road out of town for several kilometers until I see an Esso and pull into the service station, parking away from the pumps—far, far away.

"Okay," I say, killing the engine and turning to look at my best friend. "Let's hear it."

"We are going to find where the bones are buried before this day is out, I promise."

"What are you talking about? What bones?"

"Marine."

"That's not funny, Olivia," I say, my protective instincts for Xavier roused. "You have to stop implying Xavier murdered his first wife. We have no proof Marine is dead, let alone that she was murdered by my husband."

"You're right," she says. "I am sorry. I meant it more metaphorically. I had a lovely little chat with your new British friend and she told me some things about the first Madame de Maloret that have answered a few of our questions."

"What sorts of things?"

"Caro said Marine was popular in town. Girl from a humble family who marries local royalty and uses some of his fortune to host lavish parties and festivals at the château. Apparently, the locals still talk about a Christmas a few years ago when she invited all the village children to the château for a winter carnival."

"Great," I say bleakly. "How is this information supposed to make me feel better, exactly?"

"Caro didn't like her, though, and apparently she wasn't alone in her dislike. She wouldn't elaborate. She would only say Marine made her uneasy."

I am a moth to the flame, drawn to Olivia's gossip despite my common sense. I want to know more, so I move closer to the flames, hoping what she tells me next doesn't singe my wings.

"What else did she say?"

"She said Xavier used to visit her shop periodically to purchase Marine's favorite chocolates and that he was always charming and friendly. She had the sense then that he was very much in love with Marine, but he changed."

"Changed? How?"

"Caro said he stopped buying the chocolates, and when she would encounter him around town, he seemed burdened, as if he were struggling with a matter so weighty he couldn't expend the energy to engage in pleasantries. She said many times he appeared to be angry." Olivia pauses long enough to pull an Altoid out of her purse and pop it into her mouth. "That's when the rumors started."

"What sorts of rumors?"

"Infidelity."

"Whose?"

"Xavier's."

Chapter Thirty-seven

I stare out the windshield at a man in blue coveralls with a red Esso patch pumping gas into a mud-splattered Citröen and wonder if he was one of the villagers who gossiped about Xavier. The gossip didn't involve me, but I still feel angry, paranoid, and defensive.

"Caro believes the rumors were started by those snooty bitches you met on your first visit to town."

"Why?"

"They were Marine's village besties, who she spent time with when she wasn't finding the cure for cancer or jetting off to Milan to stomp a runway," Olivia says, her loyalty to me rousing her sarcasm. "There is more."

"Go on."

"Did you know the village hosts an annual festival celebrating their Celtic heritage?" She pauses, but not long enough for me to respond. "Xavier and Marine attended the festival together, around the time Caro noticed his mood change. She said Xavier drank a little too much. There was some sort of disagreement. A man stepped in to defuse the situation and Xavier punched him."

The Xavier Olivia is describing is a stranger to me, as foreign as the man in the Esso coveralls.

"You're serious?"

"Serious as a fractured jaw, which was what the innocent bystander ended up with, by the way."

I am trying to imagine what might have happened to have provoked such a violent reaction from a man I have only seen show kindness and tenderness.

"There's more."

"Lawd. How much more can there be?"

"The morning after the altercation at the festival, Marine came to town with a bruise on her cheek, the sort you might get if you were slapped hard."

The bottom drops out of my stomach. "You're not saying . . ." The idea that Xavier might have abused Marine snatches the breath from my lungs and a full minute passes before I am able to speak again. "I don't believe it. I won't believe it. Xavier has shown me respect in a thousand ways. He pulls my chair out, opens my door, walks closest to the curb. Xavier wouldn't hit a woman. He just wouldn't."

Olivia looks at me and raises her brow.

"What? Do you believe Xavier is abusive?"

"You never know what someone will do when they are pushed; besides, even you said he has flashes of temper. It doesn't matter what I believe. The fact that you are asking me what I believe tells me you have your doubts."

"Xavier arranged that lovely day for us in the South of France, remember? I can't believe someone so charming could also be a wife beater."

"Abusive men are often charming."

I don't want to fall into that despicable pattern of blaming the victim, but something about this story isn't making sense to me. It doesn't help that the "facts" of the story were gleaned from second- and third-hand gossip. I know what it is like to live in a town of gossips, how perverted and contorted a titillating story becomes as it travels down the grapevine.

"Why didn't Marine go to the police and formally accuse Xavier of abuse?"

"She disappeared the day after she showed up in town with the bruise on her face."

"Disappeared?"

"Yes, disappeared. Nobody has seen Marine. Her friends say they haven't spoken to her. It's like she vanished."

Olivia gives me time to process everything she has just told me. She pulls a small packet of Kleenex out of her purse and hands it to me.

"I don't need them."

Maybe the pain of hearing such terrible things about a man I love hasn't penetrated the numbness the gossip created, because I don't feel like crying. Or maybe my overanalytical mind refuses to accept what she has told me until all my questions have been answered. Would a man as controlled and contained as Xavier de Maloret allow himself to get as drunk as the gossips suggested? Why would Xavier, someone who values his privacy, discuss private matters in so public a forum? Who was the man who tried to intervene? Where is Marine? And why didn't she take any of her belongings—including her precious pet—with her?

"Caro did say one other thing."

I take a deep breath and exhale. "Tell me."

"Marine was raised by her grandparents. They live on an island not too far from here. I think we should go talk to them."

"Did she give you a name?"

"She said she thought it was Verity or Verite, but to ask the man who works in the toll booth leading to the island."

"There's a road to the island?"

"Yes, but only when the tide is out."

I look at Olivia aghast. "I am not driving Xavier's expensive sports car on a road that disappears with the tide. It's probably rutted and pocked with potholes. Besides, what happens if the tide comes in when we are driving across it?"

"Relax," she says, popping another Altoid in her mouth. "We will just hire some brawny sailor to take us to the island on his boat."

"A brawny sailor? Where do you expect to find a brawny sailor?"

"Caro said we follow the main road going north, and the turnoff for the road to the island is just past the docks and shipyard."

My conscience is wrestling with my curiosity. My conscience is championing for Xavier by reminding me of my promise to him to be honest. The honest thing for me to do would be to speak to Xavier directly and ask him what went wrong in his first marriage, even though I tried once before and was rebuffed. My curiosity is urging me to seek out the answers to my questions on my own and reminding me that Xavier has avoided talking about Marine.

"Freud believed that nothing happens by chance or accident, that our unconscious mental processes drive us to do things our conscious mind resists. He called it psychic determinism."

I know where she is going with her argument. "You're suggesting Xavier avoided telling me about Marine because it was too upsetting, so he arranged a trip to Dubai after our arrival, knowing someone in the village would say something? That seems complicated, doesn't it?"

"The human psyche is complicated. On some level, maybe he hopes you will hear the gossip and bring it up so he doesn't have to, or . . ."

"Or?"

"Or he murdered Marine and got creepy old Madame Vous to bury the body somewhere in the château. Either way, you deserve to know."

"I do deserve to know, but Xavier deserves my trust and honesty, too."

"You're not being dishonest by asking a few questions. In fact, you don't have to ask. I will. Then, if there is nothing to the rumors, you can forget them and you have spared Xavier the pain of having you dredge up unpleasant memories."

"Fine."

I push the engine button and carefully pull out of the gas station. The solemnity of what we are about to do is not lost on me, and it is all I can do to keep from crying in shame. Shame that I married someone I hardly knew. Shame that I am skulking around trying to uncover clues about his past. Shame that I love him, and will continue loving him, even if the rumors are true.

Chapter Thirty-eight

Text from Xavier de Maloret:

Bonjour, mon amour. I called you this morning, but you must have been sleeping. Just wanted to let you know how much you are missing from me. I am sorry this business has kept me away from you during our first weeks of marriage. I will make it up to you . . . soon.

The weather in Brittany is proving as difficult to fathom as Xavier. The early morning rains that were pitter-pattering against my bedroom window when I woke this morning disappeared by the time we finished breakfast, and the bright sunshine and cloudless cobalt skies we enjoyed on our drive into the village have been obliterated by thick-as-flannel gray clouds. I am sitting in the McLaren while Olivia speaks to a man about a boat. I decide to check my iPhone for messages.

There are two texts from Tara, asking me to call her because she wants to talk about her "castle business," five texts from Emma Lee asking if I ordered her Hunter rain boots yet and if I remembered to get the shine kit (yes and of course), and two texts from Xavier. The second text simply reads: *Where are you?* I don't know how to answer him without being duplicitous, so I decide to wait until after this business with Madame and Monsieur Verite is over.

Olivia knocks on the window and I slide my phone back into my purse. A man with a swarthy complexion is standing beside her. He is a handsome man, in a Johnny-Depp-as-Captain-Jack-Sparrow kind of way, with shoulder-length black hair, soulful brown eyes, and a nasty, jagged scar above his right eye that he probably got when he was doing something shady. He's wearing a pair of jeans with a rip at the knee, a black tee, and at least a dozen slender braided-leather bracelets around his wrist.

I get out of the car and shut the door. The temperature has dropped and the air feels moist with impending rain.

"Manderley, this is Nicabar," Olivia says. "He collects the tolls for the road to the island."

"*Bonjour*, Nicabar."

"Nica," he says, gazing deeply into my eyes, too deeply for my comfort. "Am pleased to meet you, Madame de Maloret. Was telling your *friend* the road to the island is closed today."

Besides dropping the nominative pronoun from the beginning of his sentences, he speaks with an unusual accent that is too bouncy, too rhythmic to be French.

"Nica has agreed to take us to the island on his boat," Oliva says, smiling brightly.

"Thank you, Nica. That's kind."

"Kind," he repeats, laughing. "Sure. Got money? Difficult, the passage to the island, and the weather, is not being our friend. So, pay."

"Of course. How much would you like?"

He grins. "How much worth?"

How much worth? "Excuse me?"

"I think Nica is trying to barter with us, Manderley," Olivia says, narrowing her eyes on the man. "He wants to know how much we're willing to pay for the ride over to the island."

"Oh." Heat flushes my cheeks.

"Well, alright." Oliva pushes her sleeves up and crosses her arms. "Bring it, Nica. Let's see what you've got."

"What worth?" he repeats.

Olivia names a sum. Nica laughs and responds with a sum double Olivia's offer. Furious negotiations continue until I feel a little sorry for Nica.

Olivia looks pointedly at Nica's small, shabby cottage and then at the red-and-white striped barrier barring vehicles from using the primitive toll road. A road currently very empty.

"Forgive us, Nica. It's obvious you are a busy man. We have taken up too much of your time already." She walks around the car and opens the passenger door. "Come on, Mandy, we will drive back to the docks. I saw a sign for charters."

"Wait," Nica says.

Olivia comes back.

In the end, Nica agrees to take us to the island for slightly more than Olivia's original offer plus the bottle of Chouchen she bought at Caro's shop. Before they shake on the deal Olivia makes Nica promise to wait for us while we are at the Verites and then ferry us back to the mainland. He agrees.

"Good negotiator," Nica says, grinning at Olivia.

I am wearing a simple white-and-black striped cotton sundress with spaghetti straps and my espadrilles, my hair pulled into a fishtail braid, because I didn't know when I got dressed this morning I would be climbing onto a stinking fishing boat with a nominative-pronoun-dropping toll collector who looks as if he should be living in a van, playing a guitar in some city square for spare change.

I pull my purse out of the car, tie my thin summer cardigan around my shoulders, and push the lock button on the McLaren's key. Nica leads us behind his cottage to a rickety wooden pier. A wooden fishing boat, green paint peeling from the hull to reveal several other colors of paint, is tied to one of the pilings.

Nica helps Olivia climb onto the deck of the swaying boat and then holds his hand out to me, a rakish grin on his face. I look from him to the sea, trying to measure the distance from the pier to the island, and fighting the wave of panic building inside me.

"Come," Nica says, waving backwards.

Sweet Lawd! What am I thinking? I wouldn't go sailing with Xavier, an experienced seaman, but I am going to step onto this leaking, patched-together motorboat?

"Come now," Nica says again. "Before weather comes."

A mile. The island can't be more than a mile away. I can swim a mile on a good day. No problem. It's not like we are going far from the mainland.

Inhaling, I climb onto the boat without Nica's assistance and stand beside Olivia beneath the wheelhouse awning, before I lose what little nerve I have mustered. Nica removes the rope securing the boat to the piling and we are off, *chug-chug-chugging* over choppy surf toward the island. The scrambled eggs and coffee I had for breakfast churn in my stomach.

Nica nudges Olivia. "*Kestra* is pale," he says, a scornful twist to his lips. "Think get sick from the sea."

Olivia looks at me, worried. "He's right," she says, holding my arm. "You are pale."

"I'm fine, really."

Olivia squeezes my arm encouragingly, letting me know without words she understands how difficult this journey is for me. I smile to reassure her, even as a bitter, acidic taste fills my mouth.

"Nicabar," I say, raising my voice above the noise of the motors. "That's an unusual name. Is it French?"

"No. Romani. Means one who is cunning."

He leers at me, his gaze lingering on my breasts. I pull the edges of my sweater closer together around me.

Romani.

Xavier said the French call the Romani people *manouches* and their general feeling for the nomadic group is one of distrust.

"Why visit Verites?" Nica asks, his intense gaze fixed on me. "Are friends with their granddaughter?"

"My husband knew their granddaughter."

"Husband." Nica snickers. "Knows granddaughter."

I flash Olivia a confused expression. She shrugs.

"How do you know the Verites?" Olivia asks.

Nica's answer is to stare straight ahead and keep on grinning, as if he didn't hear the question. "Take you to the dock near Verites. Short walk from there."

"Walk?" I look at Olivia.

"Apparently there is only one taxi on the island and the driver is in the hospital," Olivia explains.

"How many people live on the island?" I ask Nica.

Nica shrugs. Standing at the wheel, with the wind blowing his long black hair, he looks every bit the cutthroat pirate.

"The island has good salt marshes. Most of the people harvest the sea salt." Nica eases off the throttle and the boat slows as we approach a long wooden dock. "Are here."

A wooden rowboat tied to the dock is the only sign

that the island is inhabited by more than lichen-covered rocks and squawking seabirds.

Nica signals when it is safe for us to jump onto the dock. I am expecting him to kill the motor and lead us to where we want to go, but he remains at the wheel.

"Follow path up hill. Verites cottage close."

"You're not coming with us?"

He pulls a beanie out of his back jeans pocket and puts it on, arranging the brim low over his black brows.

"You will be here when we get back, right?" Olivia asks.

"Yes," he says, waving us away. "Go now. Storm here soon."

The sound of distant thunder rolling closer has us scrambling up the narrow path, our feet slipping on the muddy earth. We make it to the top of the hill and spot a stone cottage in the distance, surrounded by what appear to be rectangular pools of ruddy water. The edges of the pools are rimmed in a crusty grayish-white substance. In the distance, someone is raking one of the pools with a long wooden stick.

I squat at the edge of one of the pools and pinch some of the wet, gritty salt between my fingers.

"What are you doing?" Olivia asks.

I toss the salt over my shoulder for good luck and make a silent wish for the rumors about Xavier to be false.

Chapter Thirty-nine

The cottage is humble, with blue painted shutters at the deep-set windows and a roof missing a few of its shingles. I try to imagine the sophisticated brunette in the Marchesa wedding gown as a girl playing with her dolls in the small garden beside the cottage. Did she gaze out over the marshes at the sea and dream about the day she would escape the tiny island? Did she pinch salt between her fingers and wish for a knight-errant to carry her off to his château?

My chest aches for that little girl, even though I don't know her. It aches for Xavier, who loved and lost.

"Here goes nothing," Olivia says, lifting the brass door-knocker and rapping it against the door.

I reach for Olivia's other hand, childishly clinging onto it. The door creaks open and a stoop-backed old woman eyes us warily.

"*Bonjour,*" Olivia says, smiling. "*Êtes-vous Madame Verite?*"

"*Oui,*" she says, looking behind us.

Olivia introduces herself and tells the woman I am

Manderley de Maloret, Xavier's new wife. Madame Verite inhales sharply, the air whistling between teeth. She looks at me with open hostility.

When Olivia says something else, Madame Verite shakes her head and tries to close the door. Olivia sticks her foot in the opening.

"Wait!" she cries. *"Où se trouve Marine? Avez-vous vu votre petite-fille récemment?"*

"Non!"

Madame Verite shuts the door with a final, firm bang.

"What did you ask her?"

"I asked her if she has seen her granddaughter recently and she said no."

My shoulders slump. I want to curl up on Madame Verite's doorstep and cry tears as salty as the water in the marshes. I don't blame the woman for not wanting to talk to us, strangers who suddenly appeared on her doorstep demanding information about her granddaughter, the ex-wife of my husband. She can't know how much I have risked in coming to see her.

"I am not giving up that easy," Olivia says, reaching for the door knocker. "I said you were going to have answers before the sun sets, and I intend to get them even if it means I have to pull a Liam Neeson on the old broad and threaten her with my special set of skills."

"No." I grab her hand. "Maybe this is a sign that we aren't supposed to be here, prying into Xavier's past."

"Sign-schmine," Olivia says, pulling her hand away. "Don't you want to know about Marine?"

"What do you want to know about Marine?"

A stocky man with ruddy cheeks chapped and wrinkled from years of working by the sea is walking up the path, a long wooden rake resting on his shoulder.

"Are you Monsieur Verite?" Olivia asks.

"Oui."

"Bonjour, Monsieur Verite," I say, stepping closer. "My name is Manderley de Maloret."

"Manderley de Maloret, you say?" he says, his accent thick.

"Yes."

"We don't wish to pry, monsieur, but we have a few questions about your granddaughter we were hoping you could answer," Olivia says.

Monsieur Verite lifts the rake off his shoulder and rests it against the side of the house beside the door. "You already spoke to Madame Verite, I assume?"

"Yes."

"She wouldn't answer your questions."

He says it as statement rather than a question, but Olivia still answers.

"No, she wouldn't."

"Come," he says, gesturing for us to follow him. "We can talk in the barn."

We follow him into an old stone *gite* filled with rakes like the one he had been carrying, wooden wheelbarrows, and battered wicker baskets, to a scarred oak picnic table. He flips on an overhead light and invites us to sit on one of the benches on either side of the table.

"What is it you wish to know about my granddaughter"—he folds his wrinkled hands on the table in front of him—"and why have you not asked your husband these questions?"

"You're right, monsieur. I shouldn't be here," I say, guilty heat fanning over my cheeks. "I should be at home, waiting for my husband to return from his trip. It's just . . . you see, we didn't know each other long before we eloped, and my friend has heard rumors."

"What rumors?"

Olivia shares everything Caro told her with Monsieur Verite. He listens carefully, without interrupting, and then says, "In France, we have a proverb: *Dans une bouche close, il n'entre point de mouche.* It means, 'A closed mouth catches no flies.' Saint-Maturinus is full of people whose mouths are full of buzzing insects."

"Are you saying the rumors aren't true?"

"I do not pretend to know what happened between Marine and Xavier and I refuse to speculate, but you should understand something, madame. My granddaughter was *une mauvaise femme.*"

A bad woman.

"I knew something wasn't right with Marine when she was still a young girl. She seemed incapable of expressing genuine warmth. She didn't laugh and play easily with the other children on the island. She was arrogant, bossy, and at times, cruel. She would manipulate the children into giving her their favorite toys, not because she wanted them, but because she didn't want them to have more than she had." Monsieur Verite stares at me vacantly and I realize he is caught in a complex cobweb of memories. "As a teenager, she would steal money from my wallet and lie about it. Even then, Marine could not admit when she had made a mistake."

"Do you think she started the rumors?"

Monsieur Verite is still lost in his cobweb. It takes a few seconds for my question to reach him.

"It would not surprise me, madame."

"Do you know where she went after she left Xavier?"

He shakes his head. The flat, vacant look in his eyes has been replaced by sadness, and resignation, perhaps.

"My best guess is that a better opportunity presented itself and she grabbed it with both of her greedy little hands."

If there is a better opportunity than being married to a

kind, generous man like Xavier de Maloret, I don't know what it is.

"What about Coco?"

He frowns. "Her little dog?"

"Yes. She left her behind."

"Bah!" He waves his hands. "She never cared for that dog, any dog, really."

"Did Xavier give Coco to Marine?"

"Non." Monsieur Verite shifts in his seat. "Marine was never a faithful person, you see? She would tell Xavier she was coming to stay here and then go sailing with *that man*. The dog was a present from *him*."

"Xavier knew she was having an affair?"

"He called here once, worried because Marine was late in coming home. If Madame Verite had answered the phone, she would have given him an excuse, but I answered. I would not lie for Marine. She stopped visiting after that, stopped calling her grandmother."

"Poor Xavier," I say, remembering how I once likened him to a jungle cat with a thorn in his paw. He had a thorn, alright, but it wasn't lodged in his paw, it was lodged in his heart.

"Oui," Monsieur Verite says, exhaling heavily. "I am certain Marine did many things to hurt Xavier. She only married him because he was a de Maloret."

Outside a bolt of lightning zigzags across the leaden sky, followed by a drumroll of thunder.

"Thank you, Monsieur Verite," I say, standing. "I appreciate your candor."

"Go home to your husband, Madame de Maloret. Go home, put your worries to rest, and wake tomorrow grateful that you are married to a good man."

"Thank you, monsieur. I will."

We are halfway to the door when Monsieur Verite calls

after us. "If you don't want the burden of caring for Coco, you could return her to my granddaughter's gypsy boyfriend."

Olivia grabs my arm and we both turn around to look at Monsieur Verite.

"Gypsy?"

"Oui," Monsieur Verite says. "The vagrant who lives in the toll house on the mainland. His name is—"

"Nicabar!"

Chapter Forty

"Nicabar gave us the shaft!" Olivia cries. *"Bâtard!"*

We are standing on the dock, staring across the channel separating the island from the mainland, a thin rain plastering our hair to our faces.

"In hindsight, maybe we shouldn't have paid him until we were safely back on the mainland."

"He still would have left us here." Olivia angrily swipes her bangs off her forehead. "It wasn't about the money for that shady, cunning bastard. It was a way to use you to stick it to Xavier."

Normally, I would urge my best friend to give the man the benefit of the doubt, but I remember the way Nica leered at me when he learned I was Madame de Maloret and I am inclined to believe the worst of him.

"I'll call Caro and explain what has happened." I fish around in my purse for my iPhone. "I will ask her to call one of those charter captains to pick us up."

"Good idea!"

I pull my phone out and my heart sinks when I see SEARCHING FOR NETWORK in the status bar.

"We are out of range."

"What?" Olivia cries. The cool, composed woman has left the island. "What are we going to do? We can't stay on this island all night. A storm is coming. What if it is a hurricane and we are swept out to sea?"

"Calm down," I say, pulling a collapsible umbrella from my purse. "We will walk to the top of the hill and see if I get a signal."

"Good idea."

I flick the umbrella open and we huddle beneath it. We are halfway up the hill when I slip in the mud, my smooth-soled espadrilles providing no traction on the slick ground. I fall to my knees, scraping my skin on a sharp rock. Olivia helps me up. I wipe the blood-streaked mud from my knee and we finish climbing to the top of the hill.

"Still no signal."

"You have got to be kidding me," she cries, grabbing my iPhone and holding it at different angles. "What kind of godforsaken place is this? Who lives on an island without cell service?"

"Robinson Crusoe. Swiss Family Robinson."

"Funny."

"We are going to be just fine," I say, taking my iPhone from her and slipping it back in my purse. I pull a Kleenex out of my bag, dab my knee, and cover the cut with a Band-Aid. "If Leo could survive *The Beach*, you will survive this island."

Olivia slants a disgusted look my way. *The Beach* was a movie about a nicotine-addicted American video-game junkie (played by Leonardo DiCaprio) who travels to a mythical island in search of adventure. Think *Blue Lagoon* meets *Lord of the Flies* and you will understand why it gets a 19 percent splat rating on Rotten Tomatoes.

"One bad blip in an otherwise flawless career," she says, holding up her finger. "One."

"I was riling you up a bit to get your blood pumping."

"Thanks," she says, taking the umbrella from me and holding it over our heads. "We could try to find the toll road."

I look down the hill at the rising surf.

"The tide is coming in," I say. "We would never make it across in time."

"We could walk back to the cottage, but I doubt Madame Verite would let us use their phone. Assuming they even have a phone."

"And if they don't we will have wasted time."

"I am starv-ing," she whines.

I pull a granola bar out of my purse and hand it to her.

"Thank you," she says, taking the bar and tearing open the foil package. "You wouldn't happen to have a pot of coffee in that rucksack of yours, would you? Or a speed-boat?"

"I believe in being prepared."

"Okay, Eagle Scout. Can you rub two sticks together and start a fire so we can send smoke signals?"

"I have a better idea," I say, putting my purse strap over my head. "Come on."

We scramble back down the hill and walk to the end of the dock, where the rowboat is secured to a post with a rope.

"We will row ourselves back."

"You have got to be kidding me!" Olivia takes a step back, a horrified expression on her face. "You know I don't do cardio! Don't you remember what happened when I tried the NordicRower at the Beverly? I suffered a stress fracture in my rib! My body is not made for manual labor."

"Well, I am not spending the night on this dock! Xavier sent me two texts this morning and I ignored them. If he doesn't hear from me soon, he will worry and then he will call Madame Deniau and she will tell him I disappeared in his supercar. What will he think?" I climb down into the rowboat, no easy task with the waves moving it up and down, and my purse-strapped chest. "Come on, Olivia. If I can get into a boat after what happened to my father and Aunt Patricia, you can do a little cardio."

"Fine," she huffs, sitting on the edge of the dock and scooting off it until her feet touch one of the boat's wooden benches. "But only because you're a little frightening right now. Just watch where you swing that oar, Tom."

"Tom?"

"Tom Ripley split Dickie Greenleaf's head open with a paddle-thingy when they were boating together. *The Talented Mr. Ripley.* Matt Damon. Jude Law. Ringing any bells?"

"I've read Patricia Highsmith's novel. Haven't seen the movie." I sit on one of the benches, scooting all the way to the right to make room for Olivia and then lifting the oar out of the bottom of the boat and securing it in the oarlock. "And it's called an oar, not a paddle."

The thin rain has thickened to a steady downpour of fat, cold drops. I help Olivia secure her oar, pull the rope from the post, and we begin rowing.

It takes a while to get a good rhythm, rowing in sync, but even then our progress is hampered by a strong head-wind and choppy sea. We keep our heads down because the icy rain feels like needles of ice jabbing our cheeks.

The inertia of this situation is driving me to ignore the fear clawing at my insides, fear a wave will capsize our boat and we will be swept out to the open sea by a rip current.

"This is a futile endeavor," Olivia says, looking over her shoulder. "My arms already ache and we have barely left the dock."

"Don't look back," I say, pulling on my oar. "Just keep your head down and keep rowing. We will be back on the mainland soon and we will drive to the château and drink Xavier's scotch beside the fire. We will laugh about it all."

And I will call Xavier in Dubai and confess all of the sad, ridiculous details of this misadventure and beg him to forgive me for not bringing my concerns to him. I just hope he will forgive me and not see me as just another duplicitous, treacherous woman he married.

"I'm sorry, Manderley," she says, wiping her face on her shoulder. "It's my fault we are in this mess. I talked you into coming to the island. If we drown, you don't have to wait for me in the light."

"We aren't going to drown," I say.

"But if we do . . ."

"I will still be waiting for you in the light."

The island is probably only a mile, mile and a half, from the mainland. On a clear day, with no wind, we would probably be able to row across this channel in half an hour, forty-five minutes at the most, but the headwind is hampering our progress. We are also struggling against the waves. The current seems to want to take us in a southerly direction—away from Nicabar's pier. Keeping my gaze focused on the distant shore—no easy task with the sideways-falling rain hitting me in the face—I pull harder on my oar to correct our course.

My thoughts drift away from the boat and are carried on a current of memories, back, back to the day Tara called me, hysterical and crying.

Daddy took Aunt Patricia sailing early this morning

and they haven't returned. I am so worried. They should have been back hours ago . . .

When Tara phoned again, it was to say the Coast Guard had found the wreckage of Daddy's boat and that they had retrieved two corpses.

One minute, I am sitting in my dark apartment, my iPhone in my hand, praying I will wake up and discover Tara's phone call had been a terrible nightmare, and the next minute I am talking my baby sister off an emotional ledge.

After all of the practicalities had been dealt with—claiming the bodies, arranging funerals, meeting with lawyers, learning about my daddy's serious financial troubles, packing up the more sentimental items the IRS wouldn't care to claim—I plunged into a pool of grief. It felt as if my soul had been on my daddy's boat and that it, too, had drowned one hundred miles off the coast of Sullivan's Island. My body still functioned, but my essence was gone, my ability to feel deeply. I thought I would never feel again, never be happy or whole.

I still find it inconceivable that a man as big-hearted as Daddy and a woman as vibrant as Aunt Patricia have faded from this earth, but I realize my soul did not fade with them. Not really.

I recently watched a documentary on Netflix about the team tasked with restoring the frescoes on the ceiling of the Sistine Chapel. After many months of painstaking work, the restoration was complete. Years of soot and grime had been removed to reveal a far more colorful and detailed painting than had been viewed before the team's efforts.

I now realize my soul did not die the day my daddy drowned. My more colorful details, my essence, had simply been hidden beneath the soot and grime of grief.

Meeting Xavier, falling in love with him, marrying him, sticking with him even through my doubts, has restored me.

"Uh, Manderley?"

"What?"

"I think we are in trouble."

I look at the water pooling around our feet in the bottom of the boat and pray there isn't a leak.

"We are taking on some water, but I think it's—"

"No," she says, letting go of her oar and pointing out her side of the boat. "Look!"

A large sport-fishing powerboat is racing toward us, its bow raised high in the air. If the captain continues on his present course, our rickety rowboat will be shattered into a thousand toothpick-sized pieces and we will be walking into the light together . . . soon.

"I don't think he can see us through the rain."

I reach into my purse and pull out my red pashmina and iPhone. I slide my finger up the screen and tap the LED flashlight icon.

"Here," I say, handing Olivia my phone. "Aim the light at the boat."

Olivia holds the phone high in the air and moves her arm back and forth, making a wide arc, while I frantically wave my scarf, but the boat doesn't slow down.

"We are going to die!" Olivia cries.

"Keep waving the light!"

It might sound ridiculous, but I am more concerned about how Xavier is going to feel when the French Coast Guard tells him they fished his wife's bloated corpse out of the channel than I am about my impending dismemberment by boat propeller blades. And what about Tara and Emma Lee? How will they cope without their big sister around to order their rain boots and listen to their problems?

I am about to suggest we jump overboard and swim for our lives when the boat decreases speed. Olivia lets out a whoop and throws her arms around me. We are hugging and laughing, nearly hysterical with joy at having been spared dismemberment, when the powerboat pulls alongside and gives a quick blast of its air horn.

We stop hugging and look up at the ship. A person wearing a black hooded raincoat emerges from the wheelhouse and makes his way to the stern. He stands at the rail, staring down at us, rain streaming off the brim of his hood. My breath catches in my throat.

Xavier.

He removes his hood and my heart feels as if it is about to burst within my chest, so powerful is my love for him. Even from this distance, I can see the worry lines etched across his forehead and the fierce scowl pulling down the corners of his mouth.

"I am going to toss down two life vests," he says, his deep voice carrying over the waves and through the growing darkness. "I want you to put them on."

Both of the orange vests land in the rowboat, floating in the water at our feet. I put mine on and then help Olivia fasten her straps.

"Now, I am going to toss you a rope," he says. "Secure it to the eye hook on the hull and I will pull you closer."

The rope flies through the air and lands across our laps. I grab the end and climb to the front of the rowboat, threading the rope through the eye hook and doing my best to tie an anchor knot, despite my frozen fingers and trembling hands.

Xavier pulls us alongside his vessel and Olivia climbs out of the rowboat and onto the powerboat's bathing platform. Xavier helps her over the low wall and onto the deck. As soon as my feet hit the bathing platform, I feel his arms around my waist, lifting me over the wall and into his arms.

Like a frightened child lost in a shopping mall who bursts into tears only after being safely reunited with her parent, my legs begin to tremble and I bury my face against Xavier's warm neck, sobbing.

He holds me tight, tighter than he ever has before, and murmurs in my ear in French. I think he is trembling as well, but I am not sure because I am shaking violently now, my teeth chattering.

"Thank God you are safe, *ma bichette*," he says, pressing his lips to my wet forehead. "I don't want to think of what could have happened if I had not found you."

I close my eyes and concentrate on how it feels to be in his arms again, to hear him calling me his little deer, and I commit it all to memory, just in case it is to be the last time.

Chapter Forty-one

We are back at the château. Olivia has moved to a guest apartment above the stables and I am sitting on the couch in the living room, Coco curled up on my lap, her tweed blanket wrapped around my shoulders. Xavier is leaning against the armoire, rolling a glass of scotch around in his hand. We showered as soon as we arrived home. I am wearing my nightgown and a pair of Xavier's thick wool socks pulled up to my knees. Xavier is wearing a pair of dark jeans and a cashmere pullover, his wet black hair finger-combed off his forehead.

"How did you know where we were?"

It's a lame way to begin what I am sure is going to be the most difficult confession I have ever had to make, and a pathetic attempt to stall.

"Caroline Gaveau."

"Caro?"

"When I arrived home this afternoon, I discovered the burnt photograph of Marine in the liquor cabinet, beside my bottle of scotch."

"I can explain."

"Please do."

"I found the photograph of Marine on the floor in the foyer shortly after you left for Dubai. I don't know how it got there, but seeing it made me realize there was so much about you I didn't know."

"Like my marriage to Marine?"

Guilty heat suffuses my cheeks and I can't meet his gaze. I look down at the little dog nestled in my lap and stroke her soft ears.

"Yes. She looked so happy in the photograph, with Coco curled up on the pillow behind her, so in love. I told myself a love like that does not simply disappear in a week, a month, even a year. Imagining you still had feelings for her made me jealous. It sounds silly, but I thought if I got rid of the picture it would help you to forget about her."

"So you set it on fire?"

"Yes," I say, stroking Coco's curly fur. "But then I felt bad, so I rescued it from the fireplace, tossed it in the armoire, and tried to forget about it."

"You didn't leave it for me to find, then?"

"No."

Xavier sighed. "Madame Deniau left the photograph for you to find."

"Why?!"

"It was her strange, misguided attempt to communicate with you."

"What was she trying to say?" My voice wavers. "That Marine was beautiful and happy and obviously well loved?"

"No." I want him to tell me he never loved Marine, not the way he loves me, but he just gazes into his glass of scotch. "She wanted you to know Marine abandoned Coco. Madame Deniau loves that little dog, but she never cared for Marine."

"What about the stationery? Why did she leave Marine's personal stationery on the table?"

"She noticed you looked sad and thought perhaps you were homesick. She left the stationery in case you wanted to write to your family." He looks at me and shrugs. "She is old-fashioned and doesn't believe in emails. Too hurried and thoughtless, she says."

"I see."

"I did warn you she is a bit unusual."

"I was wrong about Madame Deniau."

"You are wrong about a great many things."

As Xavier stares at me I think of the day he took me to visit Thierry Lambert's farm, my fears he was involved in illegal activity or that he was a licentious playboy toying with the naïve American tourist, and how he looked when he handed me the bottle of jasmine oil. I had misjudged him. He isn't a criminal, nor is he a playboy.

"Would it make you feel any better if I told you I didn't take that photograph of Marine?"

"You didn't?"

"Her lover took it right before I caught them in bed together."

"Nicabar?"

"Oui." He narrows his gaze. "How do you know Nicabar?"

"I met him today."

"Where?"

"Olivia hired him to take us to the island. He promised he would wait until we came back from speaking to the Verites, but he took our money and left us stranded there."

"Bâtard!" The venom in his voice frightens me. "I will deal with him when we pick up the McLaren tomorrow."

"I'm sorry I drove the McLaren," I say.

"Do you really think I give a damn about the McLaren

right now?" He shakes his head. "You could have died tonight. You know that, right? You took a leaking rowboat out on the sea in a storm with eighteen-knot wind gusts."

Xavier stares into the flames in the fireplace, a muscle working at his jaw. I close my eyes and listen to the crackling logs, Coco breathing softly, the rain pattering against the mansard roof, and pray he will forgive me for invading his privacy.

"Why did you go to see Madame and Monsieur Verite?"

I look at him and realize the moment I have been dreading is upon me. I can't avoid it any longer. I pluck a fuzzy ball off the wool blanket.

"Stop fidgeting, please." He finishes his scotch and returns the empty glass to the armoire. "Is it that difficult for you to tell me what you are thinking?"

"Yes," I say, trying hard not to cry.

"Why?"

"Because I love you so, and I am afraid by visiting that island I ruined any chance I might have had for you to ever love me." I look at Coco lying on my lap, so trusting and content, and am ashamed I didn't give Xavier the same trust. "I heard rumors, terrible rumors, about your marriage to Marine. I went to speak with her grandparents because I wanted to prove the rumors false. I should have waited until you were home and asked you, instead. I am sorry, Xavier. Can you ever forgive me?"

"Can I forgive *you*?" He sits on the edge of the coffee table in front of me, his hands on my knees. "I am the one who should be asking for forgiveness. I might have spared you a lot of pain if I had just told you the truth about my first marriage. I was too proud and too afraid of what you might think if you learned the truth so early in our relationship. I intended to tell you one day, but I realize now

I should have told you sooner. It wasn't fair of me to bring you here, to Saint-Maturinus, without being completely honest. So, *ma bichette*, can you forgive me?" I am about to tell him that there is nothing to forgive when he holds up his hand. "Before you answer that, you should know everything."

He has the look of a battle-fatigued soldier, dead-eyed, a part of him still lost in the conflict, as he tells me about his two-year marriage to Marine. I listen without interrupting, resisting the urge to massage the frown lines from his brow, when he tells me how Marine fooled him into believing she loved him and how devastated he was when it became clear she had married him for his wealth. An arrow of guilt lances my heart as I remember I still haven't told Xavier about my father's shameful financial situation. I haven't told him before now because I didn't really see how it mattered, but I don't want him to think I married him for the same cold, avaricious reasons Marine married him.

"She married me for a lifestyle, not love, and she became very nasty when our reality did not match her fantasy. She thought we would be part of the idle jet set who spend their winters on the *pistes* at Klosters and their summers yachting around the Greek isles. It got to a point where I was spending more time at work than at home. Once I saw through her mask—that beautiful, manipulative, selfish mask—to the woman she truly was, I couldn't bear to be around her. She could be breathtakingly calculating and cruel." He takes a deep breath and exhales. "I didn't want to divorce her because of the scandal I knew it would create. As you have already discovered, Saint-Maturinus is a small village. As the oldest and most venerated family in the area, we de Malorets are expected to be above reproach. And there was my family to consider.

My uncles are devout Catholics. They think divorce as mortal a sin as murder. In fact, there's never been a divorce in my family. So, I made an agreement with Marine: I would pay her bills, send her to Klosters each winter and Santorini each summer, if she promised to organize and host charitable and business functions here, at the château."

"That sounds like a business transaction, not a marriage."

"Oui."

"So what happened?"

"It became too much. I grew tired of the charade and asked her for a divorce. That seemed to unleash something in her, something feral and reckless."

"What did she do?"

"She told me she had been having affairs throughout our marriage—affairs, plural—but had been discreet out of respect for me"—he laughs, but it is a harsh sound, devoid of any real mirth—"and that she was through being discreet. I would come home to find her lingerie tossed on the floor, cologne that wasn't mine left in the bathroom, empty wine bottles beside the bed."

My heart aches for Xavier. I can only imagine the pain, the humiliation that comes from such a brutal betrayal.

"When she brought one of her lovers, Nicabar in fact, to the village festival, I thought I would lose my mind. If you could have seen her that day, flirting right in front of me, in front of our neighbors, my family. I grabbed her arm to leave, but . . ."

He shakes his head.

"Nicabar got involved and you broke his jaw."

"Not my best moment, I will concede." He turns his head, staring at the flames flickering in the fireplace, a twisted frown on his face, and I know he is reliving that dreadful night. "When we got back to the château, Marine threatened to destroy my reputation if I divorced her. She said she would accuse me of abuse and infidelity. She said one of her friends was prepared to lie for her and say that we had been having an affair for months. She said she would go to my business associates and tell them she thought I embezzled money from the company. A desperate, dangerous woman grasping at anything she could to hang on."

"What did you say?"

"I told her to do her best. Then I went to bed with a bottle of scotch. In the morning, she was gone—along with my mother's jewels and a sizable amount of money from my safe. I heard the rumors, of course, that she showed up in the village with bruises on her face, weeping and whispering her tale of abuse."

"Why didn't you tell everyone the truth? Why didn't you defend yourself?"

"What was the point? Marine had already humiliated me with her behavior, and, I reasoned, anyone who believed those rumors wasn't going to change their mind because I proclaimed my innocence. I thought it better to quietly divorce her and move on with my life."

"Do you know where she is now?"

"*Oui.*"

"Where?"

"Mallorca."

"How do you know?"

"Do you remember our night at La Grotte?"

"Yes."

"Do you remember the woman who approached us as we were leaving? The one who made a scene?"

"Jacqueline."

"*Oui.*" He smiles sadly. "Jacqueline is Marine's best

friend. A few nights before our encounter at La Grotte, she ambushed me in the hotel parking lot. She said Marine was sorry for everything she had done to me, that she loved me, and wanted to come home. Apparently, her Spanish lover has tired of her."

"Spanish lover? I thought Nicabar was her lover."

"She had more than one. Marine always was greedy."

"That's what Monsieur Verite said."

"Did he?" He reaches up, brushes a lock of hair off my cheek. "I am sorry I didn't tell you all of this sooner. Omitting information is as bad as lying about it. Can you forgive me?"

"Of course I forgive you, but maybe you won't be able to forgive and trust me after you have heard what I have to tell you."

He inhales sharply and his hand drops back into his lap. "What is it?"

I take a deep breath and plunge right into the heart of the messy matter, before I lose my courage. I tell him about my daddy's back taxes and the IRS seizing his assets.

"Why didn't you tell me before now?"

"I didn't think it mattered. You see, discovering my father died in deep debt didn't change my way of life. Naturally, I was sad to learn we had lost Black Ash Plantation—a home that was built by my six times great-grandfather—but possessions have never really mattered that much to me. I was far more distressed when I realized the enormous burden my father must have been laboring under before his death, the shame that proud, honorable man surely felt knowing he had failed in his duty as caretaker of our ancestral home." My hand trembles as I brush the tears from my cheek. "My momma left me an extremely generous trust fund, which I have carefully invested. I could have helped to alleviate some of my daddy's burden, if only I had known."

"You would have done that, sacrificed your personal security to bail your father out of debt?"

I frown. "Of course, wouldn't you have done the same if your father found himself in such a distressing state? Sacrifices aren't as painful when you are making them for someone you truly love."

He reaches for my hand. "I once said that I had seen glimpses of your soul and that those glimpses were beautiful, that you were kind, honest, and selfless. I had no idea then how true those words were. You are special, Manderley. Truly."

"Does that mean you forgive me?"

He chuckles and kisses my fingertips. "There is nothing to forgive."

"Thank God!"

He chuckles again. "Does that mean you want to go on being Madame de Maloret?"

"I have never wanted anything more in my life. I would rather throw myself into a storm-tossed sea than live a day without you."

"Well, you have already done that," he says, grinning. "Fortunately, you are married to a fearless and heroic sailor who gladly risked his life to save you."

"You are fearless and heroic."

"You are biased."

"If I am biased it is only because I love you."

"I love you, Manderley, madly, deeply, desperately."

"Do you know, this is the first time you have said you love me?"

"Is it?" He frowns.

"Yes."

"Strange, I have thought it at least a thousand times since I found you standing on the edge of a cliff."

"You have?"

"Oui."

One of Xavier's socks slides down my leg, bunching up around my ankle.

"Will you say it again?"

Xavier reaches down and pulls his sock up to my knee. "I will do better than that."

He stands up, scoops me into his arms, and carries me out of the living room, down the hall to our bedroom.

"What are you doing?"

"Starting a new tradition."

"What tradition?"

"Every time you steal a pair of my socks, I am going to carry you off to bed and make violent love to you."

I look into his blue eyes, shining with happiness.

"Because you love me?"

"Oui," he says, laughing. *"Je t'aime, ma bichette.* I love you very, very much."

Epilogue

It seems to me, as I stand here on the balcony of the Christian Dior suite in the Hôtel Le Majestic that I am experiencing *jamais vu*, the wonderful phenomenon that occurs when you visit the same place, again and again, but find it as unfamiliar as the first time you visited.

On the street below, Jake Gyllenhaal is standing on the red carpet outside the Palais des Festivals et des Congrès, close enough for me to see the sun shining on his artfully tousled hair. The same spot I saw him once before, when my heart was full of unfulfilled yearnings. *That* Manderley—that sad, anxious woman ruled by responsibilities even as she ached for freedom—is practically unfamiliar to me, now.

That Manderley never imagined she would one day cowrite a screenplay that would be made into a Palme d'Or–nominated film. If Jake Gyllenhaal had stepped off the red carpet and, with the paparazzi's cameras flashing and whizzing, prophesized her success, *that* Manderley still wouldn't have believed it.

Yet, here I am, four years later, back in Cannes with

my best friend, celebrating the success of *What Is Hidden*, the screenplay we wrote together.

I sense him even before I smell his familiar, citrusy cologne, before he wraps his muscular arms around my waist, before he murmurs in my ear.

"Je t'aime, ma bichette."

"I love you, Xavier."

It is no trick of moonlight, no gossamer dream that will evaporate like mist in the morning sunshine. Xavier, my Xavier, loves me, well and true.

I do not long for those feverish first days of our love, those days of innocence and yearning, of sorrow and splendor, before my life as I now know it began. I do not yearn for them because the reality of our love is far, far sweeter than any fantasy I could have conjured.

Love the Maxwell sisters?
Keep an eye out for Tara's adventures
Coming soon from
Leah Marie Brown
And
Lyrical Books